UNDEFINED TIDES

BRIAR BELMONT

This is a work of fiction. All names, characters, events, places, organizations, and incidents portrayed in this novel are either products of the author's imagination or are used fictitiously. No identification with actual persons (living or deceased), places, buildings, and products is intended or should be inferred.

UNDEFINED TIDES

Cover Art by: María Arteta https://marosar.carrd.co/

Typography and Design by Amphi https://www.books-amphi.studio/

Map By: Isaac Jordan

ISBN 979-8-9905007-6-1 (paperback)

ISBN 979-8-9905007-7-8 (ebook)

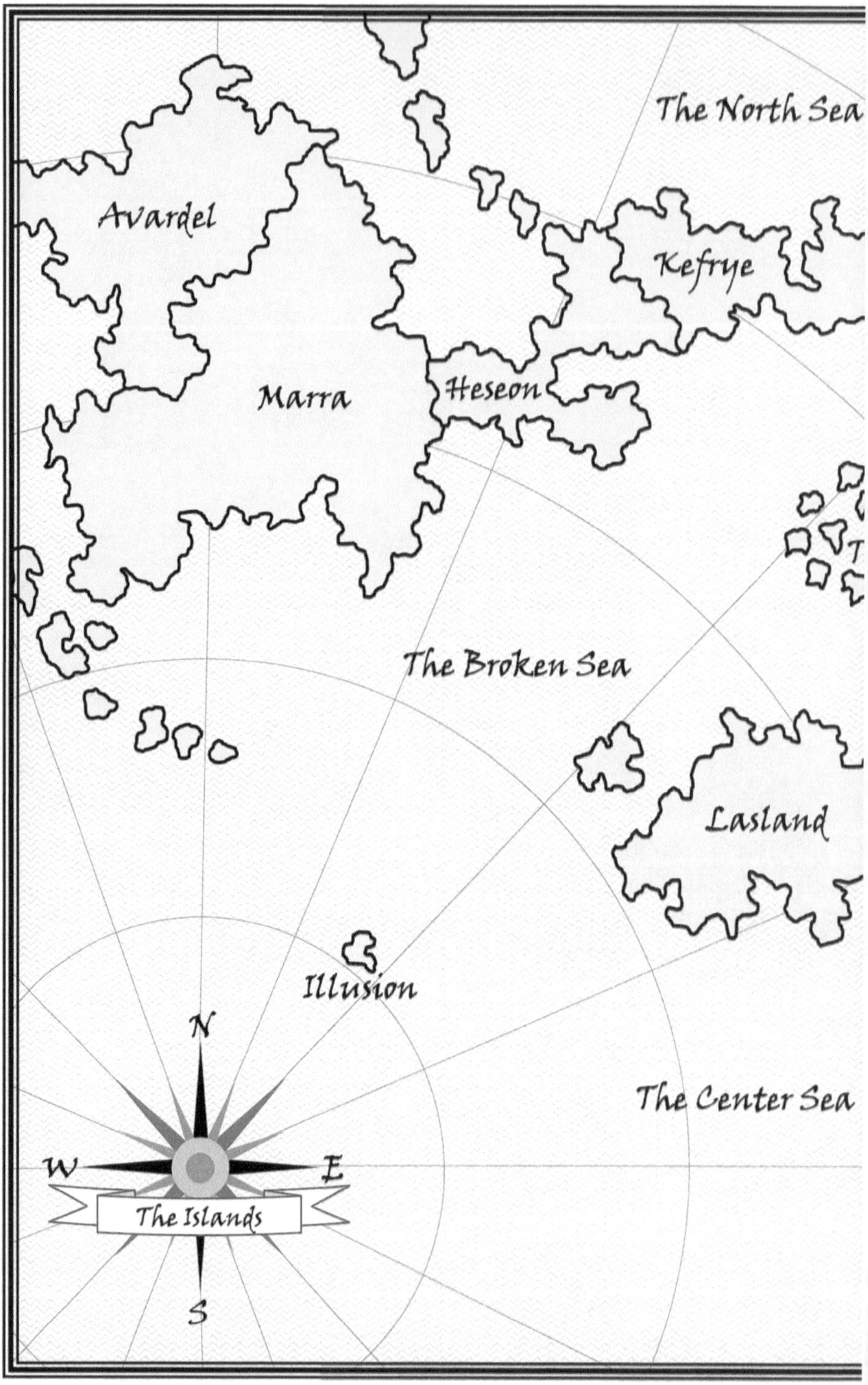

The North Sea
Avardel
Kefrye
Marra
Heseon
The Broken Sea
Lasland
Illusion
The Center Sea
N
W
E
S
The Islands

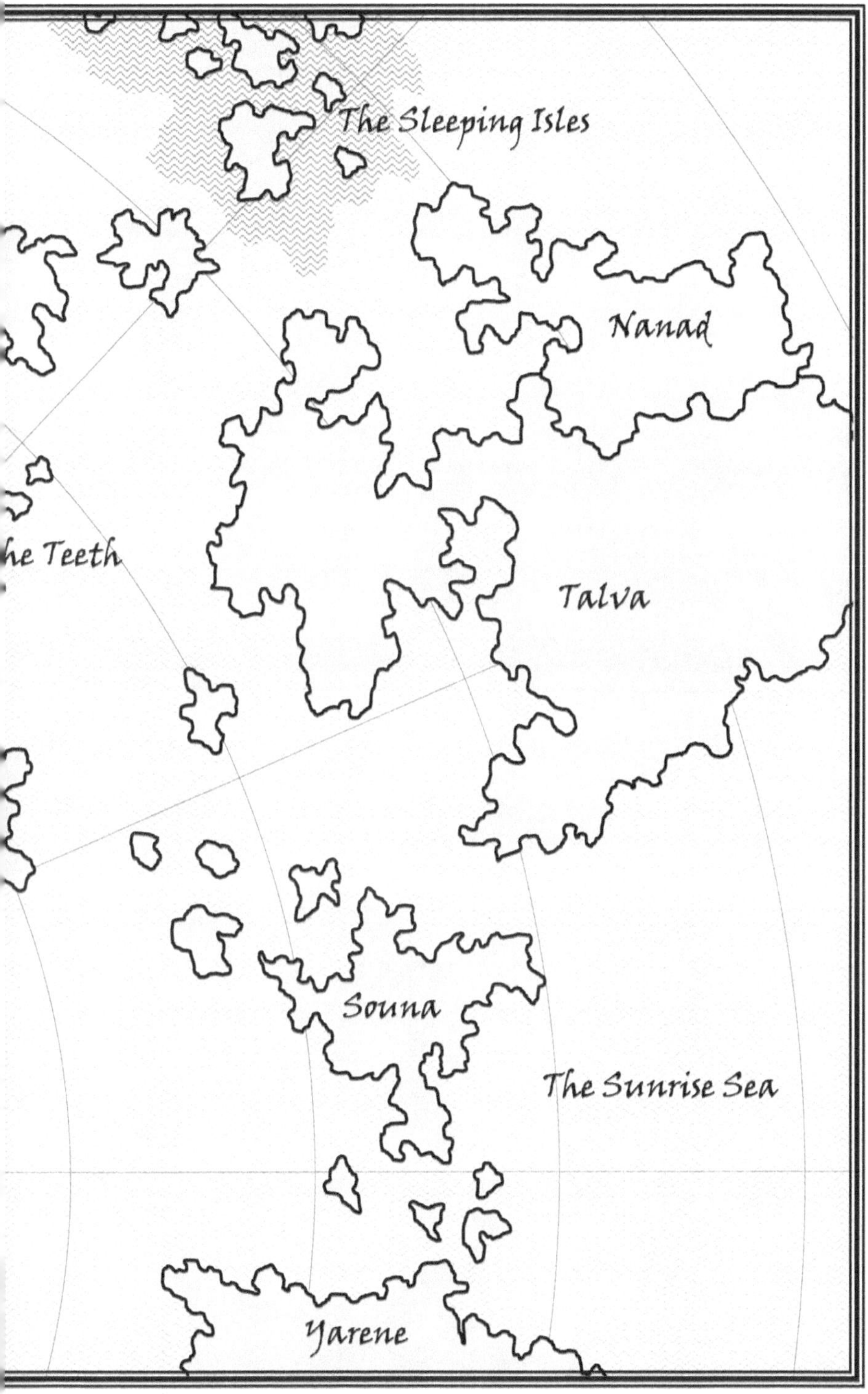

The Sleeping Isles
Nanad
The Teeth
Talva
Souna
The Sunrise Sea
Yarene

PRONUNCIATION GUIDE

CHARACTERS

- Rowan Faine: RO-ən / FAYN
- Yves Francois LeSauvage: EEV / FRAHN-SWA / Læ Saw-VAWG
- Fox: FAHKS
- Logan Crowder: LO-gən / Krow-derr
- Nephele: NEHF-ə-lee
- Henri Wells: AHN-REE / WELZ
- Gaël: GA-EHL
- John Hakon: JAWN / HAA-kon
- Robin Beckett: RAWB-in / BEHK-it
- Ana: AHN-ah
- Warrick Shaw: WAWR-ik / SHAW
- Oscar Driot: AWS-KAR / DREE-oh
- Marius: MA-RYUYS
- Laney Crowder: LAY-nee / Krow-derr
- Abel Crowder: AY-bəl / Krow-derr
- Alfred Galdwin: AL-frəd / GLAD-win
- Benedict Carlyle: BEHN-ə-dikt / kahr-LIEL

- Marie Collingwood: mə-REE / KOL-ing-wuud
- Maxwell Wallis: MAKS-wehl / WAWL-is
- Claude: KLOD
- Louis: LWEE
- Doe: DOH
- Fosse: Faa-see

COUNTRIES

- Marra: MAR-uh
- Talva: Tal-vuh
- Avardel: Av-AR-del
- Kefrye: KEH-free
- Souna: SOO-nah
- Gosoya: Gos-OY-uh
- Lasland: LASS-land
- Yarene: Yah-RHEEN
- Heseon: Hes-EE-ohn

AUTHOR'S NOTE

While the stories contained within this prequel take place before the events of *Demon of the Deep* (Book 1), for the sake of storytelling within the series and avoiding spoilers, *Undefined Tides* is best read after *Demon of the Deep*.

As always, please note that STIs don't exist in this world, and we're gonna pretend that all these pirates maintain a basic level of hygiene.

Please see the back of the book or follow QR code for Content Warnings.

ALSO BY BRIAR BELMONT

Demon of the Deep Series
Undefined Tides (#0.5)
Demon of the Deep (#1)

For Grandpa R and Grandpa P,
Thank you for always telling me stories.
Miss you.

UNDEFINED TIDES

Chapter 1

DEATH COME CALLING

YVES FRANCOIS LESAUVAGE

Winter, 1656

The human part of Yves's soul trembled as he stood on the steps before the great black lacquered door. It was the door to the Batteux estate in Saulés. The last time he'd been here, it was as a traumatized twelve-year-old boy, still fully human. Now he was different. Now a dark tide shadowed his soul. Memories of what General Batteux had done to him, what the other adults had turned a blind eye to, roiled in him. The demon raged. Hungry for revenge. Hungry for blood.

Yves pressed his palm to the smooth black wood, imagining, or perhaps actually feeling, the thrum of blood rushing through the bodies within the house.

Let me give you justice.

When he'd first woken on that sandy shore, the voice that had enticed him back to life after drowning whispered in his head, deep and echoing. He walked for months across Talva back to this spot, where it all began. With every step his thoughts and the demon's had knit together like threads into silken cloth until they became one.

But sometimes, he could still hear its voice.

Let me give you blood.

Yes, they hungered for it. Justice and blood. Vengeance. Violence. Death. He craved it.

The intangible tentacles that flowed from between his shoulder blades writhed in anticipation. At the edges of Yves's consciousness, his own death pressed in, the death he'd escaped through those undefined tides and would escape again.

I will do it for us. You need not face him.

But Yves had to face him, or that trembling child would never be still.

As he opened the door, the demon's shadows spread through him like a dark tide, reminding him he was not alone. Yet the thought of the demon taking over and using his body for this bloody task shook him. He needed to be in control.

"Hey! Who are y—" The footman's accusatory voice cut off, eyes widening in recognition of the pale, black-eyed boy in the doorway. "You..."

Yves had no time for awe. He snatched a silver candlestick from the side table with a speed that belayed his scrawny, starving frame, and bludgeoned the footman over the head. Blood gushed down his temple, and his eyes rolled back. Yves caught him as he slumped and lowered him quietly to the floor. He felt no pity for the man. He'd known what was happening and looked the other way.

All who had done so would perish today, along with their master.

A voice sounded from the breakfast room, gruff and familiar. A shiver of memory rushed up Yves's spine, chased by a wave of his own darkness, hungry to engulf it.

Vengeance.

Once he had General Batteux's blood on his hands, he would be free. Wouldn't he?

The winter morning dawned cold and clear, and as Yves stepped into the breakfast room, white sunlight slanting through the tall, east-facing windows, he froze.

The family didn't notice him at first, no doubt assuming he

was just another silent servant coming to bring them toast. His gaze swept over them. Lady and General Batteux sat, with their eldest son between them, in fine clothes and jewels on either end of the long breakfast table, laden with more food than the three of them could possibly desire this early in the morning. Bread and butter. Crocks of jam. Silver platters heavy with fruit and porcelain plates with bacon and eggs. The smell made Yves's mouth water, and he licked his cracked lips.

The younger son was away at sea, but the elder, a man in his twenties dressed in a sharp blue and green officer's uniform, finally looked up.

"Who the hell are you?" he barked, but Yves barely heard the words. A roar filled his ears as soon as his eyes landed on the pasty, square face of General Batteux.

The son jumped to his feet, drawing his service pistol as Lady Batteux screamed and the general shouted. A crack reverberated through the sunlit room like a great tree snapping in a storm. Pain sliced through Yves's gut, blood blooming on his dirty shirt. The roaring in his head deafened him, and he met the son's eyes over the smoking barrel of the gun. Quick as a striking snake, Yves snatched a silver knife from the breakfast table and launched himself over the table's heaped surface toward the son.

The dark tide surged up as the first gout of blood sprayed across Yves's face. Sunlight flashed off the knife as he wrenched it through the son's chest and turned to the others.

His vision shadowed around the edges like blinders, shielding him from anything but this. The sweet tear of his fingers rending flesh. Blood arcing across the bright windows. The persistent beat of his own death fading into the background like distant waves. But despite all his determination to remain present for his revenge, the demon clawed to the surface.

THE IRON TANG of blood coated their lips. *His* lips. His tongue flicked out to taste it. It was not the bitterness of regret that met his taste buds, but revenge, as sweet and heady as summer wine. They held his hands up to his face, fingers splayed so the blood could catch the morning light like so many glittering rubies. They pressed their fingertips to their lips, intending to lick them clean and taste more of that delectable sweetness. But some lighter part of them recoiled from it. Some part that was still, or newly, human.

Because they—no—*he* had still not found a full equilibrium between that nameless creature of the deep, and the frightened child who had just wanted to go on living. A constant tide flowed within him now. A push and pull between the two minds that occupied this once fragile body.

A sickening gurgle interrupted Yves's thoughts, and his gaze sliced up to take in the gory tableau he had created. His fingertips fell away from his mouth, the taste of revenge forgotten for now in the face of its incompletion.

A trail of bodies and blood stretched through the manor house, following his winding path from the front door to the breakfast table, to the parlor, kitchens, upstairs rooms, and back. It finally ended at his bootheels. A guard and footman, some house servants—he'd torn through them as effortlessly as a ship cutting through waves. He'd let the housemaids flee before his wrath, for some deep down part of him, the part that was still a hurt child and not a vengeful demon, knew they were the same as he'd once been.

As soon as Yves had seen the general's pink, thick-jowled face, nausea had churned in his gut, and it was as if he'd plunged back into the depths of the sea to drown. The rest was a blur. Yet he could still feel the bullet lodged in his gut, the cold metal of the ornate silver knife he'd plunged into first one body, then another and another, until it became too slippery and fell from his hand.

And he found himself back here, listening to the blood gurgle through the windpipe of the only one left alive. General Batteux. All three bodies were back in their seats, a spent pistol still hanging from the hand of the general's eldest son, his uniform staining red as he bled out. Yves's fingertips trailed through the blood pooling on the polished oak table as he rounded it and stopped at the body of Lady Batteux. His eyes never left the general as he struggled for breath. Struggled to keep living as Yves had struggled all his short, miserable life. The general gazed back at him too, those once stern eyes now full of terror, tracking Yves across the room.

Yves tore his eyes away, looking instead at Lady Batteux. She'd known, if not about Yves specifically, then about her husband's sickening appetites. Yet here she was in all her finery with not a care in the world. Two enormous rubies studded her ears, glittering as brightly as blood. Yves ran a thumb over the smooth surface of one of them. He yanked it out of the woman's ear and pierced his own earlobe with it, stashing the other in his pocket. He continued his journey toward the head of the table.

The general's eyes widened as Yves's fingertips skimmed across another silver-handled knife. Yves knew he looked like death come calling. His black hair was long and lank and soaked with blood, hanging around pale, hollow cheeks. Eyes as deep and black as the sea. He was sure his ribs showed through the blood-damp shirt. A skeleton. A dead child walking.

This body had seen only sixteen years, but inside he was fathomless.

Yves reached the head of the table, where the general still struggled for life. He was a pathetic excuse for a man, lording over his household like a king, wielding his power like a cudgel. Yves tilted his head, observing the blood pouring down the general's front from a shallow gash on his neck.

The darker part of Yves fought down the child's urge to run.

"You remember me." Yves couldn't recognize his own voice. He had not spoken aloud in so long, the deep echoes of the demon's voice almost overpowered his own.

The general shook his head minutely.

How many children had he hurt, that he did not remember?

All-consuming rage closed over Yves's head, dragging him under and letting the demon fully free.

The dark shadow tentacles writhed at his back. Yves's hand shot out, gripping the general's throat where it bled. Touching this skin again sickened him. And yet the demon had no qualms about it. Yves surrendered to the demon's lead.

"You showed me no mercy, and I shall show none." The fingertips of both hands dug into the cut and with the last ounce of his strength, the general struggled, seeing his own death in Yves's eyes. Yves did not flinch. He wrenched the flesh apart, tearing the general's throat open.

Hysterical laughter bubbled up through Yves's chest. He was free. The general no longer lingered in this world to haunt him. Could no longer hurt the innocent. Blood spatter dripped down Yves's lips and over his teeth. And he laughed and laughed until his voice grew hoarse and the bullet in his stomach had torn through more flesh.

And when he stopped laughing, he heard it. A small whimper like a frightened animal. Yves whipped around, eyes wide and searching. Had he left one alive? All the Batteuxs were dead, their blood pooling through the room. Yves moved tentatively to the hallway, spotting a trail of small footprints dotting the blood between servants' bodies. They ended at an ornate cabinet. Yves bent and opened it.

The child inside did not scream. He couldn't have been more than ten, his blond hair splattered with blood and wide brown eyes catching on Yves's stained face. He trembled in terror, mouth opening to beg for his life but no sound coming out. The warm, acrid scent of piss hit Yves's nostrils. Yves saw his own reflection in this child's tear-filled eyes. He was a ghoul, a monster.

The demon recoiled, and Yves resurfaced.

Yves grabbed the child by the arm and dragged him from the cabinet, into the breakfast room. The child's bare feet skidded over the slick floor, but he did not struggle, too terrified to try to save his own life. Yves sat him in the chair to the general's right and knelt before him.

"Look." Yves framed the boy's face with his bloody hands. "He is dead. He cannot hurt you anymore." Yves's voice came out as gentle as waves lapping a sandy beach, the demon's echo far from it. The human soul inside him found comfort in it, and he did not know whether he spoke to this boy or himself. "He cannot hurt you," he repeated.

The boy swallowed. Nodded. Yves smoothed his thumbs across the boy's teary cheeks, leaving crimson smears instead.

"Do you have a home? Family?" Another nod. "Run to them, and tell them all the general has done." Yves released the boy and stepped back, but the boy did not move. He only stared up at Yves's ghoulish countenance. Yves picked up a blood-spattered orange, cleaning it as best he could on the hem of his shirt, and handed it to the boy.

"Go."

The boy ran.

Chapter 2

SAVAGE

YVES FRANCOIS LESAUVAGE

Winter, 1657

Two months, Yves wandered. Until his feet bled. Until he succumbed to the cold and hunger but woke up the next day alive again. He was a feral thing, a demon barefoot in the snow with only the darkness inside him for company.

After slaying the general and his family, Yves had found Ana at her lodging house, materializing from the darkness of an alleyway. He felt nothing for her anymore. No affection of a younger brother for the sister that raised him. The human part of him desperately wanted that back. But the demon knew it would be impossible. So they did the only thing they could, and gifted Ana some of the riches they'd stolen from the Batteux estate. She didn't want him to go, and he promised they would see each other again. He would keep her safe, just as she had kept him safe throughout their childhood.

In the end, he couldn't save himself. He was arrested for the murders. Hanged. But thanks to the demon, he couldn't stay dead for long.

The muttered words of the crowd at his hanging still clung to him like his own ghost. *He's just a child. How could he kill all those people?* But he was not a child anymore. He was newly seventeen and had slain his monster. Now it was time to begin anew. To reach for the glory the demon had promised him and take the first steps toward fulfilling his promises to Ana.

He needed to remake himself.

Yves stepped onto the peak of a snowy ridge, observing a town arrayed below. Firelight shone through the windows onto the dark street, washing it in warmth. In the small rocky harbor, fishing vessels and small ships bobbed. Part of him yearned to dive into the freezing water and sink down to rest upon the bottom, drowning again and again until his body no longer needed breath.

But he could not do that, so he picked his way down the snowy slope, rocks digging into the soles of his feet. He strode into the first reputable inn he saw, the cold night trailing him like shadows, and plunked two gold tals onto the bar.

"A room, a bath, and a meal." His voice rasped slightly from disuse. The innkeeper eyed him suspiciously, from his lank hair, partially hiding the large ruby earring, down to his blueish, cut up feet.

"Where'd you steal this from, lad?" His eyes flicked down to the gold, then up to the ruby earring again. One of the pair he'd stolen from Lady Batteux's body. The one he'd first pierced his ear with had been stolen by the jailors upon his arrest, but the other he'd stashed with the rest of the goods and he wore now, a shining drop against bloodless white skin.

"Far enough away that they won't come looking here," Yves replied coolly. He was a thief; he had no problem admitting that. Especially considering he was also a murderer a dozen times over.

"Fine, then," the innkeeper agreed, sweeping the coins off the bartop. "You need the bath before the room. You're filthy." He led Yves through the kitchen to a small room at the back of the building. It was warmer than Yves had been in months, one wall consisting of the brick back of the large kitchen hearth and the rest lined in fragrant cedar. A stool sat next to the brick wall, and a bench at the back held a few folded towels. In the center of the floor sat a large wooden tub.

"My son Marius will bring some hot water," the innkeeper said, lighting an oil lamp on the wall beside the door. "Find my wife in the kitchen after, for your meal."

"Can I trouble you for clean clothes as well? I can pay."

The innkeeper nodded, and Yves slipped a silver coin into his outstretched hand.

"Marius will bring you some of his old ones." He left.

Yves ventured farther into the room and discovered the tub was mostly full of clean, clear water already. When he touched it, it was the same temperature as the room. Yves's skin suddenly began to itch with the grime of months on the road, and the temptation was too much. He stripped out of his grubby clothes.

A knock, then the door opened. Yves froze with one foot already in the tub. A young man, presumably Marius, entered the room with large steaming kettles in both hands and a bundle of clothes under his arm. The demon's tentacles flew to cocoon Yves's naked body before he remembered others could not see them, and to Marius, Yves appeared as naked as before.

"Couldn't wait, eh?" Marius said cheerfully. Then his gaze snagged on Yves's thin frame, lean cords of muscle clinging to bone. His protruding hip bones and flaccid penis hanging down between thin thighs. He winced at Yves's thinness, but recovered quickly, taking on his previous pleasant expression. "A good meal will set you right." He dropped the clothes on the stool where they would be warmed by the hearth. "Get your foot out so I don't burn you."

Yves backed into the corner, covering his privates as best he could with his hands and eyeing Marius warily as he poured the kettles of hot water into the tub.

Marius looked to be around the same age as Yves, though a bit shorter and a lot stockier. He had a thick shock of brown hair and Talvan pale skin slightly kissed by the sun, even in the dead of winter.

Steam rose between them as the hot water emptied into the

tub. Marius caught Yves watching. Then his gaze fell to Yves's cut up feet, which were starting to pinken with warmth.

"Are you alright? Do you need me to help you into the tub?"

"No."

Marius set the kettles by the door, but didn't leave. "I could clean those cuts for you. They must be painful."

Annoyance sparked in Yves's chest. He did not like feeling vulnerable.

"Why are you still here? Leave."

Marius's cheeks reddened. "Sorry," he muttered. "It's only, I'd much rather be in here actually helping someone than out there with the rowdy drunks." He smiled ruefully. "Sometimes they pinch my bum and say I'm too soft to be a boy."

The little spark of annoyance turned to anger. It seemed no matter where Yves fled, there would always be men like the general.

"Fine," Yves hissed. "Turn your back while I get in the tub." Marius did as he was told, and Yves sank into the scalding water, unable to keep a sigh from escaping his lips. Marius turned back around, grabbing a lump of soap and a cloth from the bench and dragging over the clothes-piled stool.

"What's your name? Mine's Marius." He seemed to be willfully ignoring how rude Yves had been to him. He dipped the cloth into the water and began to lather it with soap.

This was Yves's first chance to become a new person.

"Yves LeSauvage." He'd heard the words whispered behind hands in the last town he'd wandered through. *Look at that dirty boy. Savage.* He was a savage killer, no longer fully human, though those strangers only knew he looked like a wild thing, not the extent of his crimes or his new nature. From here on out, he would savagely chase his desires. He would claim them for his own.

"Sounds fancy. Give me your foot." Reluctantly, Yves propped his ankles on the edge of the tub. Marius handed him the soap. "Get to work on your hair."

They fell into silence, the steam rising around them. Yves

scrubbed the soap across his scalp and skin, relishing the feel of road dirt sloughing off. He flinched when Marius touched his ankle, but the cloth was soft against his abused feet. Yves knew the demon side of him would heal them before the day was out, leaving clear, unblemished skin behind. He'd even regrown the toes he'd lost to frostbite.

He grit his teeth and endured Marius's touch. Between what the general had subjected him to as a child and the rough handling at the hands of the authorities after the murder, he was loath to let anyone touch him. But the steaming water and Marius's ministrations were so gentle, Yves couldn't help but be soothed. Slowly, he began to relax into the hot water. His eyes closed, and he sank lower and lower into the bath until only his face and feet remained above the surface.

"Don't fall asleep," Marius said. "You might drown."

"It's not too bad," Yves said, without thinking.

The cloth wiping at his feet stilled. "Drowning?"

"Mm." Yves made a noncommittal noise. He did not want to share that memory with this boy. He didn't understand why he was allowing Marius to stay and help him, or why Marius wanted to.

"You must be sore from walking so much," Marius said, clearly uncomfortable exploring the topic of Yves's drowning further. Yves sat up, wary again.

"Yes." His muscles ached, but as with the cuts and blisters and every other injury he'd endured since the demon possessed him, the soreness would be gone before long.

"Can I..." Marius's fingers pinched the tendon on the back of Yves's ankle, and Yves almost jerked his leg back, but the pressure of Marius's fingers rubbed up his calf, instantly easing the tightness of his muscle.

A small moan escaped Yves's lips, and he slumped back against the side of the tub. Marius's fingers worked over his muscles, easing tension and soreness as much as the hot water did. With every inch up Yves's legs Marius's hands moved, a strange feeling stirred. He tried to stay very still, forcing himself to enjoy the touch until Marius's hand dipped beneath the water.

Yves jerked up, water sloshing over the rim of the tub.

"Sorry." Marius held his hands up, placating. "I got carried away. If you don't..." He trailed off, seeing something in Yves's dark eyes. Anger? Fear? Yves himself didn't know.

Marius's neck shone with sweat from the steam as he swallowed nervously. He was quite handsome, solidly rounded and warm-toned, where Yves was all angles and paleness. Yves sat forward, searching for Marius's intention in his open and honest face. What he found was desire, untouched by dark motives.

A thread of unease wound through Yves's chest, mingled with something primal from the depths of the demon within him. Yves's heartbeat quickened, and he forced himself to remember Marius was simply a boy, not some older abuser who would take and take with no regard for consent or the hurt he caused.

No one had ever desired Yves without cruel intentions before.

"Sorry," Marius said again. "I'll go." He stood slowly from the stool, downtrodden. Before he could think, Yves grabbed his hand.

"I was just surprised." Yves didn't know why he said it, why he wanted Marius to stay, or what he wanted Marius to do. It was as if his body moved without thought. The demon's instincts were pushing him toward this boy.

He tugged Marius closer, their eyes locked. Tension coiled in the air as thick as the steam, and no more words passed between them. Marius's other hand feathered through Yves's wet hair, pushing it back from his forehead. His eyes slid closed, and he leaned down to kiss Yves on the lips.

No one had ever actually kissed Yves before. His body tensed before giving in to the tantalizing softness of Marius's lips, the demon's primal instincts guiding him. Marius's tongue slipped between Yves's lips, and something stirred deep in his belly. The shadow tentacles that spilled over the edges of the tub twitched, and he bit back a whimper. The demon unfurled within him, and with it, his desire only grew. They pulled Marius's hand beneath the water to his hardening length. The first stroke shot tingles of arousal through their nerves, and their fragile human body arched into the touch. Shame and fear came quickly on its heels. Memories of the general threatened to surface. The demon's darkness dragged them back, sinking them deep into the shadows.

Yves had sometimes wondered if he would ever be able to accept physical intimacy after what had happened, but he was more than human now. More than Yves. The demon's shadows curled along the ridges of his mind, soft as a current and just as deadly. War waged within him. The human side of him sought connection but could not have it. The demon side demanded action. It didn't matter which side won out; in the end their desires required the same act.

Perhaps the new Yves needed this. Perhaps if he gave in to these feral cravings the way he'd given in to his bloodlust, he could heal the part of himself that had been damaged by the general. Perhaps if he fed the demon's lascivious appetites, if he awakened his lust, he could learn to love again.

Foolish. The demon's voice echoed through him like a thought of his own, repeating that undeniable truth as it had countless other times. *You will never know love.* He knew it was right. Love and lust, though often connected, were not the same. But that didn't mean he couldn't try to find his way back to some semblance of humanity.

When Yves's eyes opened, they blazed with fire.

"Take off your clothes." The demon's echo tinged his voice, but Marius didn't seem to hear it. He obeyed without question, then stood naked in the steam, as if suddenly self-conscious.

There was no need to be. Marius's body was solidly built and obviously well fed, with a soft stomach and sides. The tan skin of his face and arms faded to a paler shade on his torso. Soft brown hair trailed from his navel to crotch, his already hardening cock nestled in the curls.

Yves stood, water dripping from his now clean body. The demon didn't have the self-consciousness to care what this human body looked like, but still his heart rate quickened as Marius's brown eyes roamed over him. Marius's already pink cheeks reddened further as his eyes landed on Yves's cock.

"Gods, you're huge," he giggled.

Yves stepped out of the bath. In the small room, this brought them chest to chest. He ran his fingertips tentatively down Marius's lightly furred chest, trailing bathwater across his skin.

"Have you done this before?" Marius asked quietly.

"No," Yves answered. His eyes remained on Marius's flushed skin as his hands explored, relishing the feel of touching someone without violence, the slickness of water on his hands instead of blood. He pushed down the feeling of death that crept in at the edges of his perception, trying to focus on the sensation of skin on skin.

Yves palmed Marius's cock, and Marius gasped. He grabbed Yves's thin hips as Yves slowly stroked him, fumbling and awkward at first, then gaining a rhythm that had Marius's fingers tightening and his breath coming in little pants. Yves was hyper-aware of every place their skin touched, every puff of Marius's breath against the side of his neck. Marius canted his hips forward, the friction between their bodies eased by the water on Yves's skin.

"Do you want to fuck me?" Marius whispered between gasps. Yves stilled, though the words stoked the tide of desire high. Did he want this? All he could do was follow the lead of his body. He nodded wordlessly.

Marius released him, and retrieved a small bottle from between the folds of a towel on the bench.

"We can use this." Marius smiled nervously and uncorked the bottle. A sweet smell permeated the steam. Yves wasn't quite sure what the contents of the bottle were for, but decided not to ask. Marius seemed to know what he was doing. He dragged Marius forward with a hand on the back of his neck and kissed him. Marius poured a small amount of the liquid onto his fingers and reached back between his own ample buttcheeks. He moaned into

Yves's kiss, and Yves once again wrapped a hand around Marius's dick. After a few moments, Marius broke the kiss and dropped to his knees. He glanced up, meeting Yves's gaze, and took Yves's cock into his mouth.

Lightning crackled up Yves's spine as his tip breached Marius's lips and slid into the warm interior of his mouth. Through half-lidded eyes, Yves watched Marius's thick fingers thrust in and out of his own hole. The sight fascinated him, and his desire grew, but with it, panic rose like a tide. A sense of losing control. If he gave in to being pleasured, he would lose himself too. Anything could happen. Anything could be done to him.

Yves grabbed Marius by the hair and pulled his mouth away. Marius blinked up at him, pink lips swollen.

"Stand up and turn around," Yves growled. Marius's cock twitched at his words, and he obeyed. He bent over and braced his hands against the edge of the tub.

"I'm not quite loose enough, could you..."

The tide coursed over Yves, rising to his neck, his panicked heart thrashing in his chest to keep him afloat. He ran both hands down Marius's back and gripped his ample pink cheeks, spreading them apart to observe his hole as it clenched.

Marius whined Yves's name as his thumb traced the rim. Yves moved as if in a trance, dribbling more of the oil between Marius's cheeks and pushing one finger, then two more, into Marius's interior. Marius moaned, and a surge of hunger whet Yves's palate.

Yves couldn't let himself lose control of the situation. He had the power here. He could cause pleasure or pain on a whim, and he could push past the old memories and carve a new path for himself.

He continued thrusting his fingers in and out, clumsily at first. When he curled his fingers down, pressing to the slick walls, Marius moaned and rutted his hips back. He couldn't take it anymore—he removed his fingers and used the remaining oil to slick up his aching cock.

Marius's hold tightened on the edge of the tub as Yves pressed the tip of his cock to Marius's entrance. Yves paused, trying to get control of himself, the demon's determination twisting around his ribs, then thrust in.

Fuck, he'd never felt anything like this before. He gripped Marius's hips as he pulled out and thrust in again, harder, burying his entire length in warm, pliant flesh. The tides closed over his mouth and nose, and he drowned in sensation and memory.

Yves was not gentle. He thrust hard and fast, taking his pleasure from Marius's flesh, Marius's whimpers a distant rush in his ears. But the sensations of coupling remained purely physical. Yves felt nothing that could be mistaken for even the barest stirring of affection. In fact, the more Marius moaned and writhed beneath him, the less human he became in Yves's eyes. More like a plaything for Yves to pleasure himself with. To exert power over with every thrust. Even as, in the back of Yves's mind, he knew if he was still fully human, he may have easily been taken with Marius's friendly disposition.

Marius jerked himself off quickly, his moans reaching a crescendo, and in two more thrusts, he cried out as if in pain, spilling thick spurts of cum into the bathwater. A demonic growl rumbled in Yves's throat as his own pleasure peaked. Euphoria clawed through his nerves and something snapped, the demon pushing all the way to the surface like tentacles crawling beneath his skin and into his skull. The feeling of death wrapped him, and an urge to plunge Marius's head into the semen-filled bathwater and feel him drown as Yves fucked him almost overwhelmed him. His hand curled around the back of Marius's head. A soft caress.

With one last thrust, the clawing pleasure broke, and his cock throbbed out his orgasm, filling Marius up to the brim. Death was sated, only for a moment, enough for Yves's mind to clear. Pleasure died as quickly as it had come, replaced with disgust. He snatched his hand back from Marius's head and pulled out. Watching his own pearlescent juices drip from Marius's pink hole with revulsion for what he'd done, and what he'd almost done.

"Get the fuck out," Yves growled. He couldn't trust himself or the demon. He didn't want to kill this boy once the feeling of death returned.

Marius's head jerked up. "W-what?"

"I said get out."

Tears pricked at Marius's wide brown eyes, but he pulled his clothes on without even cleaning himself up, and left without a parting word.

Chapter 3

Birth of the Kraken

Yves Francois LeSauvage

Spring, 1657

In the northern forests of Talva, a thick layer of brown pine needles crunched beneath Yves's boots, and a carpet of spring flowers flowed beneath the trees from the direction he'd come. But it was nothing compared to the sight before him, below the cliff's edge. The rising sun sparkled red as blood across the Broken Sea, where a large Talvan warship lay at anchor in an unpopulated cove. It took Yves's breath away. The beautiful curve of the bow, the masts reaching toward the lightening red sky, as tall and straight as the pine trees Yves stood beneath. His eyes moved down the undulating curves of the figurehead's tentacles, which flowed back along the ship's prow and rails like the waves would when it cleaved them at full sail. Like Yves's own tentacles, which even now draped behind him like a cape and cast shadows between the white jewels of snowdrops.

Yves had left the inn early the morning after his bathhouse dalliance, without seeing that boy again. It was for the best. What Yves felt for the way he'd treated him was not exactly shame. But he couldn't forget what he'd almost done, even if he'd already forgotten the boy's name.

One of his shadow tentacles quested over the edge of the cliff, reaching for the ship. He felt a tug beneath his navel, a pull that made him want to leap from the cliff and swim to this beautiful ship. He needed to own it, possess it. With this ship, he could rule the seas. With this ship, he would take all the glory he desired and never be powerless again. It was meant for him. His fate.

A slow smile spread across his face, the ruby in his ear glinting in the morning sun. Within him, the demon spoke.

It will be ours.

Yves was no longer that starving boy who'd wandered barefoot through the snow. Who'd fumbled his way through his first sexual encounter in a bathhouse behind a country inn. Though that night had awakened only lust, it had eased some of the fear his human side still had of physical intimacy, and solidified his mind even further into a singular entity.

Now he stood tall in shiny leather boots and rich clothes. He was still slim, but his bones no longer showed and his cheeks were not as hollow. He'd spent the money he'd stolen from the Batteux estate to wrap himself in a gentlemanly disguise and hide the monster that lurked beneath.

Yves stood at the top of the cliff for a long time as the sun crested the blue dome of the sky, observing the sailors and soldiers in their orderly movements like a colony of ants infesting the ship. They ran a skeleton crew. Only a few dozen sailors and half as many officers and soldiers. Enough to sail the ship, but not enough to fully man the guns.

The tentacles grew restless as the day progressed, questing over the mossy ground and up the trunks of trees until Yves stood at the center of a shadowy spiderweb only he could see.

Finally, clouds rolled in as the sun descended, and mist rose from the sea as the air cooled, obscuring the bottom of the ship. Now was the time to set his fate in motion.

By the time Yves had picked his way down to the rocky shale beach, the cove had darkened with dusk, and the mist had risen thicker to obscure the water. On the ship, a few lanterns fought to keep the gloom at bay, but the light would not protect these men from what was about to unfold. Yves did not bother removing his boots or heavy coat before stepping into the sea. The freezing water closed over his ankles, knees, waist, shoulders, and then he swam, paying no heed to the cold or the obscuring mist. The ship called to him, guiding his way. Soon, he heard the gentle slap of water against wood and the dark shape of the ship loomed up before him. He pressed one blue-tinged palm against its sleek side.

"You will be mine." He imagined it shivered at his whispered words, responding to his touch like a long lost lover. He looked up through the mist, finding its name picked out in blue and green against the dark wood. K.S. *Giant Squid*. What a shitty name for a vessel as beautiful as this.

Yves was halfway to hypothermic when he found the series of small divots set with iron bars in the side of the ship. All Talvan-built ships had a discrete ladder to climb onto the deck if one knew where to look, though the iron handholds were often crusted with barnacles and the like, making them impossible to climb barehanded. Yves grasped the first shell-crusted rung and hoisted himself from the water, taking care to keep his teeth from chattering. He barely noticed when the sharp edges of the shells cut his palms. He scaled the side of the ship quickly, emerging from the mist like a drowned corpse come to life. He supposed that's what he actually was, a dead thing returned from its grave at the bottom of the sea.

"Halt!" a military voice barked as Yves finally stepped over the rail. The deck was mostly deserted but for three watchmen, one of whom ran toward him. The demon's bloodlust piqued, the unseen tentacles unfurling behind Yves like a dark corona. The watchman reached him.

"Did you fall overboard? What..." He noticed Yves's sodden, but nonetheless expensive, clothes. Clearly not a wayward sailor who'd gone over the rail. "Who the hell—"

Yves drew the dagger from his belt, the only weapon he'd brought besides his own demon-enhanced body, and stabbed the man in the throat. A warning bell clanged from the foredeck as

Yves yanked the blade back out of the watchman's neck and let him crumple to the deck.

The demon practically quivered in delight, but the feeling of death remained close. Yves had done his utmost to sate it only with carnal pleasures as he'd made his way across Talva, but it was never enough. It snapped always at their heels, demanding blood. Demanding the souls he could reap for it in exchange for his own resurrections. After so long, it was starving, and now before it lay a feast, as sailors and soldiers poured onto deck at the alarm. Its cacophony sounded like a dinner bell to Yves's ears.

Yves slashed at the next man to come near, and they all fell upon him at once. His dagger flashed crimson in the lantern light as he ducked and whirled and *killed* so quickly it left him dizzy. The mist rose as night encroached, spilling over the rails at his back as if following him into battle. He did not feel the pain of the blades that bit him. His blood sang with violence, the demon's bloodlust flooding him more and more with every life he took, until it was as if he were apart from himself, watching from the cool cocoon of mist.

He'd intended to do this properly. To sweep death elegantly across the ship with a sword in hand. But the demon had other ideas. They'd put that feral child behind them, but not that far behind.

Yves's dagger was knocked away and he resorted to fingernails and fists.

A shot rang out, bringing the melee to a standstill in an instant. They all turned to see what could only be a commanding officer, an older gentleman in a long curled wig, holding a smoking pistol pointed to the darkening sky.

Before the sailors could regain their bearings, Yves pounced like the feral thing he was deep down, tackling the commander to the deck. His teeth found the struggling man's throat and bit down, barely hearing the gurgling scream over the pound of his own heartbeat, or feeling sailors' hands desperately trying to tear him away over the metallic gush of blood against his lips. He tore a chunk from the man's throat, and the man lay still, limbs twitching as the blood spread in a pool around them, reflecting the orange lantern light.

Yves barely resisted the urge to swallow the lump of gristle, instead spitting it into a sailor's face. He drew the commander's ceremonial sword from its sheath and fought on.

Distantly, he wondered if it would ever end. If he would be like this forever. Mist swirled at his feet and encroached upon his mind, scarlet with blood. Then biting agony pierced his throat, a length of ruby steel protruding below his chin. He could almost taste its sharp edges, or maybe that was the blood filling his mouth.

The tides took him.

YVES DID NOT gasp as he resurfaced from those dark waters for the fifth time in less than a year. He floated for a moment in their embrace, somehow comforted to be borne through death again. Yet slowly his senses returned him to the mortal world. Murmuring voices all around him, a bright light shining through his eyelids.

What should we do with him?

I don't wanna touch him. You do it.

Cursed.

Not human.

Yves's black eyes snapped open. The ring of sailors that stood around him debating how to dispose of his corpse drew back in horror. A few of them made gestures to ward off evil, touching the backs of their fingertips to their right eyes, then the pads of their fingers to their lips.

Yves sat up and heard one among the crowd begin to pray fervently under their breath. Both blood and seawater had nearly dried on Yves's clothes, and above, dusk had given way to full night. Thick clouds obscured the moon, and only a single lantern lit the ship.

Yves felt the spot where the blade had pierced him, finding a smooth expanse of unblemished skin. His limbs felt heavy. Blood drunk. Sated. Death no longer snapped at his heels but slumbered soundly at his feet.

Slowly, Yves stood up. The remaining sailors drew back even more, eyes fixed on him wide and terrified, like he was a carnivore and they his next meal. They would be, if they didn't submit to him.

Yves looked at the survivors, and behind them, the scattered bodies in lakes of drying blood. He bent to retrieve the commander's sword, holding it casually, as if it were only natural he carry it. His tongue ran over the blood on his lips. Tasting. Savoring not only the copper tang of life and death but the held breaths of the survivors as they watched him.

"You all belong to me now."

"Like hell!" A burly man charged forward, and Yves did not flinch. The man stabbed, dagger sinking into Yves's right shoulder. Yves shoved his own blade into the man's soft belly with both hands and yanked it down before the man could do anything more. His guts spilled onto Yves's boots, hot and steaming in the cool night.

The man howled and collapsed to the deck among his own entrails. Yves yanked the dagger out of his own shoulder and stabbed it down into the man's spine.

They all watched in stunned silence as life fled him. Yves met the crew's horrified gazes.

"Anyone else have a craving for death? I am happy to oblige."

A collective intake of breath, a distant splash as someone leapt over the side in an attempt to swim for shore. He wanted to see what they would do. Flee? Fight?

Finally, a young man in an officer's uniform stepped forward and fell to one knee.

"We are at your command." They had seen him kill. They had seen him die. And they were afraid. Yves's dark eyes swept over them.

"Does he speak for all of you?" Nods around the circle. None of them dared disagree. He turned back to the officer. "Your name?"

The man glanced up, and Yves realized he was young indeed, no more than twenty-two or twenty-three. His dark hair was coming undone from its braid.

"Lieutenant Oscar Driot, sir."

Sir. Yves liked that. "And are you the highest rank left alive, Lieutenant?"

"No sir. That would be Commodore Fosse."

"Bring him."

There was a scuffle toward the back of the crowd, and soon enough, the sailors pushed a bewigged man in a periwinkle coat to his knees at Yves's feet.

"Please, have mercy on us, Demon." Commodore Fosse's voice trembled, and a flush of pleasure raced through Yves's chest to see a powerful man brought so low before him. The demon's dark currents surged at being recognized for what it was, though deep in the demon's memories, Yves saw that it was once worshipped as a god.

Yves felt the bottomlessness of their intermingled soul then, the hunger for power, for everything life had to offer. He knew no matter how much he fed it, they would never be sated. The ravenous thing inside him had once been a god, a monster, feared and reviled and worshipped. It had lived longer than things had names. Yet now, he and the demon were experiencing human life for the first time. Together.

"Tell me, Commodore, is there a young officer by the name of Batteux under your command on this ship?"

Fosse's head snapped up, brow furrowed in confusion. "N-no."

How perfect it would have been if Yves could have completed his revenge this very night. But he supposed he had the rest of his lives to hunt down the general's younger son.

"Then you are of no use to me." Yves had only a moment to

relish the fear on Fosse's face before he slashed his throat. The rest of the crew remained silent as they watched him bleed out, only a few whimpers of fear sounding from those at the back. When the last of the blood spilled, Yves turned back to the lieutenant, whose knee was now stained with the life force of his commanding officer.

"You, Driot, are my second-in-command. Congratulations."

"Thank you, sir." His hands trembled, but his voice remained surprisingly steady.

A small smile twitched at the corner of Yves's mouth. He could get used to this. He liked this power. Probably too much.

"Get up."

Oscar Driot obeyed, and the rest of them looked on. Yves could explain it all to them. Lay out his plans to become the most feared pirate on the seas and tell them the part they would play in it. But right now, he relished the fear and uncertainty in their eyes.

Yves took one step forward, and they all shrank away from him. All but Driot, who looked very much like he wanted to cower along with the rest of them. Yves strode dreamily toward the bow of the ship, his fingertips running over the masterfully carved tentacles that twisted around the rails. It was his. All his. This gorgeous and deadly ship would carry him wherever he wanted to go, and deal death to his enemies. His eyes slipped closed for a moment, listening to the waves against the side of the ship, inhaling the mist that enveloped them all.

"You are now the first crew of the *Kraken's Fury*." As one, the crew—full of men who were his natural enemy, and the natural enemy of pirates—bowed to him. Yves strode down the length of the deck, the crew parting before him as if he were royalty. "I am going to retire to my quarters. I expect to be underway at dawn. Prepare the ship." He glanced around at the bodies that littered the deck. "And clean this up." He opened the door that led to the room beneath the quarterdeck and paused, his dark eyes scanning the terrified faces around him. "Driot, bring me wine, and send it with someone in one of those pretty little uniforms."

He closed the door on their shocked faces.

The commodore's quarters, now *his* quarters, were rich and ostentatious to the point of gaudiness. The stateroom held a large table of charts and navigational tools. Obviously a room for receiving guests and planning. He quickly found a set of curving stairs behind a panel and made his way down to the private area of the quarters. He stepped out into a parlor lined with carved wooden panels and crystals dripping from sconces. All sorts of useless trinkets littered almost every available surface, as if one square inch of blank space would doom the owner to a life of social inequity among the poors. He'd have to change that, perhaps sell off the gaudier pieces to nouveau riche families on the other islands, who craved a taste of Talvan high society.

Above the mantelpiece at one end of the stateroom, a large portrait of the dead commodore hung in a gilded frame. Yves picked up a jeweled dagger, hefted it in his hand, then flicked it toward the painting. The tip pierced the canvas dead center on the commodore's forehead, blade quivering. The *Kraken's Fury* and all its contents belonged to him, and the rush of power provided by that thought alone had almost hysterical laughter bubbling up in his throat. The sound of it was unfamiliar to him.

The future opened before him, his for the taking farther than the horizon.

Yves ran his fingertips along a large table inlaid with a mother-of-pearl map of the Islands. Marra, Talva, all the nations the two empires had swallowed up, and all the ones they still hungered for. Yves could carve out a piece for himself, for his hunger rivaled the greediest king.

A knock interrupted his thoughts.

"Enter." The door opened, closed, and silence pervaded the room once again as Yves turned to find not an officer in uniform as he'd requested, but a brunette woman in a worn dress with a Talvan uniform jacket hastily thrown over it. She held a bottle of wine in her hands.

They stared at each other for a moment before the woman blurted, "But...you're a kid!"

This did not offend him. The woman had to be about a decade older than him, and had obviously been expecting someone who looked powerful enough to scare a ship's worth of military men. He graced her with a charming smile, despite the dry blood still rusting his skin. "I can understand your disappointment," he said smoothly.

Something about his smile made her shift uncomfortably on her feet. Had his smile put others at ease before the demon? He didn't remember.

"They told me...I am yours now," she said tentatively.

He sighed. "Give me the wine."

She hesitated, then crossed the room and set the bottle on the end of the table. Still far away from him.

"Relax. You're not what I asked for." Driot, and probably the others, had read his tone loud and clear. That was why they'd decided to send him this woman, a person they'd already stripped dignity from, instead of what he really wanted. One of them. Yves poured two silver goblets of wine and held one out to her. "What's your name?"

"They call me Flore." It was a Talvan name, but it didn't match her accent.

"But is that your name?"

She tentatively took the cup from his bloody fingers. "It's Doe."

Laslandish then, with their silly custom of naming troublesome children after animals.

"And what are you doing here, Doe?" Was it pity that tightened his gut? Or disgust for his fellow man?

"They said—"

"I mean what are you doing on a Talvan warship. I don't recall Talva allowing women in the navy, let alone foreign ones."

The blood drained from her face, and that was all he needed to know.

"Fetch me Driot." He tried to sound reassuring, but it felt wrong on his tongue. Doe downed her glass and opened the door, only to find Oscar Driot already standing on the other side.

Once they both stood at the end of the table, Yves let his anger surface.

"Is this what you think I want?" Yves snarled at Driot, jabbing his finger toward Doe in her ill-fitting uniform jacket. "A prisoner playing dress up?"

"I thought—"

"No!" Yves slammed his hand on the table, and they both jumped. "You *thought* you would save your fellow men the indignity of my bed, and instead give me someone who you've already broken." Doe's spine straightened at this, as if to prove she was not broken, only bending like a tree in a storm. Driot's hands shook as he placed them on the surface of the table to steady himself.

"There were no volunteers, sir."

Of course not. Who would volunteer to submit to a man they'd just witnessed killing dozens of their comrades in cold blood? Who'd ripped their commander's throat out with his teeth, and been stabbed through the heart, yet lived?

"And she did volunteer?" Yves's voice was deadly quiet. A viciousness had settled in him since that night at the inn's bathhouse. He'd learned in the last three months how pleasure and violence irrevocably intertwined in his psyche. Especially now that the demon lived within him, and the sense of death could be temporarily sated by carnal acts. He could not resist his own desires, nor would he inflict them upon the innocent.

"N-no, sir," Driot answered.

"So bring me an officer willing to swallow my dick. I want to fuck the Talvan Empire as hard as they fucked me." Yves took a sip of the rich red wine, savoring the warmth that circulated through his limbs. "And give this poor woman the keys to the second best set of rooms. You've put her through enough."

When Yves was alone again, he swallowed the rest of his wine and opened the door to the inner chamber. A large four-poster bed dominated the room beneath a bank of stained glass windows. On the other side, the gray mist pressed against the glass, as if trying to find a way in. Yves crossed the room and sank onto the bed, resting his head against plush velvet and silk cushions. All the weariness of the demon's ancient life seemed suddenly to slam down on him, pushing him deeper into the soft, downy mattress. His eyes slid closed, and he reached up to touch the large ruby that still pierced his earlobe. Demon, the commodore had called him. That's what he was. What he'd become. He was a creature of the deep water. A thing that lurked in the darkness. Once called a god.

He was Yves Francois LeSauvage, youngest pirate captain to sail the Islands, slayer of the Batteuxs and countless men who still laid on the deck above him, five times dead and resurrected—the Deep Water Demon.

Chapter 4

A Calling Song

Rowan Faine

Autumn, 1658

"Just a few more steps. That's it." Rowan tried to keep his voice neutral and soothing as he led Maxwell Wallis, first mate of the merchant ship, *Jackdaw*, down the blustery alleyways of Hallenburgh. The man was drunk out of his mind, stumbling over his own two feet as if he'd never walked a day in his life. He'd better be, for all Rowan had been plying him with strong drink all night, until the other crew members had left for their own beds or other entertainments. Wallis stumbled again, his shoulder hitting the stone wall of the alley.

"Where'er we goin'?" he slurred, smacking at Rowan's hands as he tried to pull him off the wall.

"Back to the *Jackdaw*, sir. I told you." Rowan bit down his annoyance. It was all according to his plan, after all. And he'd be rid of the drunkard soon enough.

Wallis cast bleary eyes around the alley as autumn wind kicked up dust in little dervishes around their feet.

"This ain't the docks."

Skies above, Rowan had given him enough liquor to fell a fucking horse, yet he remained cognizant enough to realize they weren't where they were meant to be. Rowan contemplated simply leaving him here, slumped against the wall. There was no way he'd find his way back to the *Jackdaw* in time for the morning tides. By the time Captain Gladwin noticed he was gone, and not in his cabin sleeping off a night of binge drinking and whoring, it would be too late to turn back. Especially with their recent not-so-legal cargo stashed in the secret hold. That's what Rowan had done with the other loyalists at least. Merely dumped them drunk in ditches and alleyways the night before departure. Though none of them had been this difficult or this canny.

Rowan looked Wallis over with an appraising eye. He'd lost his hat somewhere along their trek through the winding Hallenburgh streets, and his graying hair stuck up around the bald patch on the crown of his head. Rowan didn't know how old the first mate was. Certainly too old to be letting his eighteen-year-old crew member buy him drink after drink and drag him into secluded alleys.

"You're right, we're not at the docks yet," Rowan agreed. "We just need to go a little further."

Wallis narrowed his eyes for a moment, then began to hiccup. He braced a hand against the wall and puked. Rowan rolled his eyes but schooled his expression back to pleasantness as Wallis turned back toward him, wiping a bit of vomit from his chin.

"Let's get you back to the *Jackdaw*." Rowan grabbed his arm firmly. This time Wallis allowed himself to be pulled up from the wall, the fight seeming to go out of him now that the contents of his stomach were splattered across the stones. His head lolled to the side as Rowan tugged him down the alleyway. The *Jackdaw* was still a long way off in the opposite direction, but Rowan's destination lurked ahead.

They stumbled from the alley mouth into a wider street, lit by the harvest moon and little else. But still he could see the glitter of the canal on the other side.

Rowan's steps faltered. Could he really do this? He'd killed people before, certainly, but it had been a distant thing, a cannon or rifle shot toward an enemy ship. He'd even been commended for shooting a pirate captain back in his navy days. But this would be close. Intentional.

He continued on toward the side of the canal, Wallis lolling against his shoulder. Rowan's heart hardened as he thought of the 'cargo' back on the *Jackdaw,* waiting in the dark and cramped quarters of the secret hold to be sold off on foreign shores where there was no possibility of making it back or being saved.

Nausea curdled in Rowan's gut. If he'd known about the true business of the *Jackdaw* months ago, he'd never have joined up after his release from the navy. But Wallis did know. He and Captain Gladwin and their now missing loyalists were in this together. And Rowan was determined to tear them apart.

"Here we are," Rowan said. They stopped at the edge of the canal, the sheer stone wall dropping straight down into the dark, shining water at their feet.

Wallis glanced around. "This ain't th' docks!" he protested. Rowan turned so they were face-to-face, gripping both of Wallis's shoulders as he wavered.

"It's not the docks," he agreed coldly. His fingers tightened on Wallis's shoulders. "Do you know why I've brought you here?"

Wallis blinked rapidly, his drunken mind trying to wrap around Rowan's words. His breath wafted in the chilled air, foul-smelling from liquor and acrid vomit.

"Cause you're a righ' lil shit," Wallis slurred. "I know you've been gettin' th' others left behind."

Rowan laughed, surprised that not only did Wallis suspect him of the disappearances, but had the cognitive ability to remember that fact even with all the alcohol clouding his mind. A small bit of satisfaction curled through Rowan's chest.

"That's right," Rowan said. "But do you know *why?*"

Wallis didn't answer. He seemed to have no concept of the danger he currently found himself in. The dark water lapped softly against the wall, and Rowan took half a step closer.

"It's because of those people in the secret hold."

Wallis's eyes widened with bleary understanding. Rowan did

not give him a chance to defend himself. He took a deep breath and pushed.

Wallis crashed into the water and sank, then resurfaced with a shuddering gasp. Rowan tucked his hands into his pockets to keep them from shaking, and watched Wallis struggle. The splashes echoed down the deserted street as Wallis gasped and choked, sinking beneath the water again and again until his struggles lessened, and finally he did not resurface.

Rowan scuffed the toe of his boot against the street, conflicting feelings twining through his insides. Sickness and satisfaction both. He gazed into the dark waters as if he could divine his future in their drowning depths. He'd just killed a man, and there was more killing yet to be done tonight.

DARKNESS CLOAKED the *Jackdaw* as Rowan set foot on it once again. The crew was either abed sleeping off the drink, or spending the night in the arms of hired companionship. They wouldn't return until dawn when the *Jackdaw* was scheduled to catch the morning tides out of Hallenburgh. Rowan intended to be long gone by then. Which meant he had only a few hours to carry out the final stages of his plan.

"Rowan."

Rowan's friend, Warrick Shaw, approached with a shuttered lantern in hand. He'd taken a double shift of guard duty, not willing to get his hands as dirty as Rowan's now were.

"How'd it go?" Warrick raised the lantern to show his face. He was taller than Rowan by a few inches, and a year older. His light brown hair hung over one side of his forehead, the patchy beginnings of a beard and mustache dusting his cheeks and upper lip. After Rowan left the navy and joined the crew of the *Jackdaw*, Warrick had been his only friend. He was the one Rowan had told when he'd first witnessed Captain Gladwin and Maxwell Wallis loading the ship with a group of captives late at night when the majority of the crew were asleep. They'd stayed up on guard duty together night after night, talking about what they should do. In the end, it was Rowan who'd made the plans and put them in motion.

"Face down in the canal," Rowan said quietly. He still didn't quite know how he felt about murdering a man, even if that man was human trafficker scum.

Warrick briefly placed a comforting hand on his shoulder, long enough to calm the worst of his warring thoughts.

"Now what?" Warrick knew very well what the next step was, but, like the murder of Wallis, neither of them quite wanted to speak it aloud.

"Just keep to your post and make sure no one interferes," Rowan said. The evenness in his voice was hard won. He would not show weakness, nor back down now. Not when his plan was so close to fruition. Warrick nodded and retreated. Rowan made his way below.

Rowan didn't see another living soul until he stepped into the circle of orange light cast by another shuttered lantern. The guardsman glanced up, his hand curling around the handle of the loaded pistol on top of the barrel he was using as a table. His eyes narrowed at seeing Rowan, who was not part of the captain's inner circle.

"What'er you doin' here?"

Rowan lowered his gaze respectfully to the guardsman's feet, which were planted on a disguised hatch. Under it lay ten young men and women who'd been kidnapped—or perhaps sold by their parents—from all over Avardel. More than that, Rowan knew a lot of them were probably there because society had deemed them *immoral* by Avardel's strict standards.

Rowan plastered on a wry smile and pulled out a half-full bottle of brandy from behind his back. His other hand tightened around the wooden handle of the knife in his pocket.

"First Mate Wallis told me to bring you this."

He didn't miss the way the guardsman's eyes lit at the sight of amber liquid sloshing behind the clear glass. This would've all been much more difficult if Captain Gladwin wasn't predisposed to hire men much like himself. Greedy drunks whose morals could be loosened with drink and coin.

"Give it 'ere then." The guardsman's hand left the pistol to reach for the bottle. Rowan stepped forward, his boots thumping the boards above the hidden prisoners. He held the bottle out.

As the man's fingers brushed the neck of it, Rowan released his grip. The man lunged forward to catch it, and in the same moment, Rowan drew his knife and drove it up under the man's chin. It met resistance as it slid through the soft flesh beneath his jaw, through the roof of his mouth, and into the brain matter behind his eyes.

Everything became still in a second as the bottle crashed to the floor and the guardsman's lunge halted on Rowan's blade. Dark blood gushed over Rowan's hand, and he couldn't help but stare as the man's eyes dulled.

This was worse than drowning Wallis. Rowan thought he might puke. Two men dead by Rowan's hand in one night, and one more to go before he was done.

A twinge of guilt sliced through his chest. He did not even know this man's name. Yet he'd taken his life. He had to remind himself it was all to save these innocents, and gain his own freedom in the process. After eight years in the Marran navy and months under the thumb of Captain Gladwin, he could no longer stand to be ruled by the whims of other men. He would become his own master. His own captain.

He yanked the dagger back out, and the man's body slumped over the top of the barrel, another torrent of blood gushing and running down its sides to drip onto the trapdoor. Rowan waited in silence for a few moments, listening for an alarm. None came.

Only the drip of blood and the labored breathing beneath his feet broke the silence.

With great effort, Rowan pushed both barrel and dead man off the trapdoor. He felt around the edges for a catch or keyhole but found nothing. He sat back on his heels. Blood and brandy continued to trickle down the sides of the barrel, running along the cracks in the boards between the crimson smears his hands had made. They dripped down around the edges of the hatch and pooled in a knot at the center.

A quiet, fearful whimper emanated from beneath the boards. Rowan leaned forward again, digging his fingers into the knot and feeling for a keyhole. He found it, small and smooth-edged. A smile twitched at the corner of Rowan's mouth.

"I'll get you out. Don't worry," Rowan whispered. The captives below probably couldn't hear him, but it was a promise he intended to keep.

He dug the tip of the knife into the lock and with a few deft twists, it popped open. The hatch opened easily on hinges oiled with blood to reveal the face of a young woman, crimson droplets clinging to her cheeks like tears. She flinched back from him, but there was nowhere to go. The secret hold was only a few feet deep and ran beneath the floorboards, wide enough to hold a dozen grown men if they lay shoulder to shoulder.

"I'm not here to hurt you." Rowan held up his hands, then quickly lowered them again upon remembering they were bloody. He wiped them on the knees of his trousers. "You're free to go. If you go quietly and quickly." He held out a hand to her again, now only slightly bloodstained. Her eyes widened, but she clasped it and allowed herself to be dragged up as if from a grave. The rest of the captives clambered up after her, wary-eyed.

"You will go up those stairs to the deck. The guardsman with the patchy beard will let you ashore. But do not be seen by anyone else. After you step foot on land you'll be on your own, but you'll be free."

The young woman nodded silently and fled with the others.

Rowan wished he could help them more. Being alone and penniless was not ideal but it was a hell of a lot better than being sold on foreign shores.

Now, on to the last.

Only the captives' faint, hurried footsteps overhead accompanied his own as he approached the captain's door. On the other side, Captain Alfred Gladwin slept. The third man who would die tonight. The third man Rowan would kill.

Rowan pressed his palm to the dark wood of the door. Just a bit more blood, and he would be free. This ship would be his.

The brass handle turned easily beneath his hand. Why wasn't it locked? He gripped the knife tightly and entered. The room within was dark and bare. A rug. A table and chairs. And beneath the moonlit windows, the bed where the captain lay. Rowan crept a few steps into the room, careful not to make a sound. And it was this silence that saved him.

The softest shush of a footstep on the carpet sounded behind him, and he whirled as a blade slashed past the place his head had been. Rowan struck out, his own knife barely missing bare skin.

"You thought you could kill me as I slept?" Captain Gladwin growled, regaining his footing and advancing on Rowan. He hadn't been in bed at all. Rowan could see now even in the dim light that the blankets were heaped over pillows in the shape of a man. Gladwin had emerged from the shadows behind the door, barefoot and dressed in only his trousers, hair still lank from sleep. The steel of a naked blade gleamed in his hand.

"Wallis is dead, and your captives are freed." Rowan's voice did not waver as his heart did, even as he retreated back a step.

"You little whelp." Gladwin sneered. "Wallis suspected you were behind our missing crew."

"Didn't stop him from letting me buy him drinks. Funny what greed does to a man." Rowan jabbed at him, and Gladwin dodged. He was bigger than Rowan. Older, more muscled, and more experienced. Rowan swallowed down a lump of nerves. Why didn't Gladwin call for the crew? Did he think that much of himself, that another man coming to kill him in the night was something he could handle all on his own?

"And greed does not have its hooks in you?" Gladwin advanced another step, testing. This time Rowan held his ground.

"I'm greedy for more than money." Rowan lunged, slashing at

Gladwin's knife hand and missing. He had little hope of getting inside the larger man's guard. But if he could disarm him, there was a chance. Rowan silently thanked whatever luck had gotten him this far without alerting the others. How long had Captain Gladwin been waiting in the shadows? Certainly not long enough to grab a pistol and load it. Otherwise he would've shot Rowan in the back and ended it all quickly.

"You think you're better than we are?" Gladwin snarled.

His back was to the open door. Rowan knew no help would be coming from Warrick. He'd made his stance on murder perfectly clear, but Rowan didn't want to be caught with his back to the door if the other crew members came to Gladwin's aid.

Of course, that also cut off Rowan's only avenue of escape.

Rowan feinted to the left, nicking Gladwin's free hand, and Gladwin slashed back, barely missing the fabric of Rowan's shirt. He advanced until the back of Rowan's legs hit the edge of the table. There would be no more retreat—Rowan had to fight.

Gladwin lunged forward, knocking the knife from Rowan's hand and sending it skittering across the tabletop. Rowan grabbed at it, but instead found a wooden salt well and flung its contents into Gladwin's face. Gladwin hissed, one hand going to his eyes. Rowan tried to dart out from between him and the table, but Gladwin recovered quickly, grabbing the front of Rowan's shirt and shoving him back against the table.

Even with his eyes red and streaming, Gladwin was stronger than him, and Rowan couldn't break his grip no matter how he struggled. Rowan's leg came up to knee Gladwin in the groin, but Gladwin stabbed down through the meat of Rowan's hand, effectively pinning him to the table. Rowan's body didn't even register the pain at first. Too much adrenaline pumped through his veins.

He struggled, scrabbling at the tabletop with his free hand for his knife or something he could bludgeon Gladwin with, but found nothing. Not even a godsdamned fork. Gladwin's grip moved to Rowan's neck, and he knocked Rowan's head against the table. Rowan's ears rang with the force of it.

"You could've left well enough alone. Now you're gonna be the one in the secret hold," Gladwin sneered.

Fuck. That was much worse than simply dying. He'd set out to gain ultimate freedom, and now he'd be a prisoner for life.

"Just kill me," he hissed. The pain in his hand now made itself known, searing through his nerves along with the fear of his future.

A gasp sounded from the direction of the door. Was it Warrick after all? One of the other crew members? Gladwin turned, his hand still gripping Rowan's hair.

It was the young woman from the secret hold, her eyes wide and darting from Rowan to Gladwin.

"Who the fuck—"

Rowan's hand finally closed around a cold metal object. A fucking fork after all. He stabbed it into Gladwin's cheek with as much force as he could muster, tarnished silver tines sinking into flesh with a sickening squelch and hitting teeth or bone beneath. Adrenaline flooded Rowan's senses, and before Gladwin could cry out, he wrenched the knife out of his hand, and drove the blade hilt-deep into Gladwin's side. Only a wheeze escaped Gladwin, his punctured lung stealing his voice. They thumped down to the rug together, the sound muffled.

"Go," Rowan rasped to the woman. She fled.

Rowan gripped the back of Gladwin's neck as he twisted the knife deeper. Gladwin coughed, blood splattering from his lips. Rowan leaned close.

"You're right," Rowan whispered. "I'm no better than you." Gladwin stared at him, gasping as blood filled his abdomen and lungs. The captain's limbs loosened, and the life drained from his eyes. Blood spread in a pool around him. Finally, the last exhalation left Gladwin's parted lips.

Rowan sat in silence next to the body, listening for the expected commotion of the crew waking to the noise. But there was nothing. They slept like the drunken dead tonight. All the better for him.

Pain lanced through his hand as he got up. He clamped it under his opposite arm, trying to staunch the flow, and stumbled over to the bed, grabbed a discarded shirt, and wrapped it around his hand in a makeshift bandage. He tied it tight around the wound, then picked up the captain's sword and made his way up to the deck.

As soon as Rowan set foot onto the main deck, a veil lifted from his mind. The tension in his shoulders eased. He closed his eyes and lifted his face to the sky, breathing deeply of the briny sea air, chilled by the onset of autumn. His bloodied blond hair fell away from his face, and the tip of the captain's sword in his hand dropped to rest against the wood at his feet.

His eyes slid open again, gazing up at the dark shapes of the masts against the blue-black dome of the sky. His feet moved of their own accord, sword tip scraping across the deck as he walked to the rail. Fingertips whispered across the polished wood, leaving crimson streaks. And the ship whispered back to him. The creak of the ropes and groan of the timbers greeting their new captain. He looked across the harbor to the Sunset Sea beyond. The path ahead was clear. The world was his for the taking, and his freedom called him like a siren song on the soft music of the waves.

"Rowan?"

Rowan turned to find Warrick behind him, brow knit with worry.

"Did the captives make it out okay?" Rowan's voice had a dreamy quality to it, as if his mind already skimmed the waves.

Warrick frowned. "Yes, but you're covered in blood. Are you okay? Is the captain..."

"I'm fine." He could almost feel the thrum of the sea through his fingertips pressed reverently to the rail. Beckoning.

"Now what?" Warrick asked.

Rowan turned back to the moon gilded water.

"Now we sail."

• • •

As DAWN BROKE over the horizon, the crew of the newly-dubbed *Siren Song* began to wake. One by one they found and followed the bloody drag marks down the hall and up to the deck. They found a young man there. Many among them did not even know his name. Yet his ice blue eyes reflected the red sunrise at their backs and struck awe into them. He stood with his back straight, sword held loosely in one hand and a brace of pistols across his shoulders. Dried blood stained his simple clothes, his white-blond hair loose around his ears. At his feet lay the crumpled and headless body of Captain Gladwin.

"I am Rowan Faine," the young man said, his voice clear and strong. His gaze swept over them, meeting each crew member's eye one by one. "I am your captain now. And if you don't like it"—he pointed the tip of the sword toward the side of the ship, the waters stretching red with sunrise around them—"then fly away home."

Chapter 5

THE ROLLING GREEN SEA

LOGAN CROWDER

Summer, 1659

The coins of Logan's last navy pay clinked into his hand. Less than it could've been, but still enough to get him where he was going.

"Sure you want to leave?" the quartermaster of the *M.W.S. Wolf* asked. Logan hitched the knapsack full of all his meager possessions up his shoulder and smiled up at the man.

"My family's waiting."

The quartermaster raised his eyebrows but didn't comment. The whole crew knew Logan had been sold into indenture by his parents at the age of nine. Did that mean his parents didn't want him? For some, like his best friend Rowan—who'd left the navy the year before—the answer was yes. But Logan's indenture had been a last resort for his parents. His father had lost his job and couldn't afford to feed all their children. At the age of nine, Logan was the only one old enough to work. They couldn't find an apprenticeship, and then the navy had come calling with the perfect solution.

It didn't mean his parents didn't love him, despite what the rest of the crew said. His father was a good man. His mother was as caring as any mother. They were just down on their luck.

Now, on his seventeenth birthday, Logan was legally an adult. His wages would no longer go to his parents, and he was free to leave the navy. He hadn't seen his parents or four younger siblings in eight years, and hadn't heard from them in almost five. At first the letters had come every few months. His family telling him how much they loved him, missed him, how sorry they were, how much his wages were helping them in a time of need. All imparted in his father's neat, looping handwriting. And Logan was proud of that. He worked hard every day, knowing he contributed some small part in keeping his family fed.

When he hit the age of twelve, his sister Laney wrote to tell him his childhood cat had perished beneath the wheels of a carriage. It was the last letter he received. But they were still receiving his wages, and that meant they were still alive. He held no bitterness toward them, though maybe he should have. He was glad his suffering had been for something.

It didn't mean they didn't love him.

Logan pocketed the money, the first fruits of his labor he'd actually tangibly held in his hand. He saluted the quartermaster for the last time, and made his way down the gangplank to dry land. He paid a man a copper to hitch a ride on the back of an empty hay cart returning to the countryside after delivering its cargo to the dockside military stables here in Yrenmoor, Marra's capitol city.

For half a day, the cart trundled and bumped over first the cobbled streets of the city, then the dirt roads of the countryside. Its movement beneath him was oddly soothing, reminiscent of the sway of a ship. He watched the fields pass him by, green wheat heads undulating like waves between the shores of gray stone walls and hedgerows bright with summer berries. It had been the same going the other way as he sat teary-eyed in the back of the military cart with four other boys, a few days after his ninth birthday. It was wondrous really, the landscape of his childhood so closely resembled the seascape in which he'd come of age. Maybe slipping back into his old life, rejoining his family, would not be so different.

The farmer lent him a wide brimmed hat to shade his face, and the miles of dirt road disappeared behind him. A small pang shadowed his heart. He would never sail again. Never feel the salt spray on his face or watch the blue waves. He'd miss it, like he already missed Rowan. But unlike Rowan, he had a home to return to among this rolling green sea of wheat.

He thought of the last words Rowan had said to him as he stepped off the *Wolf* last year. They'd hugged tight, not willing to let one another go too soon. But Rowan had aged out and he couldn't stay and wait for Logan to do the same. He wanted freedom. Nonetheless, he'd asked Logan to find him when the time came. They could be free together. They could have adventures, the two of them against the world.

As tempting as the offer was, Logan wanted to go home. He'd offered to bring Rowan with him. But Rowan belonged to the sea; that was his home.

The wagon stopped at a farmhouse at midday, and Logan paid the farmer's wife another copper for a meal. He ate it sitting on the edge of a stone well, drinking sweet, cold water with a tin ladle from the well bucket and marveling at the softness of the bread. Ships never had soft bread. They never had good food at all. Especially if you were an indentured sailor.

"Golden Valley is just over the ridge," the farmer said, after putting away his cart and horse. "Sorry I couldn't take you all the way."

"I'm used to exercise," Logan assured him. Dusting the crumbs from his trousers, he hopped down from the edge of the well, wavering a bit on legs that were still accustomed to the roll of the sea. He offered the hat back, but the farmer bid him keep it. So Logan set off down the road, his boots kicking up dust as he went. After an hour or two, he finally crested the ridge and saw the town of Golden Valley stretching out below him.

The wheat fields that gave his hometown its name were still

green with a lively summer flush, contrasting the red brick buildings and thatched roofs. The bells of the boys' school where his father had taught tolled the hour as Logan set his feet finally on the path homeward. He wondered if his father had gotten his position back, teaching the young men of Marra's elite families.

The sun was well on its way to setting by the time the dirt road turned to cobblestone once again. His feet seemed to recognize the way his hazy childhood memories did not. He tipped his hat to a few passersby, his mood lifting with thoughts of the imminent reunion with his family. He wondered if Laney still embroidered flowers on everything, if his brothers had apprenticeships or attended school.

Logan stopped outside the gate of his childhood home. The cottage beyond, familiar despite all his distance, still had a blue door and paned glass windows. The thatch on the roof needed replacing. Maybe Logan could learn how. He was used to working high up in the rigging of a swaying ship, how hard could working on a stationary roof be?

He took a deep breath, nerves creeping in for the first time. What if his hard-earned wages hadn't been enough? What if his family was suffering? Rowan had always said he was too optimistic for his own good, but that didn't mean he didn't sometimes have doubts. Before his mind could spiral into useless circles, he quickly made his way up the front path and knocked on the door, a small nervous smile on his face.

The smile dropped when a stranger answered.

"Yes?" The plump young woman wiped flour from her hands on a white apron.

"I...um..." Nerves tightened Logan's chest. "D-do the Crowders still live here?"

The young woman peered at him. "They moved a long time ago."

"Do you know where?"

She thought for a moment, then pointed down the street to the east. "Down that way, three streets over with the green door. The curtains have flowers embroidered on them."

Logan thanked her and trudged away, trying not to let his worry overtake him. His family had gone through tough times. He'd already known that much. So it shouldn't have surprised him that they'd moved. And Laney's signature flower embroidery on the curtains could only be a good sign, right?

But the worry only increased as the houses lining the streets got smaller and more run down as he walked. How poor had they become? Were his siblings okay? Dread coiled through his chest at the thought his brothers had been shipped off to the navy too. Sure, Logan had come out of it relatively unscathed, but he'd seen battle and death far earlier than any human was meant to, and the Marran invasion of Kefrye was still active and bloody. Even as a child he'd been painfully aware that any action he took on board the *M.W.S. Wolf* could cause someone's death, whether it be friend or foe. The only reason he'd gotten through it, the only reason he'd survived at all, had been Rowan. Rowan did all the things Logan didn't have the stomach for. Rowan defended Logan against any other sailors who bullied him or wished him harm.

Logan let his mind wander toward thoughts of his friend instead of giving in to his worries. Logan hadn't seen him since Rowan's own seventeenth birthday, but there'd been stirrings and rumors among the crew of the *Wolf* that the young upstart pirate dogging the coasts of Avardel and Marra was actually Rowan. All Logan knew was Rowan planned to stay at sea, where he belonged, with big dreams of freedom in the sun and waves.

Wherever he'd ended up, Logan hoped he was okay and that someday they would see each other again.

Before he knew it, Logan reached the house the young woman had described. It was much smaller than the one Logan had lived in as a child. He couldn't imagine it contained more than two rooms. Glassless shuttered windows punctuated the face of the one-story stone cottage, topped by a moldy thatched roof. The faded door could barely be called green, but the corner of a dirty white curtain poked out from the edge of one shutter, embroidered with the little flowers Laney was so fond of sewing with whatever scraps of colored thread she could find.

The dread in Logan's chest sharpened, but he stepped up to the faded door before he could lose his nerve. His knock went unanswered for long minutes, and he knocked again. Shuffling sounded on the other side of the door, and it finally swung open.

Logan caught his breath as he found himself face-to-face with his father, Abel Crowder. They were of a height now, and Logan took a hasty step back. Somehow he'd still expected his father to be taller, the confident and smart man who'd joyfully taught his children to read, and swung Logan up onto his shoulders on summer walks through the town.

The man he found before him now was nothing like that. His skin was sallow, and the golden curls they shared were dull and greasy, a beard shadowing his previously clean-shaven jaw. His clothes were unkempt and dirty. And when he spoke, the scent of sour ale wafted from his mouth.

"What do you want?" The school teacher's proper manner of speaking Logan remembered was still there, though slurred by drink.

"I..." Logan didn't know what to say. Did his father not recognize him?

"Well? Spit it out."

"It's me, Da. It's Logan."

His father leaned against the doorjamb, eyes narrowing as they swept Logan from head to toe. Logan suddenly felt like a piece of livestock being examined for its potential worth. Any hope he'd harbored of being welcomed back into a loving family's embrace quickly dwindled to almost nothing. Finally, their eyes met once again.

"I thought we sent you to the navy," he said, his tone almost accusing.

"Y-you did. But I'm seventeen now. I got out."

"Who taught you to stutter like that? Not me." His father had always held his children to the same standard of eloquence as he did his students. But now his words were harsh. Logan drew himself up and squared his shoulders. He tried to peer past his father's shoulder but couldn't discern anything in the dim interior of the cottage.

"How is everyone? Mum? Laney? The boys?"

"So you're out of the navy?" his father asked, completely ignoring Logan's question.

"Yes." His father eyed the knapsack on Logan's back. The condition of his clothes. The quality of his navy-issued boots.

"Why are you here then? Do you have any money? Do you have a job?"

Logan blinked at him. Where had the father of his childhood gone? And who was this dull and lifeless person who'd taken his place?

"I don't have a job yet," Logan answered. He wanted to run away from this man. To go back to believing his family remained as he'd left them. "I only have my last month's wages."

His father stuck his hand out. "Hand them over then."

Logan took another step back. This man was not his father. He was Abel Crowder undoubtedly. But he was not his father. "Tell me where the others are."

Abel's nose wrinkled in distaste.

"Tell me," Logan demanded when the silence stretched on too long.

"The boys are apprenticed. Laney is married off. Your mum's dead."

All the blood drained from Logan's face. Mum was dead? Laney married? She was no older than sixteen.

"H-How did mum die? When?" he asked quietly.

Abel shrugged, as if the death of his wife, the mother of his five children, presented nothing more than an inconvenience.

"What about Laney? When did she marry? Where is she? Where are the boys apprenticed?" Tears pricked behind Logan's eyes, and he squeezed the strap of his knapsack to keep them from spilling over.

"Are you going to give me the money?"

Logan blanched. "No."

"Then why should I tell you? Your wages weren't enough to save your mum, and now you have no job, so what good are you?"

Logan's head spun. "Fine." He dug in his pocket and handed over the small pile of silver and copper. Abel counted them with narrowed eyes, then looked back up at Logan.

"Truth is. I don't remember where any of them are." With that, he stepped back and slammed the door in Logan's face, rattling the shutters.

Logan stood in front of the unfamiliar cottage, stunned, till evening began to creep across the streets. He tried not to cry. All at once, the family he'd dreamed of coming back to, of being welcomed by, was gone. It had worn away in his absence like a rock beneath beating waves. Maybe it had never been there at all, and all those warm memories of childhood surrounded by the sea of golden wheat were something he'd dreamed up to keep himself sane.

His mother was dead. His father was a drunk. But that didn't mean his siblings would be the same. He had to find them.

He finally stepped away from the cottage and made his way down the street. He caught the butcher closing up shop.

"Sir, do you know the Crowders?" He thought he recognized the man's curled mustache.

The butcher tucked the shop key into his pocket. "The Crowders? Abel and his family?"

"Yes. Can you tell me what became of the children? Where they're apprenticed and who the daughter married?"

The butcher peered at him through the growing gloom. "And why are you asking?"

"I'm their eldest son, Logan."

The butcher's expression cleared, perhaps recognizing the family resemblance.

"I don't quite know where they ended up. The boys are all in different towns. I don't know the name of your sister's husband either. I'm sorry."

The bitterness climbed to the back of his throat now. Abel had scattered their family to unknown corners, and Logan had no inkling of whether his siblings were near, or in the far reaches of Marra. He had no idea whether Laney had a say in who she had married. Logan backtracked to the cottage with the green door and knocked. When no one answered, he pounded. But his father was either ignoring him or had passed out from drink.

Full night descended by the time Logan gave up. He wandered through the town's deserted streets, wracking his brain for any ideas of where his siblings might be, or who he could ask. Finally, he found himself standing at the wrought iron fence encircling the boys' school, where all the trouble for his family had begun. Back then, his father had told them he'd been fired because of money, but now Logan wasn't so sure. Had his father been a drunk even back then? Or had he truly only spiraled after losing his job, giving up his firstborn child, and losing his wife?

Logan slipped through a broken gap in the bars, no doubt frequently used by the students to sneak out. The school's grounds were quiet and dark, and Logan found a little alcove at the back of the building. He shoved a few pieces of firewood out of the way and curled up within its shelter. He tucked his hands under his armpits and pulled the borrowed hat down over his face. As he fell asleep, he vowed to search till he found them.

Two DAYS later Logan milled about the market square, waiting for someone to drop a piece of food he could snatch up, or a vendor to turn away for just long enough. He'd given all his coin to his father and received nothing in return but bitterness. His back ached from sleeping in the alcove, and his stomach grumbled persistently. Worst of all, he'd had absolutely no luck finding so much as a lead on any of his siblings.

Finally, a pear rolled out of someone's basket. He darted from between the stalls and snatched it up. His teeth had almost pierced the delicate green skin when a shock of blond curls flashed in the corner of his vision.

Logan recognized her instantly, even though the last time they'd seen each other she'd been a child of only eight, and him nine. Laney wore a marigold-colored dress, embroidered at the neck and cuffs with those flowers he remembered so fondly, and her hair bounced loose around her shoulders. She carried a chubby baby on her hip, a half-full basket on the other arm. She breezed past him without a second glance.

He wanted to go after her, but his body was frozen, the pear halfway to his mouth. What would he say? Would she even recognize him? Would she hate him for being gone so long even though it wasn't his fault?

"Oi! Did you pay for that?" A nearby vendor grabbed his wrist.

"They dropped it. I—" Logan stuttered. He tried to wrench his arm away from the vendor. He needed to talk to Laney.

"Don't lie." The vendor shook him. "This is a respectable town, young man. A town where we don't take what doesn't belong to us." Maybe he hadn't seen Logan pick it up, or maybe he was simply that incensed by even the idea of wrongdoing.

"I'm sorry, sir. You can have it back. I didn't even bite it. See?" Logan offered the pear to him, desperate to get this over with as quickly as possible. He needed to find Laney before she disappeared and he was back to having no leads.

By now the commotion had gathered a small crowd. All of them staring at Logan as if he were the worst kind of criminal and not a hungry pear thief. Not even a thief really. He'd picked it up off the ground.

"We'll let the constable deal with you," the vendor said, snatching the pear back.

"No really. I didn't steal it. It was on the ground!" Logan protested, but the crowd didn't seem to believe him. How many of these people had seen him as a child, chattering away to his parents on a sunny market day? Now he was nothing but a lowlife thief in their eyes. This town was no longer Logan's home; his father had made that abundantly clear. He was a stranger here.

Boots tromped over the cobbles, and Logan wrenched his arm out of the vendor's grip. He had to get out of here. He turned to run, only to find a constable directly behind him. The man seized him in a much stronger grip than the vendor had. "What's going on here?" he asked in a rumbling voice.

"This young man is a thief," the vendor said haughtily.

"I'm not!" Logan protested again. But it was no use. The constable simply took the vendor at his word over the scrawny young man who'd been sleeping rough for several nights.

"Tell it to the magistrate," the constable said. Logan struggled against his grip as the constable dragged him through the crowd. He cast around for help, for anyone to defend him and say he really had just picked the stupid fruit up off the ground. His gaze met Laney's, and her eyes widened. Did she recognize him?

But before he knew it, the constable dragged him into a brick building at the edge of the market square.

"Got a thief here," the constable said to another man, who lounged on a chair tilted back against the wall.

"I'm not a thief! I found the pear on the ground!" Logan exclaimed, as the constable forced him into an iron-barred cell. The door clanged shut like a death knell.

"Sounds like thievery to me," the other man scoffed. Logan gaped at them, the last vestiges of nostalgia for his hometown shattering. He'd always been so happy here growing up, and thoughts of his peaceful town and loving family had kept him going over the hard years at sea. Now his family was gone, and he was no longer a child. He'd always held Golden Valley in a special, protected place in his mind, a safe haven he would one day return to and live out the rest of his life in peace. As it turned out, that place did not exist. His home was just another part of the wider, crueler world.

"Get him on the books for the magistrate," the constable told the other man.

"Can't." The man tilted his chair off the wall, its front feet crashing back to the stone floor. "Magistrate is on business in Yrenmoor. He won't be back for a week at least."

Logan's fingers went cold. Was he going to be stuck here for a week?

The constable groaned. "I don't wanna babysit this whelp for a week, let alone feed him." He glanced back at Logan, who still stood with his hands around the bars.

"Deal with him yourself then." The other man shrugged.

Oh, that did not sound good. Logan backed up a step, but the constable reached in and seized him by the wrist.

"C'mere boy." He dragged Logan's arm through the bars so Logan's front hit the iron. To the other man he said, "Get it."

Logan struggled futilely as the man crossed to the stove in the corner and drew out an iron rod, its T-shaped end glowing orange with heat.

Fuck, fuck, fuck. They just had that shit ready to go? No trial? No opportunity to defend himself?

"Hey, I'll wait till the magistrate comes back. I don't even eat much, I swear. Just—" The words came out all in a rush, practically incoherent as Logan struggled and the constable forced his hand open and held it in a death grip. The other man crossed the room and with no hesitation whatsoever, pressed the thief's brand into the heel of Logan's palm. Logan's scream bounced off the stone walls of the jail as searing pain raced up his arm. Little curls of smoke wafted up from where the brand met his skin. It only stayed there for a moment before the man took it away and stowed it back in the stove. The constable released Logan, and he sank down against the bars, sniffling and cradling his hand.

"You'll be released in the morning," the constable said. Neither remorse nor pleasure tinged his voice. This was simply business for him. "Best not stick around after that, boy. We don't take kindly to thieves around here."

They'd illustrated that perfectly well. Logan nodded, and the two men left him alone.

IN THE MORNING, as promised, they released him. Logan blinked as he stepped out into the light, waiting for his eyes to adjust. His hand still burned, and they hadn't given him a bandage or anything, so he held it close to his side, careful not to let the raw, seared skin touch anything. When his vision cleared, he saw her.

Laney stood on the other side of the street. She wore the same dress as before, the baby once again on her hip.

She wouldn't be here if she hadn't recognized him, right?

Logan crossed the street quickly, his injury momentarily forgotten. But when he got close, she walked away, obviously signaling for him to follow. Logan walked several paces behind her. Her baby, a rosy-cheeked thing with the signature waves of blond Crowder hair, waved its arm at Logan, fingers splayed out like a starfish. Finally, they reached a smaller, more shaded street.

Laney settled on a bench, shifting the baby to her lap. Logan hesitated, then sat gingerly beside her.

"You're back," Laney said, without preamble. Her voice was soft and calm, contradicting the tears that gathered in her eyes. Logan fought the urge to hug her, unsure where they stood.

"You recognize me?"

"Of course." Her voice broke, the tears finally spilling over her lashes. Her baby cooed at her and patted at her chin with its little chubby fingers. Logan couldn't stand it anymore, he wrapped his arms around her shoulders. She leaned into his chest, clutching the baby tight between them. Her shoulders shook, and when she spoke, he could barely hear her between the sniffles.

"Da said you were dead."

"What?" Logan pushed her back a bit to look at her face, wincing as the brand flared in pain.

"After I wrote you about Kitty"—they truly had been uncreative about naming pets as children—"Da said the navy had written to him that you'd drowned. He showed us the letter." She wiped her eyes on her sleeve, and the baby cooed again. Laney smiled down at it through her tears.

No wonder their letters had stopped. Father had told them he died. But why? The navy had still been sending them his wages. Where did they think that money came from? Or had Father hidden it from them?

"What happened after that?"

Laney told him everything. Their father had been unable to find academic work again, and refused to do manual labor that was 'beneath' him. So their mother had taken work in the boarding school's laundry, coming home exhausted every night to an increasingly bitter husband who spent so much of their meager money on drink. Laney, only a child herself, was left to care for their three younger brothers.

Then the cat had died, and a month later their father had told them Logan was dead too. At the news, their mother fell into melancholy, and was fired from the laundry. She fell ill. As their mother wasted away, Laney got a job at the tailor's cutting fabric, and when she died when Laney was still shy of fifteen, the widower tailor offered to marry Laney to his son to ease their father's burden. Laney had managed to find their brothers apprenticeships after that, not wanting them to stay with their drunken father.

"I never knew how Da could afford all that drink," Laney finished. Her tears had dried up, but sniffles still punctuated her words. "But now...I guess he must have been using your wages for it."

Logan sat in stunned silence for a moment. For the last eight years he'd toiled every day. Breaking his back in the hot sun. Cleaning blood off the deck. Climbing the rigging to the point of dizziness. Fearing he would not survive the next battle or storm. Watching Rowan take a lashing for mistakes Logan had made. But he'd done it all with the knowledge his meager wages were feeding his family.

It had all been a lie. His family had suffered along with him. All because their father's pride had driven him to drink away Logan's hard work.

It wasn't Logan's meager wages that had killed their mother. It was grief and their father's lies.

Logan tried to clamp down the righteous anger that surged through his chest. He didn't want to scare Laney.

"Are you okay? Are you happy? What about the boys?" he asked. He needed to know even if they'd suffered through all of that, they were okay now. He didn't think he could stand it if they weren't.

Laney sniffled once again and pet her baby's soft, downy curls. "I named him after you, you know."

Now it was Logan's eyes that prickled with tears as he looked down at his nephew. He reached a tentative hand to pet little Logan's hair as well.

"I thought it must have been awfully frightening to drown," Laney continued. "Naming him after you seemed like a good thing to do. I'm glad you got to meet him."

"You're happy then?" Logan's voice was awed as the baby smiled at him.

"I'm content enough. And the boys are all doing well in their apprenticeships, though I don't get to see them often. They're all so far away."

Relief washed through him, and he reached up to dash a tear from his cheek, accidentally revealing the thief's brand.

"Logan!" Laney snatched his hand, wide-eyed at the raw, burned flesh. "Is this why they released you so quickly?"

Logan nodded.

"What are you going to do? No one will give you a job with that on your hand."

Unease curdled in his gut, harkening back to his father's words a few days before. *Your wages weren't enough to save your mum, and now you have no job, so what good are you?* But no,

Laney wasn't judging his worth, worry for him etched across her brow.

Logan could spend the rest of his life trying to take care of his siblings. Trying to make up for all those years he'd been gone. All those years they'd thought he was dead. But they were doing well now, and with Logan branded as a criminal, he would be nothing but a burden to them.

"Can I write to you?" Logan asked. Laney nodded, seeming to understand immediately the path he would take.

He had to return to what he knew.

They talked for an hour more before little Logan started to fuss, and Laney had to return home to feed him and help her husband with the tailor's shop. She gave Logan a few coins to ease his passage back to Yrenmoor, and Logan hugged her fiercely, unsure when, or if, he would see her again.

Logan's feet carried him from the sea of green wheat back to the farmhouse, where he caught a ride on the hay cart again going the other direction. More than once he let tears drip down his face, heedless of the farmer driving the cart or who might pass them on the road. Until finally all his tears were shed, and he felt hollow. Golden Valley disappeared behind him, and Logan wished for his siblings to be happy and to find their places in the world. His own was yet undefined.

Late in the day, Yrenmoor appeared on the horizon, and soon enough a sense of anticipation filled up those hollow places as he stepped onto the docks. He didn't quite know where to begin searching for his future, but this seemed like a good place to start. After eight years in the navy, he had the skills to be hired on to almost any vessel despite his young age. But the thief's brand was a problem. No legitimate ship would take him if they thought he was a thief.

Many fine ships bobbed beside the docks and farther away at anchor in the harbor. He couldn't go back to the navy. He'd already decided as much. Like Rowan, he wanted no part of Marra's endless wars.

For the first time in his life, Logan had a say in where he went and what he did. But aside from returning to sea, he had no clue what to do.

He breathed in the slightly bitter sea breeze which ruffled his hair. This felt like home even more than the grain fields in Golden Valley had. So he let his feet carry him down the docks with no particular destination in mind, letting them determine whatever fate might find him.

A sharp whistle split the air as he neared the western end of the docks. Logan whirled, spotting a pretty little ship riding high in the water, unburdened by cargo. A large carved bird graced its prow, powerful wings spread, though Logan couldn't quite tell what type of bird it was.

And above the figurehead's outstretched wings, a young man leaned against the rail, watching Logan with ice blue eyes.

Logan was running before he even understood what was happening. No one stopped him as he bounded up the gangplank and up to the foredeck, where Rowan waited with arms spread as wide as the figurehead's wings. Finally there was someone to welcome him. Finally someone he could call home. He crashed against Rowan's chest so hard they both stumbled back into the rail. A joyful, disbelieving laugh bubbled up his throat as Rowan's arms closed around him.

The ship bobbed gently beneath their feet as they held each other. The movement felt much more like home than solid ground.

"I thought I'd find you here," Rowan exclaimed, pushing Logan at arm's length to look at him. Rowan's white blond hair hadn't been cut since they'd been separated and was pulled into a messy little tail. Spiky like the tuft of a ripe wheat stalk. The bridge of his nose was slightly sunburned, and he wore the widest grin Logan had ever seen.

"What would you have done if I wasn't here?" Logan laughed.

Rowan shrugged. "Like I said, I knew." He tilted his head questioningly. "Did you already see your family?"

Right. His family. "They're... My mum is dead."

"Oh, Logan." Rowan's expression was stricken on Logan's behalf. They'd spent so many nights in their hammocks, arms linked to keep from swaying apart, talking about the past, and the future. Rowan knew how much Logan loved his family.

"And the rest?" Rowan asked. "Laney?" How many times had he comforted Logan as he cried over missing his sister? Dozens.

"She's well. My brothers are well. But..." Logan had no more tears to shed today. He shook his head. "I'll tell you the rest later."

Rowan didn't pry. He knew Logan would elaborate in his own time. "So you'll come with me, right?" His sad expression turned almost giddy, his fingers tightening on Logan's shoulders.

Logan laughed again; Rowan's enthusiasm was infectious. "Where are we going? And with whom?"

"That's the beauty of it!" Rowan released Logan and swept his arms wide again. "We can go anywhere we want. We could leave the Islands altogether if we want. You're the only reason I was sticking around here anyway."

Logan's eyes widened, a curious warmth spreading through his chest. "Me?"

"Of course. I can't do this without you."

"Does this mean the rumors are true? You're a pirate?"

Rowan's infectious grin returned. "You bet your ass I am. And I want you on my crew."

There was no question. The path had laid itself out before him. Rowan was his best friend, his home. It didn't matter if pirating was dangerous or if his father didn't want him. His siblings were alive and well. And like Laney, he'd create his own family. His own life. He trusted Rowan to protect him.

Besides, he was already branded as a thief, what more could pirating do?

"Of course." There was no hesitation in his voice.

Rowan's grin widened. "Then welcome to your new home, the *Siren Song*."

Chapter 6

WANTED

ROWAN FAINE

Autumn, 1659

"Shit." Rowan stuck the pad of his thumb in his mouth as a bead of blood welled up on his skin. The metallic tang settled on his tongue, and he glared down at the offending edge of the paper that had wounded him. A woodblock print of his own face stared back at him, looking meaner and older than he actually was. As the flow of blood slowed, he took his thumb out of his mouth and tried to imitate the expression on the mean mug of this man that was supposed to be him, but couldn't quite twist his face into a configuration that felt right.

"Oi!"

Rowan looked up to find his first mate, Warrick Shaw, standing at the base of the bowsprit where Rowan sat.

"Aren't you supposed to be sleeping?" Rowan asked, swinging his dangling legs over the dark water. It was the middle of the night, and they were anchored a ways off the coast of Heseon, which had been the first country to fall to Marra's imperial war machine, long before Rowan had ever been born.

"Aren't *you* supposed to be keeping watch?" Warrick picked his way up the bowsprit and settled with his legs dangling on either side of it, facing Rowan. "What do you have there?"

Rowan held out the wanted flier to him, and Warrick squinted at it in the swaying lantern light.

"Is that supposed to be you?" he asked, aghast, his gaze flicking from the shoddy woodcut to the long list of crimes Rowan had racked up over the past year. Including, but not limited to, stealing the very ship they currently sat on.

"Sure is! Do you see the resemblance?" Rowan held up the flier beside his face, grimacing to match.

"Not at all." Warrick's laugh echoed out over the water. "You're much cuter in person."

"Cute?!" Rowan huffed in mock offense, swatting him with the flier. He ignored the little fire Warrick's words lit in his chest, which threatened to drive off the autumn chill. They'd been friends for almost two years. Warrick had always been a bit emotionally distant, but he'd supported Rowan through the shitty working conditions on board the *Jackdaw* and had helped— however little—with Rowan's mutiny scheme.

They'd grown marginally closer in the subsequent year of dodging the law. Though Rowan still knew next to nothing about Warrick's past. On one tipsy night in the early days of their pirating career, Warrick had let slip that his father had died a few years before. When gently pressed on the topic by Rowan, who was still riding the high of their newfound freedom and loose-tongued with the last of Captain Gladwin's wine, he'd clammed up. Another time, after a brush with the Marran navy, Warrick had mentioned that, like many young Kefryeans, he'd left his home country to escape the tide of Marra's invasion. That was all Rowan could glean from offhand comments and rare moments where Warrick's guard was down.

But Rowan wasn't one to judge a man based solely on his past. Rowan himself was an unwanted child from the slums. Rowan knew Warrick as smart, capable, and steady. Warrick was a stoic sort. He kept his thoughts close and didn't mingle with the crew beyond his duties as first mate. And if that was why Logan and the rest of the crew were a bit wary around him, well, they didn't know him like Rowan did. Recently though, Rowan had become very aware of Warrick's closeness at times when he used to take it for granted.

Their shared laughter rang out over the waves, as Rowan whacked him with the paper again. Warrick grabbed Rowan's chin, turning his face side to side as if to examine it from every angle, and Rowan's stomach flopped, his laughter dying into sobering silence.

"Definitely too cute for piracy," Warrick declared. "Maybe that's why the reward is a pittance."

Shit. This was no good. Why did Rowan's stomach feel like a barrel full of panicked fish whenever Warrick touched him?

Rowan jerked back, releasing the flier as he overbalanced. He had a split second to register he was falling before Warrick grabbed his arm and hauled him upright again.

"Whoa, there," Warrick said, as if Rowan were a startled horse and not a man on the brink of plunging backwards into the cold waters of the Broken Sea.

They both watched the flier flutter down to settle among the reflected stars, water spreading across the paper and running the ink. Warrick didn't let go of Rowan's arm, even though he was now firmly seated on the bowsprit.

"Where'd you get that flier anyway?" Warrick asked.

"It was on an announcement board in the last port." Rowan scowled. "I don't think anyone recognized me from it though."

"Well why would they? It looks nothing like you." He paused, glancing at the spot where the water had swallowed the paper altogether. "Still though, it's impressive you have one of those. Only pirating for a year and you're already famous."

He inched closer as he said this, his hand still around Rowan's arm, voice both admiring and contemplative. Rowan couldn't help but lean into it. The night seemed very quiet suddenly; only the shush of the waves and the breath curling up between them remained.

Before Rowan could think of something to say to break the

silence, Warrick leaned into the space between them. Their noses brushed, and before Rowan's frantic brain could register this new development, Warrick kissed him. His lips felt too warm after the chill of the autumn air, and Rowan's thoughts stuttered for half a second. He thought maybe he'd fall off the bowsprit after all. Warrick's hand moved up his arm, tracing warmth through Rowan's sleeve. His short, patchy beard chafed against Rowan's chin in a strangely pleasant way.

It was far from Rowan's first kiss, but a spark kindled in his gut. He leaned further into the kiss, almost unbalancing them again. They caught themselves, pulling back and giggling as if they weren't grown men and outlaws with prices on their heads.

"This isn't the safest place to...kiss," Warrick said. Rowan nodded, a bit in a daze. They carefully made their way down the bowsprit. When both their feet were safely on deck, Warrick grabbed his hand and kissed him again. The sparks kindled into flame, and Rowan pulled him close by his waist, deepening the kiss. Despite being taller, Warrick melted into his touch. The crispness of the air sharpened in contrast to the spots of heat where their bodies touched, barely an inch between their heaving chests. Rowan felt it intimately when Warrick shivered.

"It's too cold out here," Warrick murmured, grabbing Rowan's hand from around his waist and tugging him toward the door that would lead below deck. "Let's go warm up."

The words were unmistakably flirty, and the shiver that traveled down Rowan's spine had nothing to do with the cold and everything to do with the implications.

"I'm on watch," Rowan protested, nonetheless letting himself be led across the deck. "I shouldn't leave."

"You're the captain, remember? You can do whatever you want," Warrick said lightly. It was a suggestion very unlike him. The man was practical to a fault. So was Rowan, really. Though Rowan had taken to the role of pirate captain like he was born to it, and embraced the life of high risk, high reward with joy, he knew better than most that to be a captain was a tenuous thing.

His style of leadership was always to work as hard as the crew. So far it had succeeded, and he didn't want to jeopardize anything by ditching the midnight watch for...whatever Warrick had in mind.

Still, he didn't resist. The little flames in his gut propelled him to follow wherever his scruffy-faced first mate led him.

With one last glance across the empty deck and even emptier sea beyond, he followed Warrick through the door.

They couldn't make it all the way down the hall to Rowan's room without kissing again. So by the time they made it there, they were stumbling over themselves, eager as first-time lovers.

They kissed their way to the bed, tripping over the edge of the rug Rowan had stolen to cover up the stain of Gladwin's blood he'd never been able to scrub out of the floorboards.

None of that mattered right now. The blood, the theft, everything felt so distant in the face of Warrick's lips on his.

When Warrick's hands slipped beneath Rowan's shirt and against his skin, it was like throwing oil on a fire. His skin burned from the roots of his hair down to the tips of his toes. He gasped into the kiss, then pulled back, embarrassed he'd made such a sound just because Warrick's hands were on his bare waist. Warrick smirked, the expression much too comfortable on his face.

Slowly, without breaking eye contact, his touch trailed up either side of Rowan's waist, sending shivers across his skin. The room wasn't much warmer than outside. Though the *Siren Song* had been relatively successful in their first year as pirates, they were outlaws, and they were poor. To ensure his crew's loyalty, Rowan had made doubly sure to give them their full shares of the season's profits, even foregoing his own share to make repairs and buy supplies. So, in the spirit of stinginess, he remained determined not to light a fire in his small hearth until absolutely necessary.

Warrick didn't seem to care as much about the chill. He bent to kiss Rowan's neck, one thumb brushing Rowan's nipple beneath his shirt. Rowan gripped his shoulders, wanting to drag him closer, or push him onto the bed. Warrick made the decision for him, backing Rowan up against the edge of it. His lips moved down to Rowan's collar. Rowan squeezed his eyes shut, failing to prevent the boner that tented the front of his pants. His head felt muddled. He and Warrick were friends, weren't they? Was this just some friendly release of tension between two people starved of touch while out at sea? Or was it something deeper?

Warrick's thigh brushed up against the unfortunate hardness between Rowan's legs, and Rowan decided to surrender to whatever Warrick wanted of him when Warrick pulled back to look him in the eye.

"I like you, you know," he murmured, beard tickling Rowan's upper lip as their lips brushed. "In case that wasn't obvious."

It very much was not obvious, and in the back of his mind Rowan didn't quite believe it, even when Warrick's hands were on his bare skin here in the privacy of the captain's quarters.

"I—" But Warrick was kissing him again, and they fell onto the bed. Rowan's hips bucked up against Warrick's body, and he opened Warrick's mouth with his tongue, exploring the warm interior. Warrick groaned as their members brushed together through their clothes.

Fuck. He grabbed Warrick by the front of his shirt, concentrating very hard on not shaming himself by coming right there in his pants. His nerves already sang with need. He pushed Warrick off him, flipping their positions so Warrick splayed out beneath him.

Rowan palmed Warrick's length through his pants, and once they'd broken that barrier, they didn't stop. Rowan felt almost as if he moved without conscious thought as he tugged apart the laces at the front of Warrick's pants.

Warrick practically whimpered when Rowan's hand finally closed around his naked length. Rowan had never done this with someone else before, so he drew on his vast knowledge of covert jerkoffs in his hammock aboard the *Wolf*, then *Jackdaw*. He stroked slowly down the shaft, listening to the pleased noises Warrick made against his lips.

Warrick became putty in his hands. As his soft moans grew in intensity, Rowan set a faster pace, spreading precum down the shaft. He never let his lips leave Warrick's for more than it took for him to utter single words or wordless moans.

"Please..." Warrick gasped. And though Rowan's lips cut off whatever he wanted to say next, Rowan knew what he wanted. He trailed kisses down Warrick's fuzzy jaw and neck, and repositioned himself on the bed. He hesitated before planting a gentle kiss on the pink flushed head of Warrick's cock. He'd certainly never done *this* before, and suspected neither had Warrick. Though in the two years of their friendship they hadn't talked much about relationships, he'd never seen Warrick run off for privacy with anyone while on shore leave.

Rowan placed a few tentative kisses down the shaft, feeling out what he was meant to do. It couldn't be that complicated right? Still, a little flutter of nerves tickled his belly. Not just because he was about to do this with his friend, but also because he was the captain of this ship and Warrick was his first mate. They were about to cross lines on two fronts.

Well, technically they'd already crossed them. Rowan's lips trailed back up Warrick's shaft accompanied by his small desperate gasps. Rowan wrapped his lips a bit clumsily around the leaking tip, and Warrick let out a needy moan. Rowan glanced up to see his face flush pink. Slowly, Rowan bobbed his head down over the shaft, eyes drifting closed to concentrate on not letting his teeth scrape against the tender skin.

By the fourth stroke, he'd gotten too confident and took in too much at once. Warrick's cockhead prodded the back of his throat. Rowan resurfaced, gagging. A bit of drool dribbled from the corner of his mouth. Warrick let out a breathless chuckle that turned into a moan as Rowan resumed his ministrations more carefully this time. After a moment he picked up the pace, sensing Warrick's pleasure heightening. Warrick threaded his fingers through Rowan's white-blond hair, guiding the angle of Rowan's head how he wanted it.

Rowan tried not to gag again, regulating his breathing through his nose and letting his tongue flick along the underside of the shaft. Warrick's back arched, a guttural moan escaping his lips. His fingers tightened in Rowan's hair, making it hard for him to pull back.

"Rowan, I'm..." He spilled into Rowan's mouth. Rowan choked, not altogether pleased with the bitter liquid coating his tongue and throat. Warrick released him, and Rowan sat up quickly, gagged, and spit the cum into a corner of the sheet. Warrick's chest rose and fell rapidly as he tried to catch his post-orgasmic breath. Warrick threw his forearm across his eyes.

"Sorry," Warrick mumbled. "Should've warned you."

Rowan wiped a bit of cum from his lip with the back of his hand. "S'okay." He fidgeted, his own cock almost painfully hard in his pants. Was Warrick going to reciprocate? He didn't want to ask for it. He palmed his cock over the fabric, trying to alleviate some of the pressure.

"Hey."

Rowan looked over to find Warrick peeking at him from beneath his arm.

"Come down here." He patted the mattress with his other hand. Rowan flopped down next to him, trying not to let his desperation seem too obvious. Warrick turned onto his side and leaned in for a kiss. Rowan jerked back.

"Uh, I probably don't taste very good right now." He could still taste the bitterness on the back of his tongue. But Warrick rolled his eyes.

"It's fine." Warrick pulled Rowan into a kiss, his other hand wandering lower toward Rowan's desperate cock. Rowan's hips twitched forward, seeking Warrick's touch. He closed his eyes as Warrick slowly undid the ties at the front of Rowan's pants, relishing the lazy movement of their lips against one another, even though inside his need built out of control.

Finally, Warrick's hand slipped under his pants to close around his aching shaft. It was all he could do not to come right then and there. Rowan let out a shuddering moan, lips still caught up against Warrick's. He felt Warrick smirk again. The calluses at the base of his fingers scraped against the tender throb of his shaft as Warrick stroked it slowly. But the slight discomfort only heightened the pleasure building like a storm in his core. He clutched the front of Warrick's shirt, desperate to hold something.

"You're kinda pathetic right now," Warrick murmured against his lips, as if he hadn't been as needy and breathless moments before. A small needle of shame pierced through the pleasure. There and gone again. Warrick's hand continued to move, spreading precum down the length, and setting his nerves on fire.

Warrick chuckled when Rowan's only response was a rather pathetic whimper that proved his point. His hand left Rowan's cock, and he pushed Rowan onto his back. Warrick's lips, with their scratchy frame of beard, trailed down Rowan's jaw and neck, sending shivers down Rowan's spine. The hem of his shirt rucked up around his ribs. Warrick's mouth traveled over his bare stomach, tongue dipping into Rowan's navel. His still-clothed chest brushed against Rowan's straining cock, and even that light touch of fabric had Rowan's head swimming.

A guttural moan crawled up Rowan's throat as the heat of Warrick's mouth closed over his tip. Warrick wasted no time with teasing or hesitation as Rowan had. Maybe he was experienced after all. His head bobbed, enclosing half of Rowan's length in achingly warm, wet heat.

Gods, they really shouldn't be doing this. What if the rest of the crew found out and lost the tenuous respect Rowan had worked so hard to earn? Not because he and Warrick were both men—most people of the Islands didn't care about that—but because Rowan was the captain, and Warrick was his underling. The crew already didn't like Warrick much, any implication their captain favored him because they were sleeping together might tip the power balance out of Rowan's favor.

All these thoughts fled as Warrick's tongue laved over the tight skin of his length and he bobbed his head again. Rowan squeezed his eyes shut, knowing if he saw his cock disappearing between his friend's lips, he wouldn't last long. A tide of euphoria closed around him, and on the next stroke his hips bucked up involuntarily to meet it, flooding his senses. His mouth gaped open but nothing came out. He lost himself to sensation and didn't care anymore that this would all complicate matters. Or he wouldn't care until after.

Climax hurtled toward him and with it, panic.

"Warrick..." But Warrick seemed to read his mind. He released Rowan's cock and pumped it twice with his calloused hand before Rowan reached his peak and spilled across Warrick's fingers and his own bare stomach.

For a few moments, stars swam behind Rowan's eyelids before Warrick flopped back onto the mattress and reality came crashing back in. Rowan opened one eye a crack, watching Warrick summarily wipe cum from his fingers. Warrick glanced over at him, one eyebrow raised, and Rowan felt his cheeks heat.

"You're awfully quiet," Warrick commented. At some point he'd tucked himself back into his pants, but his hair was still mussed. Rowan grabbed another corner of the sheet and wiped the cooling spurts of cum from his bare stomach, grimacing at the thought of laundering the semen-y sheets later. He tucked his spent cock back into his pants and relaced them.

When he finally made eye contact with Warrick again, he found him watching.

"Nothing to say?" Warrick asked, with arrogance that had never been there before. Was it because of what they'd done? Or was this what he sounded like post-orgasm?

"Um...thank you?" Rowan ventured. He didn't quite know what one was supposed to say after abandoning one's post to trade blowjobs with one's second-in-command.

To his relief, Warrick laughed. "You're welcome, I guess." He ran his non-cum-stained fingers through his brown hair in an attempt to right it but it only served to increase the messiness.

Neither of them said anything more for a few awkward moments. Warrick sat up, scooting closer on the edge of the mattress.

"I meant what I said, you know," he said. There was no tenderness in it like before, but an easy confidence. "I like you more than as a friend and captain."

For what felt like the tenth time that night, Rowan's brain stuttered. He liked Warrick more than as a friend too. He was certainly attracted to him. But still that little needle of doubt pricked his guts. Things between them had already changed irrevocably, but when he thought of kissing Warrick again, scratchy fledgling beard and all, it sent warmth throughout his body, enough to drown out the prick of doubt.

"I like you too."

Chapter 7

COLD TREACHERY

ROWAN FAINE

Winter, 1659

Rowan shifted on his knees, leaning close to the hearth till his head was practically in the fireplace. He fluffed up the bit of wool and wood shavings on their bed of tinder. With shaking hands, he struck his flint and steel, watching as the spray of sparks died. His breath fogged from his lips. He'd waited too long to light the first fire in his quarters in an effort to conserve fuel, and therefore, money. But now winter had properly arrived and after he'd woken up with purple toes this morning he knew he couldn't hold off any longer. The only reason he'd even lasted this long was because he'd had Warrick warming his bed more often than not.

Rowan smiled at that, and struck the flint again. This time one of the sparks caught on the wool and Rowan leaned down to blow on it gently, coaxing the little spark into an ember, then a flame.

Once the flames had grown to a healthy orange crackle, licking at the expensive logs, Rowan sat back on his heels, relishing the unfamiliar warmth on his face. Maybe next winter he'd be able to enjoy such luxuries without worrying how much it was costing him.

Truly, he'd thought being a pirate would involve a lot more adventure and a lot less accounting.

There was nothing to do about it now; they were tucked into a little cove on the southern coast of Kefrye for the winter. It made Rowan a little nervous to stay in one place for months on end, let alone staying so close to a country Marra was actively invading, but they didn't have much of a choice. Between the bitter cold and the storms that plagued the seas all winter, it was much safer to stay close to shore. They'd resupplied in the last port, and some of the crew had chosen to stay there. With those fliers of Rowan's face and a description of the *Siren Song* plastering the town, he didn't want to risk himself or his beloved ship getting recognized. Warrick had told him of a little-used cove near the area he'd grown up, and assured them it would be safe enough for one winter.

Rowan and Warrick's relationship had only deepened in the few months since they'd first kissed on the bowsprit. The whole crew knew of their relationship by now, and it hadn't seemed to affect their view of him as captain, but it had deepened the rift between Warrick and the crew. Even Logan, who in many ways was still the same naive boy who'd first joined the crew of the *Wolf*, distrusted him. Rowan hadn't been able to get a solid answer out of any of them as to why.

Rowan held his hands out to the feebly dancing flames. An entirely unrelated heat rose up his neck when he thought about Warrick. They'd fallen so easily into a physical and romantic relationship. Unfortunately, they fell short in other aspects. Though Rowan's affection for Warrick had grown, maybe even into the early stages of love, he still knew so little of Warrick's past. Over the last month or so, Rowan's conflicting feelings between not wanting to pry and craving more knowledge of his lover had only grown muddier.

When they'd settled in this cove a week ago, Warrick had left to visit home, and not said where home was, nor when he would return.

A soft knock interrupted Rowan's thoughts. He stood slowly, knees creaking with cold.

"Warrick's back," Logan said, when Rowan answered the door. He didn't seem pleased. When their relationship had come to light, Logan had pulled Rowan aside to tell him it was a bad idea to trust Warrick. Rowan had never known Logan to be the type to judge or treat others badly, but doubt had begun to eat at him. He trusted Logan's judgment almost as much as his own, so despite the thrill that raced through him at the thought of seeing his lover again, he'd resolved to heal this rift between his first mate and his crew, even if that meant exposing whatever secrets Warrick kept so close.

"He's back?" Rowan couldn't keep the edge of giddiness from his voice.

"From wherever he went." Logan grimaced.

"Don't start again, please. I'll talk to him."

Logan shook his head, blond waves bouncing around his ears. "I have something to tell you first."

A little kernel of anxiety made itself comfy in the pit of Rowan's stomach. "What is it?"

"I looked through Warrick's cabin."

"You— Logan! I know you don't like him but why would you—"

"It's empty," Logan interrupted him. "He took all his stuff with him."

The kernel grew into a knot, heavy in his gut. "But you said he's back, so maybe he was bringing things to his family?" It sounded stupid even to his own ears, but he had to believe there was a good explanation.

Logan's mouth thinned to a skeptical line. "I know you care about him, but even if he's back..." He shook his head, as if unsure what he wanted Rowan to do.

"I'll talk to him." Rowan tried to sound confident, but Warrick taking everything he owned off the ship... It couldn't be good.

They emerged onto the deck as fat snowflakes began to fall

from a pale, cloud-choked sky. Rowan shoved his hands into his pockets, wishing he'd thought to grab gloves. Or better yet, stay inside by the new fire. He kept only a skeleton crew out here, enough to keep watch and perform the daily duties of the ship while the others remained below in the warmth. Two crew members, Berto and Melba, lowered a rowboat into the water. Through the thickening snow, Warrick's distant figure picked his way down the slope of the foothills.

The rowboat hit the water and Rowan started forward, but Logan caught his arm.

"I don't like the look of this snow," he said, hazel eyes wide on the clouds. "Maybe you should let the others go."

True, the wind was picking up by the minute, the dark water between them and the shore growing disturbed. But beyond the worsening weather, Rowan knew Logan was worried about letting him meet Warrick alone, away from the ship. Rowan patted his friend's cold fingers.

"We'll be quick. You can hold down the fort till I get back, right?"

Logan's lips pursed, but he nodded and let Rowan go.

By the time they'd made it to shore, the wind speed had increased even more, the snow fell faster and heavier, and the knot in Rowan's stomach had grown. Rowan and Berto jumped into the shallows and hauled the rowboat up the shore through the choppy waves that reached their thighs. Frigid water speared directly through his thick clothes, but by the time his water-filled boots hit the shale beach, Warrick was waiting for him. In two strides, Rowan wrapped him in a bracing hug, their embrace dislodging wet snow from the shoulders of their coats. Warmth spread through Rowan's chest, and despite his nerves, it felt good to have Warrick in his arms again.

"Did you make it home okay?" Rowan asked, when they pulled back from the embrace. Warrick's beard was thicker than it had been several months ago, though still patchy at the corners of his lips and the sides of his jaw. It had been a bit unkempt when he'd left for home but was now trimmed under a crust of frost. His wide shoulders were clad in a new wool coat.

Warrick smiled, though it didn't reach his eyes. "Yes. I'm glad to be back though." Rowan realized then Warrick didn't have any belongings with him. The knot of distrust twisted, and he glanced around the shore. Besides Berto and Melba, they were alone.

"Well, let's get you beside a fire." He could deal with his questions when they were all back on the ship. Rowan leaned in for a kiss, half to reassure himself everything was still fine. Warrick turned his head to avoid it.

"We'd better go! The wind is picking up," Berto shouted to them.

"Right." Rowan grabbed Warrick's hand. They would talk once they were safely back aboard the *Siren Song*. Berto set his shoulder against the boat's bow and began to push it back into the waves. "Let's go." Rowan squeezed Warrick's gloved hand.

Warrick freed his hand from Rowan's, glancing back toward the top of the hill, now partially obscured in swirling snow. "I'm not coming."

"What? Why?" The warmth in Rowan's chest vanished, leaving only the freezing bite of the wind through his wet clothes.

Warrick glanced at the hill again, and the knot unspooled into nauseating uneasiness in Rowan's gut.

"Are you leaving the *Siren?*" *Are you leaving me?* "Are you going back to your family?" But it felt like more than that. He felt pathetic for holding onto what Warrick had told him.

The wind blew harder, turning the snow into needles against his cheeks.

"I'm not going back to my family," Warrick said tonelessly. "They're dead."

"I'm sorry, I..." Rowan reached for him, intending to comfort, even if Warrick intended to leave him. But Warrick's mouth twisted into a disdainful grimace, his whole face transforming as if he'd been wearing a mask of affability the entire time they'd known each other, and could finally drop it.

"You don't know anything," he sneered. Rowan's hand dropped back to his side, almost mesmerized by this change in his lover's demeanor.

Warrick seized Rowan's upper arm in an iron grip.

"Captain! We've got company!" Melba shouted over the rush of wind.

Shadowy figures appeared through the blowing snow behind Warrick, materializing too quickly into Marran infantry soldiers in their black and red uniforms. They rushed down the hill with ordered efficiency despite the snow. Clearly they'd been lying in wait. Rowan tried to jerk his arm out of Warrick's grip, but he held fast. "You don't even know where we are," Warrick continued. "You were so quick to trust this was a safe place. Why? Because I said I like you? Because I shared your bed?" He spat on the snow quickly collecting at their feet. Distantly, a whistle sounded, barely carrying on the wind.

"Warrick—"

Warrick shook him roughly. "We're on *my* land," Warrick hissed. "Or it will be my land again, once I turn you in and those greedy Marrans forgive my exile."

Rowan stared at him in horror. Turn him in? Exile? What the fuck was Warrick talking about?

The soldiers were almost upon them. The front rank dropped to a firing stance and leveled their rifles at Rowan and his crew members while the rest fanned out, meaning to trap them.

"Captain!" Berto shouted in warning.

"Rowan Faine! By order of the Great Empire of Marra, surrender!"

"What did you do?" Rowan whispered. His head felt like the snow was blowing directly through it, frozen, yet frantic.

"I've been promised my title back once you've hanged," Warrick hissed. There was nothing left of the man Rowan had known the last two years. And what remained was the one thing Rowan hated most in the world, a bootlicker, and a noble one at that. His finger's tightened, vise-like, on Rowan's arm. "Once the

Marrans conquer this backwards country, my exile will be remitted, patricide charges forgotten. I'll be Lord Shaw, like I was meant to be. So surrender to these fools, and it will be easier for everyone." A sort of maniacal hope entered his expression, his eyes wide and fervent. "Maybe I'll even convince them to spare Logan's life, hm? He'd make a biddable valet wouldn't he? Maybe I'll show him some of the things his precious captain liked in bed."

At the mention of Logan's name, Rowan finally thawed, and wrenched his arm from Warrick's grip.

"Run!"

Berto jumped to Rowan's orders from where he stood in the shallows. Warrick lunged for Rowan right as the commander of the soldiers yelled, "Fire!" and the crack of rifles split the storm. Rowan slipped in the wet snow as bullets pinged around him.

Melba ducked low as she took up the oars. A bullet struck Berto in the shoulder and he went down, desperately clutching the lip of the boat, but unable to pull himself into it.

Rowan crashed into the waves, the shock of the cold driving breath from his lungs. Icy water dragged at his feet but he kept going even as bullets buried themselves in the boat's bow.

"C'mon, Captain!" Melba shouted, trying her best to keep Berto's head above the churning water but lacking the upper body strength to pull him fully into the boat. Warrick shouted something Rowan couldn't make out. He reached the boat, waves slapping at his chest, and grabbed Berto.

"Pull!" he yelled, and Melba yanked on Berto's coat as Rowan lifted. They managed to lift him enough to dump him into the bottom of the boat. Rowan hauled himself in after and took up the oar opposite Melba.

Another bullet zipped past, and Rowan grit his teeth. Warrick stood on the shale beach surrounded by more than a dozen soldiers, all taking aim right at Rowan's chest. He remembered the contemplative way Warrick had looked at the reward flier. How he had kissed Rowan soon after. Had anything about their relationship been genuine? Or had it been a ploy all along?

He couldn't think of that now. He put his head down and rowed. They made it past the breaker zone before they heard cannons over the crack of gunfire. His sleepy ship suddenly crackled with activity.

They had to get to the *Siren* as quickly as possible, but Berto was bleeding fast, a crimson pool of blood and slushy, half-frozen seawater spreading beneath him. Beside Rowan, Melba's face had gone as white and bloodless as Berto's, her eyes trained not on the receding shore and its contingent of hostile soldiers, but on her fellow crew member bleeding out on her boots.

"Take care of him. I'll row," Rowan ordered. Melba's head whipped around to look at him, strands of brown hair escaping from her knit cap to blow across her face. She seemed as frozen as Berto's blood. Her eyes flicked to the shore, then Berto, then back to her captain. No doubt trying to gauge whether they were out of range, or if Rowan would be able to row fast enough for them to get Berto safely back to the *Siren* before it was too late.

"Go," Rowan prompted, and she gave the oar over to him before slipping off the bench into the slushy blood. She pulled off her cap, folded it in half and pressed it to the gushing wound. Berto moaned, his hands shaking as he reached up to grip Melba's coat sleeve.

Still alive, thank the gods. Rowan put all his strength into each pull of the oars, focusing on the sting of the wind and salt spray, the ache in his back, what they would do next, and not on the fact that the man he'd been coming to love had betrayed him, and had maybe always been planning to betray him. So he rowed until the boom of the cannons got louder and he could hear the crew shouting.

Finally the rowboat bumped against the side of the *Siren*.

"Berto is injured!" Rowan shouted up to the deck, then turned to Melba. "Let's get him—" But Melba was staring at him with wide eyes, tear tracks striping her pink, wind-burned cheeks. Berto's empty gaze was trained on the sky with its blowing flakes. Dead. For only a moment, Rowan let the grief of losing a crew member mingle with the sting of betrayal. Then once again pushed it away.

"Let's go."

It wasn't until Rowan's feet hit the deck that he knew just how fucked they were. A Marran navy ship sat in the entrance of the cove, black, red, and white flag snapping in the snowy wind.

"There's only one ship as far as we can tell." Logan appeared by his side the moment he stepped over the rail, settling easily into the role of first mate without question.

Boom! A cannonball plunged into the sea only yards short of the *Siren*'s hull. All their gunports were open, far more guns than the *Siren Song* had.

"Damage report," Rowan ordered, and Logan rattled out only minor damage and no major injuries. "Good." It would only remain good until they tried to escape. They'd have to sail straight past the ship to get out of the cove, and who knew if more waited on the other side. He spared a fleeting glance toward the shore. Warrick and the soldiers were picking their way along the shale toward the mouth of the cove. Berto's body drifted away in the rowboat.

Boom! Another cannonball arced through the blowing snow and barely missed colliding with the *Siren*'s bow. The crew swarmed around them, making ready to sail. The only question was where they would go.

"Orders, Captain?" Logan asked.

He didn't know. His mind still reeled. But if they stayed here they'd be shot to pieces.

"Gimme a spyglass." One was placed in his hand, and he raised it to his eye, trying to make out the enemy ship's position-ing, how many guns they had and how many sailors and soldiers.

The mouth of the cove was less than two ship-lengths wide, with a cliff on one side and a sloping hill on the other. The Marran ship sat right in the middle of the opening, leaving too little room on either side for the *Siren* to slip through. Their two decks of gunports were open and ready to deliver a full broadside if the *Siren* got any closer. Even if the *Siren* managed to make it past, they'd be subject to the cannons on the other side, and whatever reinforcements might be waiting farther out to sea.

Rowan's mind ticked through the list of impossible options like the clicking of the capstan brake as the crew reeled in the anchor. Try to escape past the bow, and the other ship would be able to pursue them quickly. Try to escape past the stern, and they'd be sailing right between the stern guns and the jagged rocks. Could they negotiate? Warrick—or Lord Shaw as he'd be called if this all worked in his favor and the Marrans kept their word—had said Rowan would be hanged, but what about the rest of the crew? Was there a chance to negotiate their freedom?

He felt Logan's warmth through the woolen layers of their coats, and he remembered what Warrick had threatened would happen to Logan after he was gone.

"Warrick's not with you. Was this his doing?" Logan asked quietly.

Rowan lowered the spyglass. "Yes." Negotiation and surrender were not an option. He wouldn't let Logan or the rest of his crew fall into Warrick's or the Marran navy's hands.

So the question was, should they go left, or right?

Or straight down the middle?

"We're going to ram them."

THE BEST THING about being a pirate was Rowan could do whatever he wanted, even if it was incredibly stupid. If they were going to get out of this, it would be with bold, decisive action, and nothing could be bolder than trying to ram your much smaller ship into one that had you outgunned. But Rowan couldn't think of another option. No matter what he chose, they would be sailing through a gauntlet. So he had to meet it head on.

Logan didn't question his captain beyond a raised eyebrow

before he started issuing orders to the shivering crew. The anchors were already stowed. The sails unfurled, and caught the wind. Rowan darted below to douse the fire in his quarters, strapped on his weapons, and pulled a pair of gloves over his cold-numbed hands.

When he reached the deck again, they were well underway, speeding toward the Marran ship through the gusts of snow. The crew seemed twitchy, but none of them questioned him either. Maybe they should've. His blindness to Warrick's true motives was the reason they were in this mess. As he moved among them on his way to the quarterdeck, touching a shoulder here, giving quiet words of assurance there, they seemed to relax, and he felt more and more like a fraud.

He'd spent eight years on a Marran naval ship like this one. He knew their protocols and tactics. He knew they would try to gun the *Siren* down before Rowan got a chance to execute his plan.

But he also knew the Marran Empire was greedy to their core. They'd try to win with the least amount of damage to the *Siren Song* so they could tow it in triumph to the nearest port of conse- quence like a trophy. And they would want Rowan alive to face a public hanging as a warning to others. He was less use to them dead out here in the wintry sea.

Rowan mounted the quarterdeck and whispered his plans into the helmsman's ear.

In minutes they were well within cannon range.

"Ready forward guns!" Rowan shouted, and several crew members jumped to obey, careful to keep the powder dry in the heavy snow. They'd loaded the first six-pound ball when the thunder of cannon fire filled the air. Several shots fell short, but two ripped through the *Siren*'s rigging and one punched through the forecastle rail. They needed more speed. They needed to reach the other ship before the Marrans got a chance to get off too many volleys.

He stood quietly for a moment, feeling the direction of the

frigid wind, listening to its howl. Then he launched into action, issuing orders and scuttling up into the rigging among his crew to trim the mizzen sails to better catch the wind.

After two years sailing the *Siren Song*, he knew her abilities intimately, knew exactly the way to position the sheets, and the drag this season's buildup of barnacles would create on the hull. And so he knew, with the right touch, they could pull this off.

The report of the *Siren*'s two forward guns echoed up to him, followed immediately by the boom of the Marran cannons which seemed to reverberate off the low ceiling of clouds. The pirates hit the deck as several cannonballs raked down the length of the *Siren*, wreaking havoc in their wake. Someone screamed, and Rowan's thighs tightened on the yardarm as the impact shuddered through the timbers. They presented a smaller target by heading directly into the barrage, but a few were bound to hit.

Rowan finished tying off the line. "Keep top speed!" he shouted to the lineman next to him.

"Aye!"

Rowan climbed back to the deck as quick as he could. His joints were cold enough to crack with every movement, or maybe that was the thin layer of ice and frost forming on his wet clothes. He should've changed when he went to retrieve his weapons. He should've done a lot of things, like listen to Logan when he voiced his suspicions about Warrick. If they survived this, he'd have to let Logan scold him as much as he wanted. Then he'd officially appoint him as first mate.

The crew reloaded the forward guns and fired again, both of the six-pound balls hitting the naval ship at the second deck and punching holes in the edges of the gunports. Rowan couldn't hear the human toll it took on the other crew, but they retaliated with a full broadside that wrought tenfold the damage they'd been dealt. Twelve-pound balls slammed into the *Siren*'s hull, more raking the deck and ripping holes in the sails. Rowan grabbed Melba and pulled her down flat as a cannonball hurtled over them and burst through the quarterdeck steps.

Splinters rained around them. Someone screamed close by, and Rowan jumped up to see a man with this leg hanging on by a thread, his knee blown clean through by a direct hit. Rowan scrambled over the frost-slick deck, not sure what he was going to do when he got there.

In the end it didn't matter—the man was dead by the time Rowan got his hands on him.

Chaos reigned across the deck the closer they drew to their enemy at full speed. The bombardment thundered constantly, battering the much smaller ship and her ragtag crew.

But they were close. Rowan could see the soldiers and sailors running around the deck through the screen of blowing snow and gunsmoke. He stumbled up the quarterdeck stairs and re-took his place of command. Below, his deck was in chaos, pools of blood melting the frost and snow. The cries of his crew sliced him to the bone but this was the only way they could get out. The only way some of them would be able to survive.

Rowan brought his bosun's whistle to his lips, the cold brass sticking to his skin. He met the helmsman's eye, then focused on the pirates up in the rigging. He raised a hand and drew breath, and waited.

The *Siren* hurtled toward the larger ship. Toward freedom, or ruin.

The *Siren*'s hull ate up yards of water with astonishing speed. Fifty. Twenty-five. The Marran ship loomed over them.

"Captain..." the helmsman said nervously. Rowan cut him a quelling glance.

Rowan would not flinch. Not before his enemies did.

Another barrage of cannon fire ripped through the *Siren*. The tip of the *Siren*'s bowsprit was only a few yards from the side of the enemy ship, and the Marrans finally flinched. Their sails trimmed, rudder carving the waves and the ship tacked hard to starboard away from the *Siren*, opening a path to the sea like a doorway.

Rowan brought his hand down, whistling two long signals into the blustery air and the *Siren* tacked hard the other direction, narrowly avoiding catastrophic collision. The ship's open gun hatches scraped against the *Siren*'s side, and the *Siren* delivered a full broadside of all ten starboard guns into the Marran ship at point blank range.

The ship heeled at a dangerous angle from their sharp turn, the tips of the yardarms nearly dipping into the waves on the opposite side. Timbers groaned like a wounded animal, straining to right itself.

And then, the *Siren* was free. They broke past the naval ship, suddenly released from the bonds of combat, and sped over the waves into the white storm.

METAL SCRAPED against the boards of the *Siren*'s deck, chipping away layers of ice. Rowan grunted as he shoved the scraper they usually used to remove barnacles from the hull beneath the frozen chunks, the surface marred with swirls of blood. His back and arms ached, his palms long since blistered beneath his gloves, and his lips were chapped almost beyond recognition. For a time, the cold and adrenaline had numbed him, but he was beyond that now. Now it just hurt.

Because half of his crew was gone.

Because Warrick had betrayed him.

Because it was all his fault.

The scraper caught on the edge of a board, and Rowan huffed in frustration, his breath curling up toward the furled sails. The storm had blown hard and long enough to cover their escape, and now only a few gentle flakes drifted down from the white sky.

"Captain?"

Rowan turned to find Logan standing on the empty deck. What remained of the crew had retreated below to sleep and grieve. Rowan was supposed to be keeping watch, but he hadn't been able to keep still.

"I thought you might be cold." Logan held up an undyed wool scarf. His own neck was bare, and his cheeks were pink with cold.

"Thanks." Rowan took the scarf. Its warmth radiated through his gloves, as if Logan had warmed it by the fire before coming out here. Rowan wrapped it around his neck and chin, sighing.

"What are you doing?" Logan asked, eyeing the scraper and the pile of reddish ice shards.

"Cleaning." Really he was trying to keep the guilty thoughts from circling around in his head.

"You should rest, Captain."

No *I told you so*. No shouting and raging at Rowan's poor choices that had led them here.

"I'll rest when I'm done." He turned back to his work, but Logan stopped him with a gentle hand on his arm.

"It's not your fault. You did the best you could."

Rowan tried to force back the tears suddenly flooding his eyes. His best wasn't good enough. His best had gotten Berto and so many others killed.

Who knew freedom could be so miserable?

Logan took the scraper from his hands and set it to the side. "C'mon, let's get you warmed up."

He didn't deserve it, but he let his best friend lead him below, to the captain's quarters. He sat on the rug while Logan settled a quilt around his shoulders. A fire already blazed in the grate, burning away the precious and expensive wood. But the flames couldn't chase away the crimson shards of ice lodged between Rowan's ribs.

Logan placed a warm mug of cider between his hands, and settled on the rug beside him.

"Next time, we'll do better," Logan said.

Rowan couldn't help the bitter chuckle that escaped his lips. "You think there will be a next time? The crew won't mutiny to avenge their peers for my bad decisions?"

Logan's eyebrows drew together. "They know we wouldn't

have gotten out of there at all if it weren't for you. And death at sea is a hell of a lot better than public hanging."

"We wouldn't have *been* there at all if I hadn't blindly trusted Warrick," Rowan said miserably. That was another thing he hadn't been able to stop thinking about. Yet he could find no sense in it, and the thoughts only served to torture him further.

"Drink your cider."

Rowan could tell Logan didn't want to scold him. His own guilt and heartbreak was punishment enough. They sat in silence together before the fire as snow drifted around the *Siren*, alone on the dark waves. Next time he would only place his trust in those who deserved it. He wouldn't let his crew suffer for his mistakes. He would make his best be *the* best, and protect his ship and crew from everything that came their way.

Chapter 8

First Night, Part i

Fox

Winter, 1660

Fox giggled, bright and cheerful in the growing dark.

"The Salted Snail!" he gasped between giggles, doubling over with his arms around his middle. The laughter, visible in the cold air, drifted around his head like a halo. When Gaël didn't laugh with him, Fox sobered slightly and pointed to the sign hanging over the tavern door.

"Don't you get it?" Neither of them could actually read, but over the indecipherable words, the sign clearly depicted a snail with salt being sprinkled on it.

His best friend had a small, amused smile on his lips.

"I get it," Gaël confirmed. After so long at sea among other sailors, anyone would be hard pressed not to know every dirty joke out there. This particular one came from a bawdy Laslandish rhyme about a witch turning a sailor's penis into a snail, then salting it till it shriveled up. The tavern was practically called *The Withered Dick.*

It seemed like a great place to while away the rest of their night.

The cobblestone street glittered with the recent winter rain. Fox and Gaël had disembarked from the *Narwhal* earlier that day with pockets full of their meager wages. They'd spent the day wandering around Wave Harbor, not wanting to waste the rare opportunity to be on land and relax instead of constantly being put to work on the ship. Now the day was ending, and their pockets were lighter than they had been before.

Fox giggled again, and punched Gaël's shoulder. They'd been best friends since the age of five, when Gaël's merchant parents had been shipwrecked en route from Lasland to their home country of Gosoya. When the woman taking care of Gaël in their stead heard she no longer had the promise of pay, she put him out on the street. Fox had found him crying on the woman's doorstep.

Fox had lost his mother and infant brother to sickness the year before and had understood the other boy's grief, even if they could barely speak the same language. It had been only Fox and his pa on the farm; he might as well have been alone.

So he brought home the crying little boy who grieved parents who had actually loved him. Gaël didn't understand why the woman had put him out on the street, or why no one in the town cared enough to take him in. It was enough that he looked different and spoke a different language than them.

Fox's pa didn't care about any of that. He only cared that the boy could work.

They lasted five more years before they ran away from Fox's cruel father together, making their way to the coastal city of Carran. They slept curled together in alleyways like a pair of orphaned puppies. They stole together, got hired for odd jobs together, shared their meager food, and defended each other from the dangers of the streets. It had been a hard life, harder maybe than it would have been if they'd stayed on the farm, but they'd had each other.

Fox threw his arm around the back of Gaël's neck, dragging him close to his side. They were almost the same height, with wiry frames that came from a childhood of never being full. But in the last year, Gaël had gained more than an inch on Fox, and now that they were eating better since getting jobs on the *Narwhal*, Gaël had started to fill out in both body and face, slowly packing on muscle where Fox remained thin.

And Fox had noticed.

"Let's get a drink!" Fox said brightly, dragging Gaël toward the tavern with the ridiculous name. Gaël went along with him, as always. When they were in public, he tended toward stoicism. It was only when the two of them were alone together that he opened up his delightful, goofy self. Perhaps it was the result of five years under the thumb of Fox's pa, of being punished for any noise out of place or outward emotion. It had made him quiet, but had the opposite effect on Fox. As soon as Fox had escaped Pa's control, he'd become brash and loud, letting out everything he'd bottled up deep inside for the first ten years of his life. He wore his emotions on the outside.

Every emotion but one.

They burst into the busy tavern like a whirlwind with a stoic tree trapped in its clutches. Sailors of every nation packed the place wall to wall, and a few patrons glanced at them as Fox dragged Gaël toward the bar. Between them, they scraped together enough copper tals for two mugs of cheap, watered down ale.

Fox eyed the crowd of already drunken sailors. He practically vibrated with the pent up energy of being stuck on a ship for months with nothing much to do but learn his limits climbing in the rigging, playing dice, and getting into trouble. Here in Wave Harbor there was so much to see. So much to do. And there wasn't enough time for all of it.

He took a sip from the mug Gaël handed him. The ale tasted watery, but it was a hell of a lot better than what they got on the ship.

The back of Gaël's hand nudged Fox's wrist, brushing against the braided leather bracelet he'd woven for Fox from scraps when they were kids. He wore a matching one on his own wrist. They'd never taken them off.

"What are you thinking about?" Gaël murmured, barely audible. Fox leaned closer to hear.

"That it's great to have money for once," Fox replied with a grin. The mug of ale wasn't even enough to get tipsy, but the *Narwhal* was leaving port at dawn, so they could at least have some fun before they had to get back. And who knew how long it would be before they would be able to set foot on land again? He and Gaël had to make the most of this night.

They chatted easily about anything that came to mind. Where the *Narwhal* might go next, what countries they wanted to see. Before long, Fox joined a few sailors beside them in a bawdy rendition of *My Sweetie and the Sea*, a song about a woman waiting impatiently for her lover to come home. Fox jumped onto the bar, hoisting his still half-full mug over his head. His voice rang out louder than the rest. Joy—warm and comfortable—spread through his limbs. He stomped his boots in time with the rhythm. They were worn and too small, but Gaël had bought them for him with their first pay from the *Narwhal* a few years ago, and he treasured them. The song ended, and the barmaid thwacked him on the leg with a rag to get him down from atop the bar.

Gaël put his own drink down on the bar's surface and held out his arms to Fox. Fox let his friend grab him around the waist in support as Fox jumped down to the sticky tavern floor, managing it without spilling his drink.

They stood face-to-face, the next song already ringing through the air. The world narrowed around them, encompassing only the two of them. Gaël's hands lingered a little too long on either side of Fox's waist.

It wasn't as if they never touched. They were best friends. They'd shared a bed back at the farm and had slept cuddled up for protection and warmth when they lived on the streets of Carran. Even now that they lived on the *Narwhal*, one of them sometimes ended up in the other's hammock. It was not out of the ordinary. It was common. It happened every day.

But lately, it was different.

Fox found his gaze falling to Gaël's mouth as he talked, and now he was hyper-aware of how big Gaël's hands felt on his waist, how his pinky finger slipped beneath the hem of Fox's shirt and pressed into his skin. Fox's face went hot, and he stepped hastily out of Gaël's grip. He turned back toward the bar, avoiding eye contact, and took a gulp of his ale.

A commotion broke out near them. One drunk stumbled into another, sloshing a newly purchased drink into the other man's beard. The bearded man shoved the drunk away, and he reeled back, right into Fox. Fox stumbled, dropping his mug onto the bartop where it tipped and rolled. Gaël's arm snaked around his middle, drawing him close.

"Watch it," Gaël growled at the drunk. The man waved a dismissive hand at them, and stumbled back toward the one who'd pushed him.

But none of that mattered. The noise of the ensuing brawl faded from Fox's consciousness as Gaël's storm gray eyes turned toward him.

"You okay?" Gaël asked, concern written on his sharp features. He didn't let go this time. Gaël had always been the protector. The one Fox looked to when he got hurt.

"'m fine," Fox mumbled. Every nerve in his body sang at Gaël's proximity. What was wrong with him lately? This was his best friend. The boy he'd grown up with.

Gaël leaned closer, his arm tightening around the back of Fox's waist.

"You sure?" He caught Fox's eye, eyebrows drawn together in concern, and Fox found himself unable to look away. He was struck dumb.

"I..." He didn't know what to say. His body felt too hot. Gaël was too close. His gaze fell back to Gaël's lips as they curved into a smile, cheeks dimpling.

Oh gods. The dimples. Fox wouldn't survive this night.

"You're not drunk off only half a mug of ale are you?" Gaël asked, amused.

"N-no." He felt like it though. The heat radiating off Gaël's body through their clothes muddled his head. They were almost eye-to-eye. Gaël's lips were so close that Fox wanted nothing more than to escape their lure. Run away and never have these kinds of thoughts about his best friend again. Gaël was all he had; he couldn't risk losing him.

Gaël's free hand came up to cup the back of Fox's neck. Fox's gaze sliced up, eyes wide.

"Foxy..."

That was Fox's undoing. Every rational thought fled his head. Every worry, every fear gone in an instant in the face of his nickname on Gaël's perfect lips.

It was impossible to know which one of them leaned in first. Their lips met, soft and sweet as warm honey, and Fox knew.

He was in love with his best friend.

He didn't know how long it had been. When the love of friendship, of brotherhood, had turned into this. Maybe it had always been that way, simmering beneath the surface of Fox's consciousness, waiting for a catalyst like this to make itself known.

The fear surged back all at once, and Fox broke the kiss. He lowered his head to Gaël's shoulder, clutching the front of his shirt in balled up fists. Fox's whole body shivered as love opened up in his heart like a whirlpool, consuming everything that had come before and would come after. There was no going back. Even if they laughed and chalked this up to a drunken mistake. Fox was startlingly sober. And for him, nothing else existed but Gaël.

Had he just ruined their friendship? Thrown everything from childhood till now down the whirlpool? His fists shook, convinced Gaël was about to push him away. He couldn't stand to look up and see the rejection that surely marred Gaël's beautiful face.

But Gaël didn't push him away. He held Fox close, cheek resting on Fox's hair.

"You didn't know." Gaël's voice was low and awed beside Fox's ear.

"Know what?" Fox whispered, still not able to bring himself to look up.

"That I'm in love with you."

Fox's head snapped up, almost headbutting Gaël in the face.

"What?" He must be dreaming. His love-addled mind was playing cruel tricks on him. He searched Gaël's handsome face for answers. His high cheekbones, stormy eyes, pouty lips, every line of him held affection.

"I love you, Foxy. I always have, and I always will."

Distantly, Fox heard ringing. He was losing it. This really was a dream. He stared at his best friend, dazed.

But no, those were the midnight bells ringing somewhere off in the town.

"I-I..." The whirlpool in his heart spun faster, devouring his thoughts.

Gaël's thumb brushed over the side of Fox's neck. The light in his eyes dimmed slightly.

"You don't have to say it back. We can stay friends."

Fox wanted to, but for once in his life, he was at a loss for words. He'd spoken without thinking too many times to count. Now he was thinking too much to speak. So he did the only thing he could do. Fox rose up on his toes and kissed Gaël again. His fists tightened in the front of Gaël's shirt. He never wanted to let go of this moment. No matter what happened, Gaël loved him. And that was enough.

Gaël groaned low in his throat. He tilted his head, tongue slipping between Fox's lips.

"Get a room, kids!" the barmaid shouted. A few nearby patrons laughed and hooted.

Fox felt Gaël smile against his lips. He turned so Fox's back pressed to the edge of the bar. Their inexperienced lips moved together like the push and pull of the tides that governed their lives. Fox's body responded to Gaël's touch, heat pooling in his stomach.

The peal of the midnight bells faded away, and Gaël broke the kiss, leaning his forehead against Fox's.

"It's late. We should get back to the ship," Gaël said reluctantly.

"Y-yeah..." Fox's brain was still not functioning properly. He needed to say he loved Gaël back before it was too late.

Neither of them moved.

Gaël dipped his head and planted another lingering kiss on Fox's lips. Then they were hand in hand, Gaël dragging him between the packed bodies toward the door. Fox tripped over the boot of a drunk passed out in his chair. He spotted something glittering on the tabletop next to his hand which still clutched a mug handle. Fox swiped it. Old habits died hard.

Silver moonlight glittered on the rain-wet cobblestones when they left the tavern, frost starting to creep along the edges of buildings. Fox pulled up short, breath pooling in the air. He held the stolen object up to the light, his other hand still in Gaël's.

A key.

Fox grinned, his eyes sliding to the exterior stairs that ran up the side between two buildings to the guest rooms above the tavern. He squeezed Gaël's hand.

He didn't want this night to end. He wanted to sleep in a proper bed for once, wanted to show Gaël how much he loved him.

Gaël's eyes went wide, but he followed the tug of Fox's hand, letting himself be led up the stairs. They found the correct door and stumbled into the dark room together.

The door had barely closed before Fox's lips found Gaël's again, drawing out a breathless moan. No fire had been laid in the grate, but it didn't matter. They could keep each other warm. They always had before.

Fox backed Gaël up against the door, never breaking the kiss, hands slipping beneath the hem of his shirt. The whirlpool spun faster and faster, taking Fox's mind with it. He could feel himself growing hard. His hands roamed over Gaël's fevered skin, eliciting wonderful sounds. Fox wanted to please him, wanted to do everything for him, to keep him until his mind calmed enough to say the words.

"Mmh...Fox..." Gaël pushed him away slightly. His eyes roamed over Fox's face as if trying to read his mind. There was nothing to read. Fox's whole being was filled only with him. "What are we doing?"

Fox pressed his body tight against Gaël's, making sure he could feel the hardness of Fox's cock.

"I want you," Fox said breathlessly.

Not the right words. Not the ones he needed to say.

Gaël seemed to be barely holding himself together, and now Fox could feel Gaël hardening as well. Gaël crooked a finger under Fox's chin, tilting his head up so their eyes could meet in the silver moonlight streaming in from the small window.

"I've never..." His voice trailed off meekly.

Neither had Fox. He knew all about it, both of them did. It was hard to live in the back alleys of Carran or the close quarters of a ship without unwittingly witnessing intimate moments, let alone the endless dirty jokes and sailors who were all too eager to explain any and everything. Besides, the mechanics of it couldn't be that difficult to figure out.

"Me too," Fox said.

Gaël smiled, dimples deepening with shadow. "What about that girl last spring?" he asked, amusement feathering his voice.

"I've never even been kissed," Fox laughed. He'd always been a hopeless flirt, but he'd never let it go further than that. Now he knew why.

"What about—"

"Gaël." He laid his hands on Gaël's chest, feeling the heartbeat hammering beneath. "It's only you. I saved myself...for you..." He didn't realize the truth of the words until he'd spoken them. He'd always belonged to Gaël, whether either of them had known it or not.

Gaël's entire body stilled, shock evident on his beautiful face. How long had he known he was in love with Fox? How long had he been waiting? Watching Fox shamelessly flirt?

One of Fox's hands slipped down to brush over Gaël's straining cock.

"Do you want me?"

"Gods, yes." Gaël's voice was raw.

"I'm yours."

Something in Gaël finally seemed to snap. All the yearning that had been silently building between them for years finally wearing away his self-restraint. He surged forward, kissing Fox hard on the mouth, his arms wrapping around Fox's thin waist. They stumbled a few steps to the bed and tumbled onto the patchwork quilt. Fox's hands shook as he pulled Gaël's shirt off over his head. This was happening. This was real. He was lying in bed beneath Gaël.

Fox pulled back a little to admire him. His frame was still a bit wiry, beginning to recover from the hungry years on the streets, and bulk up with muscle from their work on the *Narwhal*. They were long past adolescence, but it had taken them both a long time to catch up to their well-fed counterparts. Gaël had grown into his strong features, becoming the man he was always meant to be.

Fox's eyes flicked up to Gaël's face, only to find Gaël gazing lovingly back at him.

"You're beautiful, Foxy," Gaël whispered. He gently swept a lock of brown hair out of Fox's face. Fox felt a blush creep up his cheeks and hoped Gaël couldn't see it in the dim light. He ran his hands over the honeyed skin of Gaël's chest.

"You're not so bad yourself."

Gaël kissed him again, slower this time, savoring it. Fox breathed in the smell of his skin, so familiar yet so sweet. Fox wrapped his arms around the back of Gaël's neck and returned the kiss with enthusiasm. Their movements became more fevered with every passing moment. Fox let his fingers run lightly down the center of Gaël's back, eliciting a small moan. Gaël's back flexed, his hips rolling involuntarily to rut against Fox's body.

Heat flared beneath Fox's skin. He sat up, tearing his own shirt off over his head, and capturing Gaël's lips again. Despite the cold room, he felt hot with desire and Gaël's body heat. His fingers dipped beneath the waistband of Gaël's trousers. Gaël leaned into him and pushed him back down to the bed, caging him between strong arms. His mouth wandered away from Fox's lips, over his cheek, his jaw, and down his neck. Tingles spread over Fox's skin with every touch, ratcheting up his need. He was almost painfully hard now, and he strained toward Gaël's touch.

Gaël pulled Fox's trousers down his legs with one hand, his mouth sucking a mark into one jutting hip bone. Fox gasped as his aching cock sprang free.

"Touch me. Please," Fox whined.

Gaël's calloused hand closed around Fox's length. The leather bracelet that marked their relationship up to this point brushed Fox's balls. Gaël stroked him slowly. Clumsy with lack of experience. But to Fox it was exquisite.

Gaël watched him closely, gray eyes taking in Fox's expressions. He lowered his head, lips finding the tip of Fox's cock, never taking his eyes from Fox's face.

Fox whimpered as the tip breached Gaël's perfect lips. Bliss swirled through him, and he tried his best to hold it together, to not fall apart in Gaël's mouth. Gaël took him in as far as he could go. Which wasn't much. But to Fox it was the best thing he'd ever experienced. His abdominal muscles tightened. He tried to breathe deep, to regain his composure as Gaël withdrew, then took him in again, a little bit deeper. And again, a little more each time until Gaël's hot mouth almost completely enveloped him. Gaël rubbed circles into Fox's thighs with his fingers.

His tongue swirled over the tip on one down stroke and Fox almost lost it right there.

"Gaël, please," he choked.

Gaël withdrew, climbing up the bed with a fevered look in his eye. The faint moonlight silvered his black hair as it fell across his brow. Fox took Gaël's face between his hands.

"Please, please... I want you inside me. Don't make me wait anymore."

Gaël froze, brow furrowing.

"Are you sure?"

"Yes," Fox practically sobbed. "I'm yours."

Gaël visibly swallowed, throat bobbing.

"Do you know how to..." He didn't seem able to finish his sentence. His own cock strained against the front of his trousers. Fox roused a little from his pleasured stupor.

"We need lube," he declared. He sat up and looked around the room. Spotted a chest of drawers next to the bed. "Take your pants off."

Fox rolled to the side of the bed and fumbled through the top drawer. Nothing but a small prayer book and some old matches. He tried the bottom drawer, and came away with a small glass bottle the previous occupants must have left. He uncorked and sniffed it. A sweet scent wafted into his nostrils.

"Coconut?" Gaël asked.

They grinned at each other.

Some of the tension between them eased, and with it the twinge of anxiety that had still nagged at Fox relaxed. Gaël was still the same Gaël. Even if this changed things between them, it would only make them better. They still had the same easy banter, the same camaraderie. That wouldn't change if they slept together. It could only bring them closer.

Fox rolled back toward a now fully nude Gaël, his cock standing at attention and already beading precum at the tip. Fox dropped the corked bottle on the bed beside him and captured Gaël's lips in another kiss. He would never tire of this. Each time their lips met it felt like the first time all over again, a thrum of pure love and excitement echoing through his entire body. He palmed Gaël's cock lightly, and Gaël bit his lower lip, letting out a desperate groan. Fox rutted against his hip, growing more restless with each passing moment. He wanted Gaël inside him. Now. He couldn't wait much longer.

"F-Fox," Gaël stuttered. His eyes were glazed over. "I want you."

Fox thumbed the slit of Gaël's throbbing cock.

"Come and get me," Fox teased.

Gaël's eyes darkened for a moment. He drew Fox tight against his chest, and even though they were almost the same size, Fox felt treasured and protected in his arms.

"Don't tempt me too much," Gaël murmured low in his ear. "I don't know how much self-control I have when it comes to you."

A shiver rippled through Fox's body, and he vowed to tempt Gaël as much as possible for the rest of their lives.

Gaël rolled Fox onto his back, and Fox's thighs fell open invitingly. He ran a hand up the inside of one of his own thighs and over his cock. Allowed a small gasp to escape his lips at the contact of his own hand. Gaël watched him with eager eyes.

Fox reached out, his fingers catching on the braided leather around Gaël's wrist, and drew Gaël's hand to his entrance.

"Do you know how to prepare me?"

"I..." Gaël stared in wonder at the place where his fingers touched Fox's puckered rim. Fox uncorked the bottle and dribbled a bit of the sweet-smelling oil over where Gaël's fingers connected to him. Gaël looked up at him, unsure.

"If you're nervous, we can stop," Fox reassured him. Gaël nodded again, drawing close so their bodies pressed together, He dropped a kiss to the corner of Fox's pouty mouth. One finger prodded Fox's hole gently.

Fox tensed. It felt strange, but it didn't hurt. Gaël withdrew quickly.

"Maybe we shouldn't."

"I want this," Fox whispered. "Just go slow."

Gaël ran his finger around the rim, getting Fox used to the pressure. His dick twitched against Fox's thigh.

Gaël's finger sank slowly into Fox's tight pink hole. Fox hissed at the intrusion, eyes squeezed shut.

"You okay?" Gaël murmured in his ear.

Fox nodded, eyes still closed.

Gaël's finger continued moving, fumbling, but gaining confidence with every push. It didn't feel good, but it wasn't bad either, just different. Fox opened his eyes.

Gaël's tongue was tucked between his teeth, concentrating. Despite how hopelessly turned on he was, Fox giggled.

"You're cute."

Gaël looked up at him, cheeks dimpling with a smile. His finger pressed forward and curled, sending a bolt of lightning straight to Fox's head.

"Mmph." His back arched; his cock throbbed with renewed vigor.

"You like that spot?" Gaël asked. He stroked it again, eliciting a pathetic whimper from Fox.

Gaël's smile only widened. Encouraged, he circled the tip of his finger around the spot, then continued stroking Fox's clenching walls. Before long, he withdrew. Gaël reapplied the lube and went back in, this time with two fingers. His tongue tucked back between his teeth, unfairly adorable as he slowly opened Fox up for their first time. Fox couldn't help but sink into his heart's whirlpool a little bit further. He loved this man. He would do anything for him. He wanted him so badly it hurt.

"I'm ready," Fox whispered. He couldn't stand to wait any longer. He needed to be connected to Gaël, filled up with his love and his cock.

Gaël leaned over him, their eyes locking. His fingers danced through Fox's insides, slowly stroking him toward unimaginable pleasure.

"Gaël..." Fox pleaded.

Gaël kissed him, all the heat he had been holding back as he prepared Fox coming through in the hard line of his mouth, the stroke of his tongue. His fingers withdrew, and he rolled onto his knees between Fox's legs. He dribbled more oil over his cock and leaned over Fox's heaving chest, lining himself up at Fox's entrance.

"Are you ready?" he asked, his voice raw with emotion and the struggle of keeping himself restrained.

"Yes," Fox answered.

Gaël pressed in slowly. Fox gasped at the unfamiliar intrusion, but didn't stop him. His back arched off the bed as Gaël slid in. Fox's insides stretched painfully around his girth, but he didn't care. His own impatience had won out. Gaël was inside him, and he would never let him go.

Gaël made it halfway before the last thread of his self-control snapped. He groaned. His hips bucked forward involuntarily, penetrating Fox up to the hilt. Further than his fingers could have reached. Fox cried out in both pain and pleasure, the sensation of being filled like nothing he'd ever experienced before.

"S-sorry." Gaël gathered Fox into his arms, feathering kisses across his freckled nose and cheeks. Fox held him tightly, and neither of them moved for a long moment.

Fox blinked. There were tears in Gaël's stormy eyes, and it took Fox's breath away. The whirlpool in his heart spun faster. Faster. Swelled to an unimaginable roar.

"I-I love you," Fox gasped.

Gaël's beloved face broke into a brilliant smile.

"I never thought I'd be lucky enough to hear those words from you."

Fox laid a hand over Gaël's hammering heartbeat.

"I'll tell you every day from now on."

A tear slipped down Gaël's cheek. Such adoration lit his eyes that Fox almost forgot Gaël's cock was seated deep inside him, until Gaël's hips pulsed forward gently.

"Can I move? Are you okay?" Gaël asked.

"I'm fine," Fox replied. In truth, he was a bit overwhelmed.

With love. With relief. With the painfully delicious stretch of Gaël's cock inside him. But he definitely didn't want to stop.

Gaël pulled out halfway, and slowly rolled his hips forward again. His arm slipped from around Fox's shoulders to his waist, lifting Fox's hips to get a better angle.

"So soft," Gaël groaned.

Fox let his hands fall to the quilt beside his head. His cock throbbed, begging to be touched. He wondered what it would be like to be inside Gaël. How soft. How tight. How exquisite it would be to fuck him. Maybe next time he would get to top.

The next thrust snapped his mind back into focus. This new angle had Gaël hitting all the right spots. Fox's fingers fisted in the quilt, and his insides clenched around Gaël's cock. A long moan escaped his lips, unbidden.

"If you do that again, you're gonna make me come," Gaël panted. But he rolled his hips forward again and again, picking up speed and confidence with every well-placed thrust. Tingles of pleasure crashed through Fox's body, building with every moan and whimper Gaël pulled out of him. He clenched again, a small needle of pain tumbling among the waves. But he found that it only served to heighten the pleasure by contrast. And he liked the way it made Gaël go wide-eyed and breathless.

Gaël bent to plant a line of sloppy, open-mouthed kisses along Fox's collarbone. His thrusts grew shallower, and Fox wrapped his legs around Gaël's hips.

Fox's untouched cock bounced against his stomach with every thrust, weeping precum. He whimpered, craving friction, pain, anything that would bear him through the waves of ecstasy to sweet release.

"Harder," he gasped. Gaël abandoned his attention to Fox's chest, and sat back on his heels. He unwound one of Fox's legs from around his waist and threw it over his shoulder. The change was slight but on the next thrust he hit Fox's prostate, and bottomed out all at once, his hips smacking against Fox's ass.

"Yes!" Fox cried out as stinging pleasure shot through him. "Right there... Oh gods..."

Gaël obeyed him, powerful legs thrusting harder and harder until Fox saw nothing but stars surrounding Gaël's beautiful face. One of Gaël's hands tightened on Fox's hip bone, keeping him in place as he pounded into him. The other hand closed around Fox's neglected cock, stroking him lightly in heady counterpoint to his almost violent thrusts.

The whirlpool in Fox's chest coiled and tightened, making it hard to breathe. Still, he couldn't stop the tumble of words that fell from his lips.

"Ah...aaah...Gaël...please...I'm..."

"You're so beautiful Foxy," Gaël panted back. "Come for me. Be all mine."

Every muscle in Fox's body tensed, his vision going white and sparkly for a moment as intense, unimaginable pleasure crashed through him like a raging storm. Cum spurted onto his stomach. At the same time Gaël cried out, finally surrendering to the bliss of Fox's body sucking him in and enveloping him. One more thrust and his lips contorted into a snarl as his cock throbbed out his orgasm deep inside Fox's clenching hole.

Tears pricked hot behind Fox's eyes. He was suddenly overwhelmed again, as the whirlpool of his heart began to slow and unravel. He let out a choked sob, then clapped his hand over his mouth when Gaël's head snapped up.

"Foxy?"

Fox shook his head, hand still over his mouth. If he spoke, he would break completely. But the tears came anyway, running down his cheeks into his sweat-dampened hair. His whole body shook with the release of both emotion and tension.

"Fox." Alarm threaded Gaël's voice. He attempted to pull out, but Fox stopped him, reaching up and pulling him down to cradle against Fox's chest.

"D-did I hurt you? Talk to me," Gaël pleaded.

There was no going back. But Fox didn't want to. He wanted to stay like this forever, locked together with Gaël.

Fox pressed his cheek to Gaël's, hoping that would somehow be reassurance enough until he could speak again. Gaël seemed to accept this. Some of the tension went out of his body and he reached up to smooth Fox's wavy brown hair away from his face.

They stayed locked in their embrace for a little while longer as Fox's tears and breathing slowed, cocks softened and cum cooled on their skin.

Fox shivered as the chill of the winter night crept back across his skin. Gaël's softening cock slipped out of Fox's sore backside.

Fox sighed, contentment overtaking him. Gaël planted a light kiss on his cheek.

"Are you okay?"

Fox returned Gaël's concern with a lazy, glassy-eyed smile.

"I'm sorry. I was... I just love you too much," Fox said.

Gaël's stormy gray eyes searched his face for any hint of sadness, of hurt. But now the euphoria of being in love was returning. Fox reached up to cup Gaël's face in his hands, leather bracelet slipping down his arm, and drew him down into a kiss.

"I love you too," Gaël murmured against his lips. Fox grinned.

Fox woke in the best mood of his life. Even if his back hurt a little bit, he floated on a cloud of bliss. He and Gaël had slept together. He loved Gaël, and Gaël... Fox turned over, his hands searching out his best friend-turned-lover.

Gaël wasn't there.

Fox blinked sleepily for a moment. They'd decided to get out of here before the room's rightful occupant, the drunk down in the tavern, came back, but he'd fallen asleep in Gaël's arms instead. At some point he must have rolled over. The other side of the bed was clearly rumpled. It hadn't been a dream.

He touched the spot where Gaël had slept. It wasn't even warm.

Fox sat up and rubbed his eyes. Where was Gaël? Had he stepped out to use the toilet? Or get food? Fox's stomach growled loudly. That must've been it. The room was still cold and dark, but he didn't want to put on his clothes yet. He wasn't above pulling Gaël back into bed in this stolen room for one more romp before they had to slip away back to the *Narwhal*. Fox wrapped the blue and purple quilt more tightly around himself and waited.

And waited.

The sky began to lighten—the *Narwhal* would be sailing, and Gaël hadn't returned. With every moment Fox grew more and more anxious. Where was he? Was he coming back? Was he hurt? Fox was beginning to feel like an abandoned puppy who didn't know its master was never coming back.

Finally the anxiety and cold grew too much to bear. He got out of bed and dressed. His worn out boots sat neatly on the floor near the foot of the bed. Gaël's were not beside them.

The whirlpool in his heart spun and spun, dragging all the perfect memories of the night into its depths. Gaël hadn't...left him, had he? He wasn't capable of something like that. He'd always been by Fox's side.

Fox bent to pick up his boot, wincing as his lower back twinged with a residual ache, reminding him of last night. The room lightened further, and Fox froze. Sitting on the toe of his other boot was Gaël's braided leather bracelet, untied and half unraveled.

No.

With shaking fingers, Fox picked it up. They'd never taken their bracelets off since the day they made them, but here Gaël's was perfectly placed for Fox to find. Fox's heart dropped, cracked, shattered. The whirlpool consumed itself, becoming a great aching pit. Neither of them could read or write—Gaël couldn't have left him a note—but this message was as clear as day. Gaël would never take this off. Not unless he was leaving for good.

The bracelet was a goodbye.

Fox sank to his knees, unable to hold himself up. He couldn't breathe, and great wracking sobs threatened to shake him apart. He pressed the unraveled bracelet to his heart, as if by some miracle the old leather strands could lash the broken pieces together again.

Gaël had kissed him, accepted the gift of Fox's virginity. Gaël had said he loved him.

But Gaël had left him.

Chapter 9

THE BEAST OF WHITESTONE REEF

JOHN C. HAKON

Spring, 1661

The sun descended, golden and warm over the bright Kefryean waves as Lieutenant John C. Hakon stepped back onto the *M.W.S. Bear*, the lead warship of the Marran navy's northeastern flotilla. His unit dispersed to their rest, tired from the scouting mission they'd just returned from. John was in a foul mood. After several days of wading through brambles and getting sand in his boots, he wanted to give his report and be done with it. The thought of actually being able to sleep in his bunk tonight lifted his spirits only slightly. Admiral Lowe wouldn't be happy with his report. It meant all the work of getting here to Whitestone Reef was pointless. They'd have to pack up the operation and move along.

Because Whitestone Reef wasn't a military target at all, but a town full of civilians going about their lives, unsuspecting of the invasion force hiding out of sight. During their reconnaissance, John and his unit hadn't seen a single piece of evidence that there was a military presence there. He was returning to the *Bear* confused, but confident that once the admiral heard his report they would call off the attack and move on to their next mission.

He went directly to the admiral's quarters and knocked.

"Enter."

John stepped into the sumptuously decorated office. The decor was too ostentatious in John's opinion, especially when they were at war.

"Report, Lieutenant," Admiral Lowe ordered, without glancing up from his paperwork. His teeth clenched tightly around the stem of an ivory pipe, pungent tobacco smoke wreathing his bewigged head.

"Our intelligence must have been inaccurate, sir," John said, standing properly at attention. "The port is only full of civilians. There is no fort, nor is there a military presence in or around the town."

Admiral Lowe looked up at him and frowned, the embers in his pipe bowl glowing faintly orange against the bottom of his nose.

"Your unit was sent to assess defenses. Why are you telling me this?"

John kept his expression carefully neutral, though his confusion only deepened.

"There are no defenses, sir. The target is not military." Maybe the admiral hadn't understood him the first time?

Lowe took a puff on the pipe and slowly let it out.

"The target is the target, Lieutenant Hakon. These are our orders. You would do well not to question your superiors."

"Of course not, sir. But..."

"It makes no matter whether the target has a military presence," Lowe snapped. "We are at war, and they are our enemy."

John's throat tightened. "Are we not going to call off the attack, sir?" His voice was barely restrained. He must be misunderstanding. The rules of engagement clearly stated civilians were not to be intentionally harmed.

"We will continue as planned. It is vital that we establish a foothold in this area. It is to be our base of operations for the push toward the Gray Mountains. Reinforcements are arriving in less than a fortnight, and we must have that rickety old town cleared out before then." He puffed on his pipe again, the smoke curling into his immaculate wig.

"Cleared out, sir?" The admiral couldn't mean what John thought he meant. There was nothing here but a small collection of buildings surrounded by an ancient earthwork. Barely enough to slow a modern invasion force. Barely even high enough for children to slide down in the winter. If Whitestone Reef was to be a base of operations for not only the northeastern flotilla, but an entire branch of the Marran operation, the townspeople would have to be pushed out.

Or killed.

"I'm sorry, sir, but what do you mean, cleared out? Surely..."

"You're getting dangerously close to insubordination, Lieutenant." Lowe set the pipe down in a green porcelain dish on his desk.

"Surely you don't mean to push them out. That town isn't big enough for a base of operations."

"Push them out?" Lowe laughed, but there was no humor in it. Nothing that would indicate the next words out of his mouth would be assurances. "This is war, Lieutenant. You think we'll ask them nicely to let us take over their town and homes? You think we'll let them run to the fort down the coast and tell the generals exactly where we are? No. We must establish a foothold fast. We must establish total rule before the reinforcements arrive. It does not matter whether they are civilians. They are Kefryean, and they will submit to our rule or be killed. It's as simple as that."

Any faith, any patriotism John had left in Marra fled in an instant. He'd learned long ago that war was not gallant and heroic as he'd been raised to believe. But up until now he'd remained a good soldier. He'd diligently worked his way up the ranks. Even if this war was driven solely by the Marran king's greed, it was still the country of John's birth, and before now, he'd never had cause to question the orders of his superiors.

Horror gripped him. The townspeople would resist, of course they would. But they were a bunch of herders and fishermen. And they'd be no match for the superior numbers and weapons of Admiral Lowe's force. It was clear to John now that Lowe had no qualms about putting down every man, woman, and child in that town to get his way.

Anger rose up in him, hot and fiery.

"That town is full of children!" he shouted, taking one threatening step forward, not knowing yet what he intended to do. "We can't just—"

"You're out of line, Lieutenant!" Lowe barked. Behind John, Lowe's door guards burst into the room. "Arrest him."

The guards grabbed John by the arms as he surged forward, wrestling him into submission.

"You can't kill civilians!" John shouted as the guards dragged him back.

"Take him to the brig," Lowe ordered. His cold gaze settled back to John. "We'll let the court-martial deal with you."

All the fight went out of John's body. Years of loyal service to his country, and for what? To be punished for disagreeing with his superiors? For refusing to take part in the murder of innocents?

HE WAS THROWN UNCEREMONIOUSLY into the brig. A cold room lined with wood and iron-barred cages. He scrambled to his feet as the door guards slammed and locked the bars behind him.

"This is wrong!" John shouted, but they ignored him, and laughed as they left the brig. He smacked the bars, growling in anger.

The attack would happen in the morning. The flotilla had moved into final position after the town's fishermen had returned to shore that day, and would attack before they could take to the sea at dawn and discover the flotilla hidden around the curve of the cape.

In a few hours it would be dark, and everyone but the night

watch would be abed, getting much needed rest before they had to be up to move the ships into position.

What would his fellow soldiers and sailors do when they attacked, and realized only innocent civilians lived in the town? Would they feel as horrified as John did? Or would they simply carry out their orders, still believing in the wisdom and rightness of their superior officers?

John leaned his forehead against the bars. He'd worked so hard to gain this position. He'd been the perfect soldier. He'd followed all his orders until now. And because he disagreed with the admiral, his career was over.

The door opened, admitting two of the men from his unit, Barber and Massey. If he had friends here, they would be it.

"I didn't believe them when they said you'd been arrested, Lieutenant." Barber frowned, scratching his scalp, hair still dirty from the mission. It seemed neither of them had been able to settle in before the news reached them.

John glanced at the door, but no guard had accompanied them, or seemed to be listening. "Barber," he hissed. "Lowe plans to go ahead with the mission. You have to..." But what could either of them do? Barber and Massey might be fine soldiers, but they were just that, soldiers, with no more influence over Admiral Lowe than John had. "Lowe plans to massacre the civilians," John finished.

Barber and Massey exchanged a troubled glance. They'd spent days together tromping through the countryside, assessing the town's defenses. Massey had crouched in the scrubby brush with John, hiding as a young mother and child from the village picked their way over the coastal cliffs, searching for early season blueberries. Nausea rose in John's throat. What would happen to them if the admiral wasn't stopped? If they resisted, they would die. If they lived...John didn't even want to think of what occupation might mean for them.

This was John's first active post. His first taste of real war, and he found it bitter on his tongue.

"But the rules of engagement..." Massey started, at the same time as Barber said, "That's just what war is, Lieutenant." They glanced at each other again warily.

"Maybe you misinterpreted his intentions," Massey said to John hopefully.

John shook his head. That woman and child were trying to live a peaceful life. This war had nothing to do with them. They would be another casualty in the unstoppable wave of the Marran Empire's expansion.

"You have to tell the rest of the unit. Tell everyone. Maybe we can stop this." Even as he said it, both Massey and Barber were shaking their heads.

"There's nothing we can do, Lieutenant," Barber said. Massey looked down at his hands as if ashamed to be agreeing. "Orders are orders."

John's hands tightened on the bars, anger engulfing his nausea again. He couldn't let this happen.

THE AFT BELL rang the change of watch high above John's cell. In a few minutes, the old watch would be abed and the new would be groggily at their posts.

John swung the cell door open on silent hinges. He internally thanked whatever ship boy had kept them well-oiled, and the admiral's guards who hadn't bothered to search him before throwing him in here. Maybe it was laziness. Maybe it was the fact that Lieutenant John C. Hakon was known to be a loyal and upstanding soldier until today.

Or they hadn't searched him because officers facing court-martial were typically sent home to their wealthy families in disgrace. But John hadn't had the privileged upbringing most of the other officers had. Best case scenario he would be demoted back to a grunt, but more likely he'd be relegated to the prison work units, all for simply saying they shouldn't kill innocents indiscriminately.

What he did have was his grandfather's thin whittling knife that he always kept in his pocket.

After Barber and Massey left, he'd made short work of the brig's simple lock. Now, he padded to the door and peeked out into the hall. No guards, as he'd expected; everyone was resting up for what they thought would be a battle in the morning.

During his few hours in the brig, John had thought long and hard about what to do. He'd had no doubt he could escape this cell. He'd thought about trying to kill Lowe, but Lowe's second-in-command was a stern and vicious man. John had watched him flog a sailor for accidentally dirtying his illustrious officer's boots. Lowe's death alone would not stop his plans.

John had thought of simply escaping, trying to make it to the town and warn them of the imminent attack. But would they even believe the word of an enemy soldier? And what could they do to defend themselves against an entire flotilla of the Marran navy? It would be a massacre.

He had no choice but to stop the attack altogether.

On silent feet, John stole down the hall and up several flights of stairs toward the weapons hold. It was ironic that the same skills the navy had so thoroughly beaten into him over the years would now be used to take them down.

He only saw a few patrols in the halls, easily avoided by ducking into side rooms and around corners. Despite his outburst earlier, there didn't seem to be any additional security set. Admiral Lowe seemed confident he commanded the most powerful entity in these waters, that nothing could harm them.

With every step, John's anger grew. Contempt for those who so carelessly threw away the lives of innocents slowly replaced the pride he'd once had in working his way to an officer's position. Everything he'd worked for up to this point was a lie. It had all been for nothing.

The storeroom was dark when he entered. He gathered what

he needed by memory and slipped back out, going only a few doors down to his final destination. A single guard leaned sleepily against the heavy door labeled *black powder* with a black X slashed below it, warning of the room's dangerous contents. A small smile twitched the corners of his lips.

John stowed his supplies at the edge of the hall, and peered around the corner at the guard. He hadn't seen any patrols in a while. Would they come down this hall? If he took the guard out, would they discover him before John could execute his plan? He had to take the chance.

John fished a coin out of his pocket and whipped it around the corner so it pinged off the walls at the other end of the hall. The guard startled alert, turning to peer into the gloom where the noise had come from. John rushed him, and before the man could even shout an alarm, John clobbered him over the head with the heavy, unlit lantern he'd gathered from the storeroom. His eyes rolled back in his head, and John caught him by the collar as he crumpled, took the key from his belt, and dragged him into the powder room.

John took a moment to light the now dented lantern before gathering his supplies and shutting the door behind him. Barrel upon barrel of black powder lined the walls, two deep and two high. This was only one of several identical rooms on board the *Bear*, all of them stuffed full of black powder. But he wouldn't have to visit all of them. One spark in one storeroom, and it would be over.

John set the lantern carefully by the door next to the guard's unconscious body. In his other hand he carried a coiled bundle of fuses, and tall clock candles with their hours marked out in thin black lines against the white wax. He had to time this right. There were two other ships in the flotilla besides the *Bear*, disabling only one of them wouldn't do, and he couldn't give them any time to understand what was happening before all three went up in flames.

Fire was the most expedient and complete way of dealing

with things like this. Ever since the granary in his hometown had gone up in flames when he was a child, he'd always been fascinated by it. It was the reason his grandfather had taught him how to carve wood, hoping idle hands would reach for the whittling knife and not the flint. It was ultimately the reason his parents had encouraged him to join the military. They hoped it would give him a constructive outlet for his fixation.

It might have worked if he'd joined the army, but he'd ended up in the navy instead. And fire was the enemy of ships.

John made quick work of binding the guard's limp wrists and ankles with lengths of rope, then turned toward his true task. The plan formed so naturally in his mind, he could see it clearly as he bored holes in the appropriate place on each clock candle and placed them atop the explosive barrels around the room. He made the round again, feeding one end of the fuses through the hole and the other end into the barrels. When the candles burned down, their flame would light the short fuses which in turn would set the powder alight and the rest would be history.

He lit the candles carefully, and stepped back out into the hall, locking the guard into the deadly room behind him.

Security was sickeningly slack. This was a time of war. Yet after ditching the lantern, John had little problem evading the night watch, and the boat he and his unit had returned on blessedly still bobbed in the water. He paused, wind sliding through his auburn hair. It wasn't too late. He could turn back. Blow out the fuses and lock himself back in the brig.

Something caught the corner of his eye, a blue flicker of light up the coast. There and gone again. John shook his head, dislodging his doubts. His grandfather had taught him not to hesitate. A decisive stroke made for a cleaner cut. It was true whether fashioning a bird from a poplar block, or planning the destruction of all you'd ever known.

He slipped his bag full of candles over his shoulder, threaded the loops of fuse rope through his belt, and climbed silently down the ladder.

Waves lapped gently against the side of the flotilla's second ship. He secured the rowboat to the ring next to the ladder and climbed. A lantern at the prow cast a circle of light around a pair of watchmen, gambling their wages away. Their wooden dice rattled across the lid of the barrel, loud on the sleeping ship.

John rolled his eyes, and slipped through the darkness to the deck below. He found the black powder room near the center of the ship. Again he positioned the candles and fuses and set them with a shorter time. He lit them with a lantern he'd procured on the way down.

With every step of this plan that he went unchallenged, John grew more and more disillusioned with the institution he'd been raised in. Had those surrounding him always been so lazy? So disorganized? Not only were they completely unaware of the true nature of the battle to come, but they were also incompetent to the point that one lone man would be able to take them down.

It disgusted him.

The second fuse set, he made his way back up. He peeked out onto the deck, but the watchmen were no longer at their post. Were they doing rounds? If so, it would be the perfect time to sneak back onto his boat.

After a few more seconds, John ventured out into the dark.

"Who goes there?"

John whirled to see one of the watchmen stalking down from the quarterdeck above. John's muscles tensed, ready to run. But he was still wearing his uniform. He could talk his way out of this. John tried to put on an air of dignified sternness.

"Lieutenant John C. Hakon," he identified himself. The watchman squinted as he approached. Then, seeing the red laurels on John's black uniform collar, saluted.

"Pardon me, Lieutenant, I don't recognize you. What are you doing here?"

"I've just rowed over from the *Bear*," John said, "I had a

message for your captain from Admiral Lowe, but I'll be on my way now." He sidestepped toward the starboard rail, where his boat waited below.

The watchman frowned.

"Why didn't you announce yourself when you came aboard, sir?" His eyes slid to the coil of fuses over John's shoulder. "Why do you have—"

The watchman's hand went to his rifle, but John was quicker. The crunch of the watchman's nose beneath John's fist rang loud on the silent ship, accompanied only by the lap of waves. The watchman reeled back, his rifle clattering to the deck. John made it almost to the side before the watchman caught up with him. He tackled him and they both crashed into the rail, John's breath wheezing out of him as the hard wood caught him in the gut. He pushed back off the rail and grappled with the watchman. John had been hoping to settle this without one-on-one violence, but now that wasn't an option. If they continued this struggle, others would wake and come running. He'd be caught.

He'd killed enemy soldiers before. And with this plan he'd kill again. But that was war, and the prospect of killing a fellow Marran soldier with his bare hands left a sour taste in his mouth.

The watchman shouted for help, and John had no more time for his personal qualms. He punched him in the side of the head. The watchman grunted, wavered, and pushed John back against the rail. Far below, the rowboat bobbed in the dark water. Pain blossomed in John's side as the watchman hit him with a closed fist. He tried to push him off but the watchman hooked a leg around his, unbalancing him. The vast chasm of the sea yawned wide and dark beneath him.

John grabbed the watchman by the front of his jacket to keep from being pushed over the side, but it only served to unbalance them further. They toppled over the rail.

They plummeted together, hitting the water with a ferocious splash. John's breath rushed out of him with the impact, and for a moment he sank into the dark and freezing depths, stunned.

Salt stung his eyes as he regained his bearings. He'd released the watchman as they fell, and the man was nowhere to be seen. John kicked to the surface.

Gasping as his face hit air, he swam a few strokes to grab the edge of the rowboat. No commotion came from above. Had the watchman's shout not alerted anyone?

The watchman resurfaced a few feet away, coughing and sputtering. He grabbed John by the back of the uniform, and tried to wrench him away from the side of the boat. What was this idiot doing, trying to drown them both? John kicked out, and twisted in the watchman's grip.

Blood streamed down the watchman's chin from his broken nose. John hit him there again, forcing him to release his grip. John gripped the lip of the rowboat with one hand and pushed the watchman away with the other. He shouted, scrambling to keep his grip on John's clothes. John steeled his resolve, fisted his fingers in the man's hair, and pushed his head beneath the water. The man struggled, arms flailing and slapping ineffectually at John's arm and face as panic gripped him. The splashes echoed loudly in John's ears, but he held firm. Soon the watchman's struggles slowed, and he went still. John released the locks of soaked hair, and the man slowly sank beneath the waves.

John stared at the empty water for a moment. He took a deep, steadying breath, and hauled himself over the side of the rowboat. He'd wasted too much time. The first candles would be burning close to the fuses by now. He didn't have much time left to complete his self-imposed mission.

He thought for a moment about simply running away. Leaving the last ship intact to watch their fellows burn, and escaping with his life. But no. If he left them in fighting shape, there was a chance the attack might go ahead as planned. It didn't matter that he was throwing his own life away for this; the stakes were larger than his own fate. There were innocent lives on the line, and he'd never been an innocent to begin with. This is what he had decided, and he would see it through. A decisive stroke.

His muscles burned as he took up the oars and rowed to the third and final ship.

It too was eerily dark and quiet. John secured the boat and climbed, soaked hair and uniform dripping back down into the rowboat. He'd lost the fuses and candles in the water, but they'd be useless wet anyways. He'd have to improvise.

He swung one leg over the rail. Had no one on this ship or the last heard the scuffle? How long until the other watchman returned to his post and found his comrade gone? How long till a patrol walked past the first powder storeroom and found it unguarded?

For the third time, John stole across the deck and down into the hold. He grabbed a rag and a lantern from the hall, and tore the rag into strips as he made his way to the powder storeroom, leaving a trail of seawater on the floor.

Like the other storerooms, John made short work of the guard and lock. He pried the lids off several powder barrels, and stuffed the ends of the torn up strips of rag into the explosive substance. These short, ragged fuses wouldn't give him much time to get away.

He lit them and ran.

BOOM!

John braced himself for a fiery end but it never came. The explosion hadn't come from the storeroom behind him, but one of the other ships. The force of it shivered through him. And suddenly he felt very heavy. He'd killed before, but never comrades, and the weight of his choices hit him like an aftershock.

There was a beat of silence before the aft bell started clanging an alarm. John dragged his heavy body into motion and ran.

He made it all the way to the main deck, darting among other confused sailors.

"Hey, you!" A soldier grabbed John's arm, and he wrenched it away. Across the water, the *Bear* burned. He sprinted across the deck, soaked boots squelching.

"Seize him!"

Another hand grabbed him, ripping the shoulder seam of his uniform.

BOOM!

Fire bloomed across the deck of the second ship. A huge hole opened up in the side, and the ship began taking on water, but it did nothing to extinguish the fire steadily climbing the upper decks. The ship began listing to the side, the dark forms of surviving sailors swarming to escape, silhouetted by the orange flames.

He had to get out. He had to get to the rowboat before this ship went up too. It didn't matter that he had nowhere to go if he escaped. That he would be a criminal with a bounty on his head. He was going to fight.

John lurched forward, the sleeve of his jacket ripping clean off in the soldier's grip. But he didn't get far; a wall of comrades-turned-enemies stood between him and the starboard rail. He whirled, only to find the same on the other side.

He was cornered.

John's muscles tensed, his lips pulling into a snarl. These men didn't know him. Didn't know what he was capable of, or what was coming. The soldiers closed in.

BOOM!

The deck bucked, throwing everyone off their feet. Flames licked across the boards all around them, climbing the rigging with astonishing speed.

John scrambled back to his feet and made a break for the side. But he was snared, a beast caught in a trap.

So, like a trapped beast, he fought.

With a roar to rival the flames, he barreled into the line of soldiers. Several of them scattered, either fleeing the flames or running to put them out. But enough held firm. Two of them caught John and wrestled him to the ground, bashing his skull against the deck. Hot blood gushed down his forehead. He bucked them off, landing a hard blow to the side of one's head. That soldier went down, but two more took his place. John's vision blurred as blood flowed into his eyes.

Across the water, another explosion rocked the *Bear* as fire reached its second powder storeroom. The ship groaned, in its death throes. The crews of all three vessels were now abandoning ship instead of trying to save them.

The soldier bashed John's head against the deck again, forcing him onto his stomach and wrenching his arms behind his back. Cold iron closed around his wrists.

IN THE END, the sinking of the flotilla did not prevent the Marran navy from invading the town at Whitestone Reef. But it did prevent a massacre. The townspeople heard the explosions, saw the swarm of rowboats heading their way, and by the time the small contingent of soldiers had landed on their shores, the Kefryeans had fled into the foothills at the base of the Gray Mountains.

Just as well—the soldiers were in no condition to fight. Less than a third of them remained, and they all knew the deaths of their comrades were on John's head.

Or, more accurately, around his neck.

Once making land, the soldiers had wasted no time taking over the abandoned town, and John was thrown unceremoniously into a seaside shed full of fishing nets. The door was barred behind him and a man posted there to prevent escape, but not before the men in charge of John's imprisonment had taken it upon themselves to give him a good beating.

His brain sloshed in the confines of his skull like bilge water, the still sluggishly bleeding wound on his forehead leaking onto the packed dirt floor, and granules stuck to his face. His body ached all over, and he knew beneath his clothes, bruises would soon be blooming. If he lived that long.

John pressed his cheek to the ground, trying to reorient himself. His hands were still shackled but at least they were in front of him now.

The shed smelled of salt and fish, but that was the least of his worries. Even in his probably concussed state, he was under no illusions about what his future held. The soldiers hadn't dragged him from the burning wreck and brought him to land out of the goodness of their hearts. The Marran navy was overly fond of hangings, and that was the only thing John had to look forward to. He almost wished they'd left him to burn or drown. It might've been better than waiting here in this stinky shed, wondering when they would come for him.

His head ached. His shoulders ached. And he wanted to sleep. If he wasn't a murderer before, he'd definitely earned that title now. He'd watched from the landing boats as all the ships burned down practically to the waterline. He was fairly sure the second two sank, but the *Bear* had come unmoored and drifted closer to shore, caught on what could only be the dead reef that was the area's namesake. How long would it burn? How long would its charred remains stay there at the mercy of the sea, crashing against the reef? Would it outlive him before it broke up and became just more flotsam in the waves?

Two DAYS, John waited, and no one came for him but to throw in a crust of bread and a skin of foul tasting water. He could hear the soldiers out there. Hear the crash of the waves and call of the gulls. But his concussed brain barely registered these things. He knew only pain. Hunger. Thirst. He began to wonder if they intended to let him die of dehydration instead of bothering to hang him. That wasn't very sporting of them. They could at least do him the courtesy of the rope.

On the third morning, the door opened, and it was like looking into the shining lights of the afterlife's gate, until a man in a

Marran uniform stepped through. John blinked back the tears that had formed in his eyes from the sudden light.

"Lieutenant John C. Hakon?" a gruff voice asked.

John managed to nod, though he felt as detached from that name as he'd ever felt from anything. He was no longer a Lieutenant in the Marra Royal Navy; he'd become a low creature that lay in the dirt to starve.

"Take him," the man commanded.

Two soldiers entered the shed and hauled John up to his feet, unshackled his hands and secured them behind his back once again. He wavered and almost fell, but they dragged him out anyway, his limp form hanging between them.

The first thing he saw was the newly constructed gallows in the middle of the town's grassy square. Goats grazed beneath it, unconcerned with anything but the grass between their teeth. So this was what his captors had been doing for the past two days, constructing a proper gallows for him. He was almost flattered.

The soldiers hauled him up the few short steps to the platform where the man with the gruff voice waited. Somewhere in the back of his mind, John registered that the man wore a captain's uniform, silver laurels crossed with a red anchor stitched into his black collar. If only a captain was going to be announcing his death, that meant no one of a higher rank had survived. Admiral Lowe was surely dead.

John almost wanted to laugh. If only the admiral had listened to him, they could have left this place in peace and continued on their merry way to war with an enemy that could fight back. They could have lived. But the admiral hadn't listened. He'd wanted to raze this quiet town. He'd wanted to kill that mother and child picking blueberries on the clifftops.

A crowd of surviving soldiers gathered around the platform as the guards forced John to the center. He pointedly averted his eyes from the instrument of death awaiting him. Instead he looked out at the crowd. He recognized Massey, who glared back at him hatefully. The crowd whispered.

He fought like an animal.

He was always too quiet.

He's a beast.

The beast of Whitestone Reef.

"John C. Hakon," the gruff-voiced captain boomed. John noted he had dropped the military rank. John was just an animal now. About to die. "You are charged with willful destruction of the Crown's property, treason, and murder. For these crimes you are sentenced to hang by the neck until dead."

Short and to the point. John supposed there was no reason for greater formality on foreign shores in a deserted town square. There had been no trial. No questions, and no defense. He was going to die and that was that.

John finally looked up to the loop of rope hanging menacingly above his head. He wanted to go to his death with dignity, but his body had other ideas. His knees gave out, and it was only by the strength of the soldiers on either side of him that he remained upright.

Weak. He had never been weak. He'd promised himself he wouldn't be.

Someone came up behind him and looped the noose over his head, tightening the knot at the back of his neck. The soldiers still held him up, they wouldn't move away until the trapdoor dropped out from under him.

John closed his eyes.

"Sails, Captain!" someone shouted from the direction of the beach. John opened his eyes, and looked with the rest of them toward a soldier running up the sandy path.

"Sails?" the captain said. "What nation? One of ours?" It could have been Kefrye, come to take back their land. Or Talva, come to wrest control of the mines from their mortal enemies. Or even the Marran reinforcements, arriving early.

"No, sir." The soldier stopped at the foot of the platform, out of breath. "They fly the pirate flag, sir; it's the De—" A rifle shot rang through the square, and the soldier dropped to the grass, bleeding from the temple. Every military eye swiveled from the distraction of the pirate ship to the new, more present threat. An ambush.

Chaos broke out across the square. The goats bleated in fright and took off in all directions, getting underfoot of the soldiers running to take up arms. The captain shouted something unintelligible beneath the noise.

More shots. The soldiers holding John abandoned him and ran. He sagged in the embrace of the noose, unable to keep himself upright. The rope dug into his throat, and he choked. His hands were still shackled behind him. He couldn't get free.

He barely registered the report of gunfire, the shouting. The soldiers scattered to cover, and between their fleeing forms strode a young man in a white coat. He took his time, unconcerned with the danger around him as the soldiers began firing back. Blood bloomed upon his shoulder like a rose, but he barely flinched.

John's vision narrowed, the slow strangulation of his body weight in the noose choking out what life he had left. Surely this young man was Death coming to claim John's soul.

The young man leapt onto the platform, bullets kicking up the dirt all around him. He smiled at John. Too handsome. Too calm. His black eyes glittered with mirth as he leaned down to look John in the eye.

"Are you the beast they've been whispering so much about?" he asked, as if John was in any position to answer. The man's dark gaze swept over him. "You don't look like much. But I suppose even a beast must be spared occasionally." He stepped back, drew a long, ornate saber from his belt, and slashed the rope. John crumpled to the boards, gasping for air.

The young man crouched next to him, still heedless of the chaos and violence around them. The soldiers' tenuous position was already being overrun by pirates, men and women who looked suspiciously like townsfolk bringing up the rear. John's vision curled into darkness around the edges.

"Before you go, I should thank you. I thought I'd have to take on the whole lot, but you burned them down to a nice, bite-sized piece." His teeth clicked together on the word *bite*. John fought against the darkness threatening to pull him under. The man reached out and smoothed John's hair back from his blood-caked forehead. "So thank you, John Hakon. You did well."

It was no use; John's vision went black.

Chapter 10

THE DEMON'S RIGHT HAND

JOHN C. HAKON

Spring, 1661

John woke with an aching throat and a cotton-filled head. He groaned, his mouth tasting sour, as if he'd drunk too much. It was not a hangover that ailed him this time, but the residual effects of the hanging he'd barely survived. He rolled over onto his hands and knees, retching. Nothing came up, but he wiped his mouth on the back of his hand anyway.

Looking around, John realized a metal-barred cell in the bowels of a ship once again enclosed him. He still wore his dirty officer's uniform with its missing sleeve. The other cells were empty, and a single tallow candle guttered in a sconce on the wall, casting long shadows across the brig. Fuck. He was back where he started, imprisoned and hopeless. What was the point of saving him if they were going to throw him in the brig? The man had known his name, but who was he?

Well, no point in sitting around here to find out. His grandfather's knife had been confiscated before the fishing shed, so he felt around the floor until he found a large splinter in the wood and pried it up. His body protested, but he wasted no time in reaching through the bars and fitting the thin end of the splinter into the lock. It was a long shot, but it wasn't as if he had anything better to do. He jiggled the piece of wood around in the lock, trying to catch the tumblers.

The brig darkened further, and a man emerged from the shadowed corner, black eyes gleaming like a hungry shark. The same man who'd walked through a hail of bullets at Whitestone Reef and cut John down from the noose. His bloodstained white coat had been replaced by rich green velvet. His ebony hair hung loose around his ears instead of slicked back as it had been before. He looked infinitely softer than he had in the square as bullets zinged around him. Like a spoiled gentleman. But John still got the impression this was a man many feared.

"I admire your tenacity," he drawled. "But that's not going to work."

The man produced a key from his pocket, and the metal door swung open between them.

"Who are you? Why did you save me?"

The man flipped an elegant hand in the air. "Is this hostile questioning the thanks I get for saving your life? Perhaps I should have left you in the gallows." The deep tones of his voice smoothed the sharp edges of a refined Talvan accent.

"And you promptly threw me in the brig," John countered, crossing his arms.

A ghost of amusement twitched at the corner of the man's mouth. "Come, we will discuss things in a more savory atmosphere." He turned his back on John without a second thought, as if John, still armed with the splinter, was no threat at all. John had no choice but to follow.

He observed the man's broad shoulders as he followed him down a series of dark corridors. The man had a few inches on him, with long graceful limbs and an air of detachment now that there was no imminent violence. The farther they walked, the more John came to realize how massive the ship must be, almost as big as the *M.W.S. Bear*. Finally, they reached a dark oaken door, and the man opened it, stepping aside to let John enter ahead of him.

An elegantly appointed parlor met them on the other side,

clearly an antechamber to the captain's private quarters. On one side, a golden candelabra sat atop a large wooden table meant for war meetings, casting the only light in the windowless room. And on the other, a pair of velvet armchairs sat facing an unlit fireplace.

The man, clearly the captain, closed the door behind them, and strode past John to settle into one of the armchairs. He crossed his legs, and poured himself a glass of dark red wine from a crystal decanter. When John remained by the door, he gestured to the chair across from him.

"Take a seat Mister Hakon."

John grimaced, but did as he was told.

"Wine?"

"Are you going to answer my questions?" John asked, his voice a bit raspy from the unsuccessful hanging.

The captain poured him a glass anyway. A rich fruity scent wafted to John's nose as he abandoned his splinter on the table and accepted it. John narrowed his eyes as the captain took a delicate sip of the dark red liquid. He was undoubtedly Talvan, but clearly not a military man. The clothes were too expensive for a smuggler, and a merchant wouldn't have risked getting on the wrong side of the Marran navy. That left only two options: a Talvan-endorsed privateer, or a pirate.

This revelation did not strike fear into John. In his six years in the Marran navy, he'd dealt with his fair share of pirates and privateers both, though never this close and personal before.

John took a large gulp of the expensive tasting wine.

"Now." The captain set his glass on the table between their chairs. "You seem not to know who I am."

"Should I?" The alcohol burned past John's sore throat, straight into his empty stomach, where it felt almost as if it evaporated straight to his head. John realized suddenly that all he'd had in days was a hard crust of bread and dirty water. His stomach growled loudly, and the captain raised an eyebrow.

"You were imprisoned for quite some time. Would you like something to eat?"

John's empty stomach tried to answer for him, grumbling loudly again, but he wanted information first.

"Tell me who you are and why you saved me."

"Very well. I am the pirate they call the Deep Water Demon, and you are currently on my ship, the *Kraken's Fury*."

John's stomach clenched, a small spark of fear lighting for the first time since he'd woken up in the brig. He knew of the Deep Water Demon, everyone did. The legends of his strength and brutality were told throughout the Islands. He had the biggest bounty on his head of anyone currently sailing.

"I see you know me by name, if not by my face." The Demon seemed pleased. And John got the sense this man reveled in the stories told about him, the more outrageous the better. To be perfectly honest, John was surprised none of the stories mentioned his looks. He was handsome beyond belief, his face sculpted from ivory, starkly contrasting his dark hair and eyes.

John tried to school his expression to neutrality, and took another gulp of wine. The rich alcohol hit his empty stomach like a cannonball.

"I've heard of you," John finally said. "Why would you save me? If you're planning on collecting a bounty on me, I hope you left a few of them alive." He was a criminal now. A mass murderer and traitor. And the Empire would want him back, if only to turn around and hang him.

"It's nothing like that." The Demon smiled slightly, and leaned forward, elegant fingers interlacing before him. "As I said before, you helped me, though you didn't intend to. I've been hiding out near Whitestone Reef. I wouldn't have been able to sail out of there without being spotted. After your treasonous little stunt, I rallied the townspeople. Your surviving comrades are now prisoners of war, and the people of Whitestone Reef owe me a favor. You saved me from a costly battle. That would have been inconvenient." His dark eyes flashed. "But you. You accomplished it all on your own, and that is impressive. Did you know they're calling you the Beast of Whitestone Reef?"

He did. He'd heard it whispered through his delirium from the other side of the fishing shed walls, and from the crowd who'd come to watch him hang. From Massey's own mouth. He wondered distantly if Barber had survived.

John had already mourned the man he used to be as he lay concussed on the dirty floor of his prison. He'd mourned the fellow soldiers he'd killed with his actions. And he hadn't wanted to die, but some part of him felt he deserved it. Being called a beast by the men he used to lead, the men he used to entrust his life to, was the least of the punishments he deserved.

After some silence, the Demon continued. "I'm curious, just how beastly are you? Why did you blow up those ships?"

"They were going to kill all the villagers," John answered, a bit breathlessly, caught in the snare of the Demon's intense eyes. The wine was definitely affecting him more quickly than it should have. Or was it the dizzying weight of his actions finally starting to crush him?

"How noble," the Demon drawled. He sat back again, as if his interest in John had suddenly died upon learning John hadn't blown up an entire flotilla for the fun of it.

The Demon was somewhat of an enigma. He had the refined manners of a gentleman, but something feral lurked in him as well. A violence beneath his perfect ivory skin. And for some reason John's stomach dropped. He had the distinct impression this man would dump him off the side of the ship without a second thought if John failed to serve the purpose for which he'd been saved.

But he still didn't know what that purpose was.

John couldn't decide what to say next. Should he plead for his life? Or would that only heighten the Demon's disinterest? He seemed like a man who would not be swayed by such displays. No doubt he'd been begged for mercy so much by now he was sick of it. John rubbed his jaw with his knuckles, realizing a beard had sprouted up in the days of his captivity.

The Demon's head quirked to the side, a lock of raven hair falling across his brow. "You think I am going to kill you." It was not a question.

"It crossed my mind."

"I'm not as monstrous as the stories say."

"Somehow I doubt that." To this, the Demon only downed the rest of his drink, so John continued. "Why did you bring me here, Captain? I doubt you went through the trouble of saving my life because I accidentally helped you."

"Very astute." The Demon's tone was mocking.

John stood, patience running thin, but the wine roiled in his stomach, and he swayed. "Answer the question and quit playing games," he growled.

The Demon surged to his feet, grabbing John by the front of his dirty uniform and hauling him forward. His eyes flared with anger so intense John's fear spiked, both emotions almost palpable between them.

The Demon's nose wrinkled in distaste, and he loosened his grip. "You stink. Perhaps a bath is in order before I tell you why you are still alive."

John's head spun at this change of mood. "What?"

"Come, the bathwater in my chambers will be cool enough by now. We will get you cleaned and fed before we discuss this further." When John only gaped at him, the Demon released his shirtfront and grabbed him by the wrist instead. In a daze, he let himself be led through a door on the other side of the room.

A bank of stained glass windows lined the entirety of the opposite wall of the bedchamber, and for the first time since he woke, John saw the outside and realized it was early morning. The light shone gentle and blue over the open water. Beneath the windows lay a huge bed, sheer curtains hanging down around its corners. Plush, jewel toned rugs layered the wooden floor, and a copper tub gently steamed before the unlit fireplace. John took a deep breath, the room smelling of sex and lavender.

Upon the bed, a figure rolled over, exposing one delicate ankle. John stopped short, and the Demon dropped his wrist.

"What..." John began to say, but the figure sat up, covers falling away to reveal a naked woman. She rubbed her eyes, her hair mussed with sleep.

"I am sorry to wake you, my dear, but I need the room," the Demon said, nothing like affection in his voice. The woman climbed out of bed. She moved like a noblewoman, all refined grace, yet heedless of her own nakedness in front of a stranger. She retrieved a floral dressing gown from the end of the bed, and made to leave. "Bring some breakfast for our friend here, if you're so inclined," Yves said, but it felt more like an order than a request. The woman nodded and walked past both of them, not sparing a kiss nor lingering touch for her supposed lover. She closed the door behind her.

"Now." The Demon turned toward John, pointing to the bath. "Get in so you can quit stinking up my rooms."

John blanched. "I'm not bathing in front of you!"

The Demon rolled his eyes. "Fine." He pushed John toward the tub and drew a silk paneled folding screen between them. John could still see the Demon's silhouette against the light from the windows, but he supposed he had no choice in this matter.

"I don't stick my neck out for just anyone," the Demon said from the other side of the screen, as John shucked off his blood and filth crusted uniform. He rubbed his thumb over the ripped sleeve for a moment, a symbol of his disgrace. Then discarded it to the floor and quickly sank into the warm embrace of the water. It smelled heavenly, a little sachet of dried lavender floating on top. "The truth is, I think you have something I need."

"And what is that?" The uncommon luxury of the warm water combined with the wine to relax him far past what should be reasonable, given he was currently in the bedchamber of one of the most notorious and violent pirate captains to ever sail the

Islands. John sighed, and leaned his head against the back of the copper tub.

They both fell into silence as the door opened for who John assumed was the woman again. He'd seen no other people but her and the Demon. A dish clinked on a tray, and the Demon murmured something to her. She left again.

The Demon drew the screen aside, and John sat up with a start, covering his privates.

"What the hell—"

"Oh please." The Demon rolled his eyes, and set a tray of food on a small table beside the tub. He did not retreat behind the screen again, but leaned against the wall as if all of this were perfectly normal.

"Do you mind," John said peevishly. He couldn't have gotten himself into a more vulnerable position than sitting stark naked in a tub with his natural enemy looking on.

"I thought you wanted to know why I saved your life," the Demon said.

"Spit it out then."

All the Demon's supposed anger had gone, replaced by amusement again. "Clean up, and eat your food."

John glowered at him, but his stomach betrayed him by growling again, and his tight muscles were beginning to loosen as the grime leached off his skin in the lavender scented water. He reached for a date off the laden plate and popped it into his mouth, then picked up a cloth from the edge of the tub and began scrubbing

"My first mate is dead— I didn't kill him," the Demon interrupted himself as John's eyes sliced to him. He took a step forward, testing, but John's eyes remained on him.

"How did he die?" Now that he'd eaten something, John's hunger sharpened, and he shoved more food into his mouth.

The Demon's tongue pushed against the inside of his cheek in annoyance. "You interrupt a lot for someone who's desperate for answers." When John remained silent, he continued. "It doesn't matter how he died. The point is, I am without a first mate, and I want you."

John startled, dropping a date into the bathwater. "Me? Why the hell—"

"Shut up, and let me speak!" The Demon barked. John shrank back against the side of the tub, but as quickly as his anger had flared, the Demon settled back into graceful nonchalance. He stepped to the end of the tub, his eyes never leaving John's face. John drew his knees up, as if that would protect his vitals in this horribly vulnerable state. The Demon swirled his fingertips lazily in the bathwater.

Fuck, why was John allowing this? How had he even let himself get into this position? But the Demon's eyes lit with ferocity now, mesmerizing, and John couldn't seem to move.

"I am beginning a new venture, one that my current crew is not suited for. I must do away with the ruffians who know nothing else but pirating, and build a crew I can be proud of. Who will carry me to further greatness. To do that, I need a first mate by my side that will be loyal to me. I need someone practical and tough. Someone who knows when it is time for violence and time for peace. I need someone capable of curbing my more violent tendencies when there is a need for it." During this speech he'd crept closer to the head of the tub, his fingers trailing the surface of the water, and now crouched to John's eye level. John couldn't move, entranced by the Demon's words.

"And you think that's me? That I'll be loyal to you? You don't even know me." John's voice came out quieter than he intended.

"I know enough of you, and I would know more of you." The Demon's knuckles brushed the side of John's knee, and John tensed. His stomach churned with unease. Could he really refuse an offer like this? He'd already sunk his military career along with the rest of the flotilla, and soon enough he would be a wanted man if any soldiers survived to make it back to their commanders. He'd be a fugitive for the rest of his life, even if he fled far from the shores of Marra's Empire. What other option did he have but to take the Demon up on his offer?

"You're wondering whether to take your chances with me or the world," the Demon said.

John nodded.

The Demon reached up, his gaze dropping to John's throat. His graceful fingers feathered across the bruising there. Contemplative. John tensed again, and the Demon's touch slowly moved down over his collarbone and chest. Had John not been one glass of wine deep on an empty stomach, and probably still concussed, he might not have allowed it. But as it was, he felt like he was drunk on the fear the Demon elicited in him.

"What must I do to prove myself worthy of your loyalty?" the Demon murmured, his voice deepening. His hand moving ever lower.

Loyalty. John had always assumed that pirates, especially a man with as brutal a reputation as the Deep Water Demon, ruled through fear or even a sick sense of mutual greed. John swallowed past the lump in his throat.

"I don't know."

The Demon's hand dipped below the waterline, trailing down John's tense stomach and over the soft hair beneath his navel.

"You must learn not to fear me, John. I need someone to tell me when I am being monstrous." It was as if he was goading John to tell him off, to refuse him, and tell him he was being monstrous in this very moment. His hand closed over John's cock, which John had not noticed hardening until now.

"Fuck," John groaned, powerless to refuse the Demon's advances even if he'd wanted to.

The Demon's eyes lit with intrigue. "Oh, I do love a challenge."

He stroked down John's length, and before John knew it, he was being pulled out of the tub and guided toward the bed with a firm hand clamped on the back of his neck. The Demon pushed him onto the edge of the bed, and his exhausted legs folded easily.

When his hand closed over John's dick again he arched into the touch, fear turning to lust in an instant. He didn't understand why the Demon was doing this, or how it had gotten this far, but if he was going to die anyway, he may as well get something out of it first.

There was no kissing, nor gentle touches of a lover. John's mind briefly flit to the naked woman who'd exited this bed only minutes ago. Would she take revenge on him? Or was the Demon free to take as many people to bed as he wanted?

The Demon's hand was replaced by his warm mouth stretching over the considerable girth of John's dick. He sank down quickly until the entirety of John's cock was encompassed in its wet heat. John fell back, clutching the sheets as the Demon's long tongue roved over his shaft.

Pleasure built low in John's gut as the Demon deepthroated him, hands roaming over his thighs, and massaging his balls. A groan escaped John's sore throat, and the Demon hummed in satisfaction.

In his life before this, John had dedicated almost every waking moment to his career, climbing the ladders of the military designed to keep commoners like him in the lowliest positions. He'd had little time for affairs of the heart or flesh. Still, he'd slept with his fair share of comely men and women, and none of them possessed the skills the Demon currently displayed.

The Demon set a voracious pace, taking the entire length of him with every stroke of his enticing mouth. John propped himself up on his elbows to watch him, head spinning with panic-edged euphoria. There was no coming back from this, just as there was no coming back from destroying the flotilla. This was much more pleasurable, but no less dangerous.

John buried his fingers in the back of the Demon's ebony hair, his hips twitching up to thrust deeper down the Demon's throat, chasing whatever pleasure was left to him in this life. He'd made up his mind. The Demon moaned in turn, as if fellating him was a great pleasure. His nails dug into John's thighs, and his pace increased. John's head swirled at the sight of the most notorious pirate on the sea's pink lips stretched around his cock.

John tensed, a moan escaping his lips, and with one last flick of the Demon's deceptive tongue, he spilled hot and hard down the Demon's throat. The Demon swallowed it all without difficulty, milking John's exhausted body for all he was worth. John's arms went weak, and he collapsed back onto the bed, staring up at the ceiling in a daze. The Demon released him and stood, gazing down at him from the end of the bed.

"Fuck, Captain. You'll have to teach me how to do that," John groaned.

"I think we are on a first name basis by now, John. If you can trust me not to bite your dick off, I think you can call me Yves." The Demon paused for a moment, then said, with that slight edge of amusement in his voice, "Does this mean you've agreed to be my second–in-command?"

John managed to sit up. "Yes." It was his only option. Better than being on the run. And he didn't know why, but the events that had unfolded in this room had kindled a strange sense of loyalty in him.

"Good." Yves smoothed down the hair John had grabbed in his ecstasy. "Now get back in the bath, you're still filthy."

Chapter 11

THE KRAKEN'S KINGDOM

YVES FRANCOIS LESAUVAGE

Spring, 1661

The scent of lavender had drifted out into the parlor, where candles burned low on the table. Yves slumped into one of the chairs, staring into the wavering orange flames. The taste of cum still hung heavy in the back of his throat, and he poured himself another goblet of wine, drinking deep of its heady aroma.

John Hakon was gone, led to the first mate's quarters by Yves's current paramour, Kristina, to sleep and collect himself before being introduced to the crew. Yves sighed, running his hands down his face. He hadn't actually intended to seduce John Hakon at first, but Yves's appetites had grown so ravenous that at this point it was almost inevitable. He inspired only two emotions these days. Lust or fear. Sometimes both.

Yves downed the rest of the goblet, rich liquid washing away the bitterness of John's cum. He lowered his head to rest on his hands on the table, images of childhood flashing briefly behind his eyes. The weeks he'd spent in General Batteux's household. There and gone. A different, distant encounter in a bathhouse behind an inn. A slow breath shuddered out of him. The memories, no matter how brief, always came after. Reminding him of a past he'd sooner forget.

Despite the darkness physical intimacy still roused in him, he used his otherworldly beauty to seduce without care for who it was or how it would affect either of them. It was like a compulsion, an insatiable need to bed as many as he could.

Perhaps he sought to overwhelm the memories of his past. Perhaps knowing that inhuman darkness inside him made him incapable of love, he sought to prove his own nature wrong.

Yves sat up again. There was no use wallowing in self-pity. He needed only to press forward as he always had. It wasn't only the Deep Water Demon that townspeople spoke of in fear and awe in dockside taverns these days; another young pirate had come onto the scene. A pirate who laughed in the face of danger, then disappeared like mist. A pirate who carried a hunting hawk on his shoulder.

All the more reason for Yves to solidify his power before others could swoop in and take hold. From the corner of the table, he retrieved a yellowed parchment, embossed around the edges, and heavy with old ribbons and seals. His fingertips ran reverently over the now familiar words, much softer than he'd touched John. This was the future he'd been working toward since the day he'd murdered the general and his family. The future that would protect Ana. The future John C. Hakon, the Beast of Whitestone Reef, would help him build.

Months ago, he'd returned one more time to Saulés to retrieve the last of the loot he'd stolen from General Batteux's mansion. Buried beneath a pile of old jewelry in a small wooden chest, he'd found this parchment. The deed to a long forgotten island to the west of Lasland. His fingers ran over the scrawled coordinates.

This was where he would build a home. His kingdom.

Chapter 12

First Night, Part 2

Fox

Summer, 1662

Fox winced as the man's knuckles connected with his ribs. He danced away on light feet, too small boots rubbing at his blisters. The same boots Gaël had bought him all those years ago. A gift of care and love. At least that was what Fox had thought at the time.

All that was over now. Gaël had abandoned him, and he'd grown out of the boots.

Even after finding Gaël's bracelet, Fox had hung around the Salted Snail for days, waiting for him to come back. To say it was all a misunderstanding, and he hadn't meant to leave. Fox had searched the docks and met a fellow sailor who'd been discharged from the *Narwhal*. He'd seen Gaël sign on to another ship before dawn. He'd not been kidnapped. Or killed. Or anything else. He'd left Fox willingly.

Gaël was dead to him. But even after a year and a half of being stuck in this godsforsaken town, Fox still grieved him.

Fox ducked under another swing, landing a punch to his opponent's guts. The man was middle-aged, and had about fifty pounds on Fox's own scrawny, underfed form. He'd been nice enough at the beginning of the night, offering to buy Fox supper when he'd come up a few tals short at the tavern. Unfortunately for Fox, that good deed had come with invisible strings.

Strings that had become all too obvious when it came time to part ways and the man had become handsy and demanding. When Fox resisted, the man had tried to drag him into an alleyway. So Fox resisted harder.

Once again Fox found himself in an all-out brawl on the streets of Wave Harbor. He didn't want to fight, but trouble always seemed to find him anyway. A crowd had formed around them, curious to see who would win out: the man, or the scrawny gutter whelp with the too long hair.

The torches lining the street guttered, barely keeping the night at bay as Fox took another hit to the torso and landed one on the side of the man's head in return. The onlookers jeered, unsure exactly who to root for. Fox's eyes scanned the crowd, searching for a gap, some avenue of escape that wouldn't end with him and this man alone in another dark alley. His gaze landed on a lone figure standing half shadowed in the mouth of the alley Fox had almost been dragged into. The figure didn't cheer. Didn't move. He watched Fox with a cool, assessing gaze.

A shiver ran up Fox's spine, but he couldn't afford to get distracted.

His opponent roared, drink-swollen face turning red, and barreled toward him. Fox sidestepped, one leg snapping out to catch the man in the ribs with his knee. The man's breath came out in a pained *oof*, and he crumpled to the cobblestones. Here was Fox's chance. He whirled, searching for an exit.

Sharp pain sliced into his side, and he stumbled back, almost doubling over. He pressed his hand to the spot and it came away crimson. The man jumped on his feet again, still winded, but with a bloody knife in his hand.

The creepy bastard had stabbed him.

Fox's legs suddenly felt heavy, and he stumbled again, pressing his hand hard to the wound in an attempt to staunch the bleeding.

"Got you," the bastard sneered. His eyes raked over Fox's wounded form, and he licked his lips. "Since you can't use your mouth for anything nice, maybe I'll cut you a new hole for me to play with."

What the fuck—who brought a knife to a fistfight? That was just rude.

Fox regretted not thinking of it himself.

His head was getting fuzzy, and he found himself on his knees, blood dripping between his fingers onto the dirty street. The bastard grinned, switched the knife to his right hand, and stepped toward him.

Shit. Fox was gonna die. Were all these people really going to watch him get gutted in the street?

"That's enough." The figure from the alleyway stepped between them. He must have been about Fox's age. Early twenties at most. His short blond hair stuck up at all angles and gray feathers hung on a long strand behind his ear, which glittered with gold rings. He stood before the knife casually, one hand in his pocket, the other loose at his side.

"An' who'er you?" the bastard spat. "This gutter trash owes me—"

The blond man moved so fast Fox didn't even see it happen. One moment he stood there, as casual as could be, the next, the barrel of a pistol pointed squarely at the bastard's chest. The gray feathers in his hair fluttered in the breeze.

Now bringing a gun to a fistfight, that was vastly outside the realm of fairness, but Fox could get behind it.

"If you don't already know me, you don't wanna know," the blond man drawled in a lowland Marran accent. "You already took your pound of flesh, so move along before I put a bullet in your gut."

"Little whelp, I'll—" The bastard took another step forward, knife raised, but halted in his tracks as the blond man cocked the pistol.

"Move along," he repeated. "It would be inconvenient for me

to catch a murder charge on my first night here." He tilted his head. "Though they might thank me for putting down a rabid dog like you."

If the bastard took offense to that he didn't say. He stuck the blade back into his boot and slunk off like the cur he was, grumbling about spending money for nothing.

Their entertainment over, the crowd began to disperse. The blond man waited until most of the bloodthirsty onlookers had gone before he uncocked and holstered the pistol. His eyes turned for the first time toward Fox, startlingly blue even in the dim torchlight.

He strode over and knelt beside where Fox lay bleeding on the street.

"Here, let me—"

Fox swatted his hand away, baring his teeth like his namesake. He wasn't going to trade one debt for another. Even if this man had saved his life.

The blond man reached into his coat, and fished out a large handkerchief.

"Staunch the bleeding with this. I have something to ask you, and I'd prefer it if you didn't bleed out in front of me." He held the cloth out for Fox to take, and after a moment of eyeing it suspiciously, Fox snatched it and pressed it to his wound.

"I'm not a whore," Fox spat. This man had obviously seen enough to know how the fight had started. And Fox had been mistaken for a prostitute before. That was all anyone ever seemed to want from him. So it was better to make himself perfectly clear from the start.

"It's got nothing to do with that," the blond man assured him. He had a self-satisfied smirk on his face that was both off-putting and intriguing. "You might have heard of me. I'm Rowan, captain of the pirate vessel *Siren Song*. I saw you fight just now, and I want you to join my crew."

Fox stared at him for a moment. The stab wound in his side burned, and his brain blurred from the combination of blood loss and coming down from the adrenaline of the fight. At least the flow seemed to be slowing. He probably wouldn't die. At least not today. Infection, however, was a distinct possibility considering the knife had come from that dirty bastard's boot.

"I lost, though."

Captain Rowan shrugged.

"What's the catch?" Fox asked warily.

"Nothing. You work for me. I pay you. It's a job. You have had one of those before right?" He thought for a moment. "Well, you might die, but given your current situation, pirating might actually be safer."

Fox almost laughed, but his body hurt too much. He sat up a little straighter.

"Why...why would you want me on your crew? I'm just a scrawny kid."

Rowan raised an eyebrow. "So am I. Like I said, you're a good fighter, and I need people who will be loyal."

"Who says I'll be loyal?" Fox had no idea why he was arguing so much. He wasn't in danger of passing out here on the street, but it was probably better to skedaddle as soon as possible before the creepy bastard decided to come back.

"You don't seem like the type to bite the hand that feeds you," Rowan said.

"That guy fed me," Fox pointed out.

Rowan rolled his eyes. "It's a metaphor, kid. Do you want the job or not?"

Fox didn't really have the option to mull it over.

"Yes."

THE *SIREN SONG* was no grand warship, but it had a quiet elegance about it that could only come from expert craftsmanship and meticulous care. Some of the tension in Fox's body eased as soon as his sore feet hit the deck. Captain Rowan boarded after him.

"Home sweet home," the captain said, a wry smile playing on his lips.

Now that they were a bit further removed from the violence of the street, Fox realized his new captain had a sort of brash, boyish handsomeness about him.

Another man, who looked younger than both of them, hurried over.

"There you are! It's so late I was about to send out—" He caught sight of Fox with the bloody kerchief pressed to his side. "Did you stab him?" he asked, more incredulous than accusing.

"What? No!" Captain Rowan looked affronted. "He *got* stabbed, and I prevented him from being stabbed more."

"Bringing home another kicked stray then, are we?" The younger man gently chided, and though Fox would usually have taken offense to being called a stray, the man's demeanor was so gentle, he found himself soothed by it instead.

"We're all strays, Logan," the captain replied easily, "that's why we're pirates. This is..." His voice trailed off. "Sorry, I didn't catch your name."

"Fox."

"No surname?" Logan asked.

"No." He didn't remember it.

"Stray indeed." Logan laughed.

"As if you have a stellar pedigree," Captain Rowan teased.

The easy banter between these two was putting Fox more and more at ease. He chided himself not to let his guard down so quickly.

"Take him to the infirmary while I get the book," Captain Rowan told his comrade.

Logan brought Fox belowdecks to a room lined with empty cots, and retrieved an old man from the adjacent room.

"Old Joe will stitch you up." Logan's eyes dipped to Fox's bloody shirt and the rest of his shabby clothes. "We'll have to find you new clothes."

Fox nodded, dazed.

Despite his apparent advanced age, Old Joe made quick work of cleaning and stitching Fox's wound. It wasn't as deep as Fox had feared, but it had sure bled a lot.

"Leave it to a creepy bastard to have a shallow prick," Fox muttered under his breath. His head twitched to the side, habitually looking for Gaël to share in the joke even after all this time, but of course the space next to him was empty.

All patched up to Logan's satisfaction, he led Fox to a small storeroom. When he opened the door, Fox was amazed to see it stuffed full of clothes of every size, color, and quality. There were even a few gowns thrown in the mix.

"Where'd you get all this?" Fox laughed.

"Stole it of course. Pick something that suits you."

Fox pawed through the pile, selecting a pair of blue trousers, a white shirt with an open collar, and a short padded jacket. He was so giddy to finally have new clothes he began to strip off the old ones right there in the hallway. Logan grimaced as Fox pried off his worn out old boots. Fox looked down, realizing his raw and blistered feet were on full display.

"New boots too, I reckon," Logan said, bending to retrieve Fox's old ones.

"No!" Fox snatched the boots back before he realized what he was doing.

"They're clearly too small for you," Logan said, raising his eyebrows.

"I know but..." Besides the bracelets, which he kept in his pocket but couldn't bear to look at, they were all he had left of Gaël. "I want to keep them."

Logan sighed as if dealing with an unreasonable toddler.

"Fine, but you're not going to wear them, you hear? We can't have you crippling yourself out of stubbornness."

Fox clutched the boots to his chest and nodded. He felt foolish for hanging onto them when they were literally falling apart as well as hurting him. But it was a hurt he had to hold onto for a little longer.

He padded barefoot after Logan to their next destination.

The captain's quarters.

A spike of anxiety lanced through his middle. Worry that it was all a setup after all. He had no reason to trust these men, despite—maybe because of—their supposed kindness toward him. He felt almost like a lamb being cleaned up for slaughter. He'd learned long ago that you never got something for nothing. Unfortunately, his foolish heart kept forgetting.

But when Logan opened the door, only Captain Rowan sat at a small table with a leather-bound ship's log open in front of him.

"Sit."

Fox obeyed, sliding into the chair opposite while Logan, obviously second-in-command, stood at his captain's shoulder. Captain Rowan turned the book to face Fox.

"This is the crew contract. You will receive a wage equivalent to two silver tals a week, minus one-half tal a week for room and board. Once a season, you will receive an equal share to other crew members of whatever plunder is left after the captain and first mate's combined shares of thirty percent, and twenty percent for ship's expenses. You are free to leave at any time. However, if you leave without notice before the season is over, you forfeit your share, and will not be considered for rehire." He speared Fox with an icy glare. "I don't permit drunken fools or violence between crew members."

Fox's mind reeled. That was a lot of numbers, but if he understood it correctly it was more than fair compensation. After a year and a half of eating scraps on the street and barely any wages on the *Narwhal*, these numbers seemed astronomical.

"If this is agreeable to you—" Captain Rowan flipped a few pages further into the book to a page that contained two columns of words. He held out a quill to Fox. "Then sign."

"I can't," Fox said.

"The terms aren't agreeable? Or you can't write?" Captain Rowan asked.

"Or read."

"We'll have to remedy that," Logan muttered, as if making a mental note of all the ways he would have to whip Fox into shape.

"No matter. I will write your name, and you can leave your print," Captain Rowan said.

Fox nodded.

The captain took the pen back and scrawled two words on a new line. He pushed an inked sponge in a clay container toward Fox.

Fox leaned over the book, his eyes flitting over the unfamiliar symbols.

"What's this say?" He pointed to the first word in fresh ink.

"Fox."

"And this?" Fox's finger followed the line to the second word.

"It says 'crew.' That's your position until we see what you can do."

Fox nodded. He inked his thumb on the sponge and pressed his thumbprint onto the page beside his name.

Business done, Logan led Fox away, found him a pair of boots, and escorted him to a small cabin that contained a pair of bunks, one of which had a pillow and blanket folded on top.

"This one is yours for now. We might have to double up once we hire more crew. Get some sleep."

With that, they left Fox alone, which was his least favorite thing to be.

He slumped onto the edge of the lower bunk and rubbed his still ink-stained thumb across the worn leather of his old boots. This was to be his new home, and so far it was good. He almost felt safe, and that made him anxious. The last time he'd felt this way, he'd woken up to the worst day of his life.

Fox stood quickly, the wound on his side flaring in pain, and the boots dropping to the ground with a thump. His nerves prickled uncomfortably. This situation was out of his depth. When Gaël left, the whirlpool of Fox's emotions had turned into one that devoured anything good and spat out only bones in return. New clothes, safety, and kindness? Those things hadn't existed in his world for a long time. He had to make this into something he understood.

He was sure to be quiet as he left his new room, and padded barefoot down the hall.

He knocked on the captain's door.

After a moment, the door opened.

"Logan, how's our stray settling—" Captain Rowan's eyes lit in surprise. "Oh. It's you."

Fox twisted the hem of his new shirt between his hands, hoping it portrayed just the right amount of vulnerability to be alluring, not pathetic. He bit his lip, looking up at the captain through thick brown lashes, even though they were almost the same height.

"Um, can I come in?"

Captain Rowan frowned but stepped aside to allow Fox entry. Fox followed him in, closing the door behind him.

"So what can I do for—"

Before Fox could think anymore, he grabbed the captain by the front of the shirt and kissed him.

A startled sound escaped the captain's throat. His stubborn mouth softened for a moment before he grabbed Fox's shoulders and forced him away. Fox's back hit the door. A mixture of anticipation and trepidation wormed its way through his gut, followed closely by sharp rejection, then relief when Rowan didn't continue kissing him.

"What's this?" Captain Rowan demanded. He sounded angry. Fox's anxiety spiked higher.

"I-I'm sorry. I know you said...but I thought..." Fox hadn't really thought this through fully. He'd simply given in to the antsy energy crackling across his nerves.

"I meant what I said," Captain Rowan said firmly. "I didn't hire you because you're pretty."

Fox's lip trembled, but this time he wasn't putting on an act. Getting scolded by a man he'd just met shouldn't have hurt, but it did. He wasn't used to being turned down, nor anyone finding value in him beyond sex. In the end, that was all Gaël had wanted him for too. But Captain Rowan glared at him as if regretting bringing him onto the ship, and was about to throw him back onto the streets, or to the fishes.

"I'm sorry," Fox gasped, tears brimming.

The captain's eyes softened.

"Look, you should know now that I don't sleep with crew members. I don't care if you sleep around while you're on this crew. Just...do it because you actually want to, not for any other reason." His fingers tightened on Fox's shoulders. "I saw you fight like hell today because some creep thought you owed him. It's not like that here. You're safe here. You belong to yourself, and you don't owe me anything but the work I'm actually paying you for."

Embarrassed tears slipped down Fox's cheeks at the words. He'd known that, deep down. But he'd fought and scrapped and suffered for a year and a half alone on the streets of Wave Harbor, and somewhere along the way he'd forgotten what it was like to have someone who actually cared.

A profound wave of relief washed over him, tumbling him through its undertow.

Captain Rowan's grip slackened, and he stepped away.

"You can stay here till you've collected yourself. Then go back to your quarters. And *do not* lie and tell people we slept together, or I'll void your contract immediately."

"Aye, Captain."

"Call me Rowan."

They settled on either side of the table, and Rowan dealt out a hand of cards without saying another word. He pointedly ignored Fox's tears until they dried up with several minutes of residual sniffles, during which Rowan trounced Fox in two hands in a row.

Fox wiped his nose on the back of his sleeve. The warm room and sudden release of tension that had been building and building throughout his miserable day made his head heavy. He propped his chin on his hand, zoning in and out of the card game before him. He'd close his eyes for a minute while Rowan mulled over his next turn.

Fox woke from a dream about floating on fluffy clouds to find himself in a wide, cozy bed. Sunlight streamed over the blue quilt tucked around him.

For a moment, he didn't know where he was, and his hand reached out to the other side of the bed, seeking Gaël's warmth.

But the other side of the bed was cold and untouched. Fox's mind plummeted back to the Salted Snail, reaching out and finding Gaël gone. Renewed grief enveloped him, sucking him down into the whirlpool.

A rough snore broke the silence, and Fox remembered where he was. He sat up quickly, scanning his surroundings. He'd fallen asleep in the captain's quarters? Had Rowan lied after all?

His eyes landed on the captain's form, draped uncomfortably over one of the wooden chairs, head tilted back, mouth open and snoring.

Warmth spread through Fox's chest.

Finally, someone who kept their word.

Chapter 13

CROCUSES ON A GRAVE

HENRI WELLS

Spring, 1663

The sun beat down on Henri's head as the priestess intoned the last lines of the burial prayers. Henri didn't hear them. The priestess's voice mixed with the droning of insects in the foliage around the perimeter of the small cemetery, and farther off, the crash of waves on the rocky shore. The day was beautiful, though much too hot for spring.

It seemed like yesterday that Henri's mother had woken from her fevered slumber, insistent that the snow was melting and the crocuses would be reaching their small purple heads toward the sun. She'd talked and talked and talked about them in her once rich voice, now raspy with illness, until Henri gave in. He bundled her frail body into as many blankets and shawls as he could find in their little two room apartment above the bakery, and carried her down the stairs to the village green, ringed in still dormant oak trees. Sure enough, the purple buds of spring crocuses were poking through the gaps in the melting snow. Not yet ready to open and show the delicate yellow threads within.

Henri had crouched down, his mother cradled in his arms, no heavier than a bird now. She'd reached out to touch the purple petals, the snow, and her fingertips came away wet.

"Back home," she said, her voice no more than a shiver, "the snow was always long gone by the time the crocuses bloomed." She smiled. "But there's something about life bursting through that—" Her words cut off in a fit of coughing, and Henri swiftly brought her back inside.

She never finished what she had to say. Too weak to get the words out. She was gone four days later. Henri's name, the last word on her tongue. By that time the snow had melted, and with her death, spring had burst forth in all its riotous glory of life.

But snow still clung to the contours of Henri's heart, spring not yet daring to poke its buds through. So he did not register how beautiful the day was, nor that the priestess had finished her prayers, and waited for him to speak. He could not take his eyes from the simple pine box as the baker's boys, Claude and Louis, lowered it into the grave. It seemed impossible that his mother lay within, washed and dressed in her best clothes by his own hand. Her only child. He'd tucked a bouquet of crocuses with their bulbs into her thin brown hands, and he couldn't stop thinking about what she might've meant to say that day in the snow.

The pine coffin hit the bottom of the grave with a soft thud. Gentle fingers brushed Henri's arm, and he finally wrenched his gaze away from his mother's coffin to find the priestess standing beside him. She dropped a handful of grave dirt into his hand, still cold with the last dregs of winter. He stared at it a moment until the priestess gestured him toward the open grave. On the other side of it, Claude and Louis, only a few years younger than him, waited with shovels, looking properly somber. He'd grown up with them, the closest thing he had to brothers.

A memory rose unbidden to his mind as he stepped toward the edge of the grave with the cold brown dirt in his hand. His mother in her rocking chair by the fire in their tiny apartment, bouncing Louis on her knee as Henri and Claude played on the braided rug at her feet. His father had recently left for a season at sea, and she'd been pregnant, though it had never come to fruition.

The smell of baking bread wafted up through the floorboards where the brothers' parents toiled in the bakery below.

Henri's mother had raised the baker's boys as much as their own parents, trading child minding duties with their mother as the two women switched off working in the bakery. When the boys got older, all three of them worked as well.

Did they feel even half of the grief that lay like a blanket of snow over every part of Henri's world now? Even a tenth?

The toes of Henri's boots met open air, and he stopped on the edge of the grave. He looked down at his mother's final resting place beneath his feet. Breathed in the warm, honeyed smells of spring which did not quite reach his dulled senses, and dropped the soil into the grave.

It landed with a thud. Jarring. Claude and Louis picked up their shovels, Louis wiping a stray tear on his sleeve, and began to fill in the grave. Each thump of earth on the coffin lid was a heartbeat. A reminder that life still went on, even if his mother was dead.

The priestess appeared at his side again, looking up at him expectantly. He stared back. Vacant.

"My fee?" she finally said, the heartbeat of soil on wood punctuating her words.

Henri blinked at her. "I...I used the last for..." he trailed off, thinking of the two copper tals he'd tucked in among the crocuses, now being buried.

The priestess frowned, her eyes flicking to the knapsack that had rested by his feet as he listened to her prayers, now fallen over in the new grass without his legs to lean against.

"Your bag looks heavy." He didn't miss the accusing tone. *You seem to be leaving. And you must have something left.*

But he didn't. The bakers had stopped collecting rent for the little apartment after Henri's mother had become too sick to work. But Henri's wages alone weren't enough, and he'd slowly sold off their meager possessions over the last few years to pay for medicine. The last of it had gone to buy the coffin. He hadn't been able to stand the thought of his mother's frail body in the ground with only a shroud to protect it.

"I'll pay," Claude said, digging into his pocket and handing over a few coins. The priestess bowed in thanks, and left without another word. Henri took up a shovel.

Between the three of them, the grave filled in no time.

"So you're still set on leaving," Louis said, when the last shovelful of dirt settled.

"Yes."

"Where are you going?"

Henri shook his head as if to clear it. He hadn't cried yet. It was all frozen inside him. He touched the brass key hanging on a leather chord beneath his shirt. The last thing his father had given him. Right after his mother's illness had taken a turn for the worse two years ago, his father had shown up alone in the dead of night after an absence of nearly three years. And when he saw the state of his wife's health, his eyes had grown distant and haunted, and he'd turned away without going to her side. He'd pressed the key into Henri's hand, saying all manner of things Henri didn't understand. And when Henri asked after his half sister, who sailed with him, his father had no answer.

"I'm going to try and find my father." He was searching for more than that, but couldn't tell them.

The brothers grimaced but said nothing. They'd discussed this before. Heard Henri and his mother arguing over his desire to find his father and sister, who hadn't returned from sea since. Most of the town had long assumed them dead.

"We think you should stay," Louis chimed in, always the softer brother, doted on by his parents and Henri's mother. "You know Maman and Papa will let you stay in the apartment, and you'll always have a job in the bakery."

Henri shook his head. He didn't want to stay. He couldn't continue living in those rooms where every little thing reminded him of her absence. Even the few days since her death had been a torture of loneliness. On more than one occasion he'd turned to ask her a question, or made too much food, and remembered all over again that she was gone.

"I can't," was all he could say.

"Here." Claude dug into his pocket again and pressed two silver tals into Henri's palm.

"Thank you." Henri didn't quite know what to do now. He knew if he lingered here, knelt beside the grave and touched the earth above her head, and said goodbye...he might never get back up.

A hammock waited for him aboard a merchant ship down in the harbor, and he had to go. So he slung his knapsack over his shoulder.

"We'll plant some crocuses for her this fall," Louis said. "We know they were her favorite."

"Thank you," Henri said again. They said their goodbyes, and Henri turned away from his mother's grave, hoping that this time next year it would be blanketed in purple.

Chapter 14

THE FOX'S PATH

GAËL

Summer, 1663

Gaël's breath fogged in the cool, earthy air as he ran, bare feet digging into the leaf litter and dirt, leaving a path of where he'd been. But a path stretched ahead of him too, his own footprints leading out into the gloom as if he'd been here before. No matter what he did, there was no deviation. He could not change it, only follow.

A streak of copper flashed between the tree trunks. There and gone. Always elusive. Always out of reach.

"Wait!" Gaël reached for it. His feet pounded against the earth, heedless of sharp sticks and rocks. No matter how fast he ran, no matter how hard he tried to follow, his feet only landed in his own predestined prints. The copper streak flitted in and out of his vision, never close enough for his outstretched hand to touch.

"Please," Gaël begged, but it didn't stop. It led him deeper and deeper into the woods like a will-o'-the-wisp. He didn't care if it led him to ruin, only that he needed to...

The trees opened suddenly, revealing the edge of a high cliff with the sea crashing beyond. The fox stopped at the edge, turning to look back at him as he stumbled over roots and logs. Its shining copper fur ruffled in the wind rushing up off the water.

"Please wait," Gaël sobbed. No matter how fast he ran, he never got closer. The fox tilted its head as if trying to understand his words, its tail swishing peevishly. This had never happened before. His path had always led him through the tangled woods. No footprints told him where to go now.

"I'm sorry, Fox. Please."

The fox stood up, and looked out over the waves below. Then, with a springy hop, it jumped over the edge of the cliff.

"No!" Whatever invisible force kept him in place vanished, and he ran to the edge of the cliff in time to see the fox plunge into the blue sea. Gaël only hesitated for a moment before he followed.

Air rushed past his face, stinging and cold, before he hit the water. Like the rocks and sticks that cut his feet, the impact didn't hurt. He sank like a stone beneath the waves. Freezing water punched the breath from his lungs. He struggled toward the surface, but as in the forest, he made no progress.

A pale figure emerged from the watery gloom, materializing into Fox. The real Fox. His brown hair floating around his face, freckles stark against pale skin. Gaël reached for him, more desperate for him than air. Fox swam closer, green eyes glittering and flashing in the filtered sunlight from above. His lips moved, words lost in the water. Gaël reached for him, needing to pull him close, needing to apologize over and over until Fox understood how sorry he was. But Fox remained beyond his reach. Fox was screaming at him. Raging. In all Gaël's dreams, he'd never caught up with Fox before. Yet here he was. So close.

Gaël's lungs burned, and he opened his mouth to tell Fox he loved him. That he was sorry. But cold seawater rushed in instead.

Fox's eyes widened. Was he afraid for Gaël? This was only what he deserved, to be the subject of Fox's anger. To suffer.

Fox turned away from him.

Gaël woke with a gasp, sitting bolt upright in his hammock, overbalancing and falling face first to the floor of the *Seahorse*.

"Pipe down!" someone grumbled from across the room. Gaël remained face down on the dirty floor, trying to steady his ragged breathing and fight off the dregs of the dream. His hands trembled.

He'd dreamed of Fox again. Another dream where he could never catch up. But this time Fox had waited for him, even if he couldn't touch him.

It had been three years since the night Gaël left Fox sleeping soundly in that slightly uncomfortable bed at the Salted Snail Inn. Anxiety had gripped his chest like a vise, squeezing away the deep well of love he had for that beautiful man, his best friend. As he watched his chest rise and fall with even breaths, the anxiety turned to all out fear. What had he done? With Fox in his arms, all those years of pining had coalesced into one shining moment of bravery. He had kissed him, and that kiss had turned into so much more.

But the fear that gripped him was too great for even love to overcome. What if he'd messed it all up? What if he'd hurt Fox, and when Fox woke he'd say it was all a mistake, he didn't love Gaël like that, and they could no longer be friends? Gaël couldn't endure that.

As if in a trance, Gaël had brushed one last kiss across Fox's forehead, slipped out of bed, and unraveled the leather bracelet from around his wrist. His heart beat so fast it hurt. But it would be better for him to leave now, and hold this bittersweet memory in his heart, than to stay and put them both through the heartbreak of the life they'd built crumbling because of Gaël's foolishness. It would be better for both of them.

Fox had *cried* while Gaël was inside him. It was terrifying. He never wanted to see Fox cry again.

He could still feel the press of Fox's skin on his lips as he boarded the first ship out of Wave Harbor. When the morning dawned, he knew Fox would be waking alone, confused at finding Gaël gone. His heart would be breaking. Gaël's heart broke along with him. Gaël knew he was a coward, and he did not deserve

Fox's love. But the fear had carried him until Wave Harbor shrank to a speck on the horizon. After that, he'd known he'd made a mistake. But there was no going back.

Now, laying on the floor of the crew quarters with the dreamy memory of Fox so close, Gaël's heart was broken still. By the time he'd finally made it back to Wave Harbor, Fox was gone, and Gaël had been searching for him ever since. It had become the undercurrent of every thought, the catalyst of every action, and every time he dreamed of chasing Fox, he knew he needed to change his path.

He needed to leave the *Seahorse* at the first opportunity. Find a different ship with a different crew that might have once met Fox. Sail a different course that might lead back to him. It was all Gaël could do—keep searching forever.

No sooner had this thought crossed his mind than cannon fire rocked the ship. Gaël sprang to his feet. Crew members woke all around him. Gaël pulled on his boots and rushed up the steps.

The main deck had already fallen to chaos, crew members rushing around half dressed and sleepy. Off the starboard bow, a huge warship with a tentacled figurehead flew a pirate flag. Gaël went cold as if he'd plunged back into the freezing water of his dream. He knew that ship, every seafarer in the Islands did. The *Kraken's Fury*, captained by the dreaded Deep Water Demon. Some said it was crewed by the hungry ghouls of the Demon's victims. Others said if you surrendered easily, the Demon might grant you mercy.

The *Seahorse*'s crew didn't seem inclined to throw themselves upon his mercy. Nor did the Demon seem to be in a merciful mood. The *Kraken* fired a second volley straight into the side of the *Seahorse*, cannonballs punching through the hull. Gaël didn't have time to think, didn't have time to wonder how pirates had gotten so close without an alarm being raised. He sprinted across the deck, and joined a group of crew members working to load the main deck cannons. But it was no use; terror ruled the crew. His hands slipped on dew-slick tools as the

Kraken's cannonballs thundered all around them in the gray dawn, tearing apart the *Seahorse* with startling ferocity. Gaël's gunner crew finally managed to finish loading, and got a single shot off. It arched across the water, missing the side of the *Kraken* by mere feet.

On the back foot and already damaged, they were no match for the Demon's might. The *Seahorse*'s captain ran up a white flag of surrender, and as quickly as it had started, the battle fell into stillness. The *Kraken* prowled closer, as if its figurehead would come to life and seize the *Seahorse* in its tentacles. Instead, grappling hooks took hold and drew the two ships together. Pirates swarmed across the lines with swords and axes held between their teeth. Not ghouls, but flesh and blood. The weaponry was unnecessary—the crew of the *Seahorse* was too terrified to fight.

A pirate forced Gaël to his knees among the other crew members. They huddled in the center of the deck as the Demon's pirates broke into the hold and began looting their cargo. Gaël stayed as silent as the rest of them. The Demon had a reputation for cruelty, and Gaël would have preferred to fight to the end rather than rely on a slim hope for mercy. But now, if Gaël was to have any shot at living long enough to find Fox, he couldn't draw attention to himself. He kept his eyes trained on the deck between his knees as the pirates swarmed through the ship, stealing all they could and destroying anything they couldn't.

Beneath the sound of the ransacking pirates, there was a persistent roar. Gaël focused on it, unable to place it at first. Until, with dawning horror, he realized water was rushing into the lower decks. Even if the Demon didn't kill them outright, the *Seahorse* was going to sink.

The man beside Gaël flinched, and a frightened whimper sounded from somewhere else in the knot of the crew. Gaël raised his eyes to find a tall, elegant man striding across the deck. He wore a long dove gray coat, his black hair slicked back from an aristocratic face, and carried an ornate saber in his right hand.

He stopped a few feet from where Gaël knelt, issuing orders

to his crew in a calm, deep voice. A dark aura seemed to engulf the *Seahorse*'s crew, suffocating any fight they might have had left.

This was the Deep Water Demon. It had to be.

The *Seahorse* lurched. The pirates below deck yelled and began to scurry back topside. The Demon didn't move a muscle as others stumbled. It was sinking, and Gaël felt the awareness of that fact ripple through the *Seahorse*'s crew. If the Demon left soon enough, would the *Seahorse* be able to limp to shore? Or were they doomed to sink beneath the waves?

The pirates finished loading the last of the loot and began to disengage the *Kraken* from her prey.

"Orders, Captain?" a pirate asked, over the roar of the water pouring into the lower decks.

The Demon's dark gaze swept over the ship until it landed on the gathered captives, on Gaël himself. Was it bravery that kept Gaël from averting his eyes as the others did? Or was he simply a prey animal unable to take its eyes from a carnivore?

"Disable the boats," the Demon ordered. The man beside Gaël began to weep. The Demon gazed at the captives dispassionately, then turned on his heel and strode back to the *Kraken*. The pirates smashed holes in the hulls of the landing boats, cutting off any escape for their victims.

Fuck, Gaël didn't want to die. He couldn't leave this world before he saw Fox again. He'd never gotten a chance to say he was sorry.

The *Kraken* drifted away as the last pirates retreated from the *Seahorse*'s decks, small looted trinkets in their hands. Below, the water continued its onslaught through the lower decks, the roar almost deafening. The demon had left them alive only to be engulfed by the sea. No land could be seen in any direction, and even if they could cling to the damaged landing boats or the debris of the *Seahorse* itself, they would have no supplies, and no way to get to shore.

Hopelessness swept through the *Seahorse*'s crew like a plague. A few sailors began to deploy the wrecked landing boats anyway, desperate to escape the deathtrap their ship had become. Some sailors stayed on their knees as the *Kraken* drifted farther away, too terrified to move. Gaël's eyes landed on a single wet footprint on the deck.

Gaël had to live. He had to forge the path that would lead him back to Fox. Maybe it was a coincidence that he'd dreamt of Fox right before this attack, but this time, Fox had waited for him. Fox had been close. If Gaël was cursed to search the seas for the rest of his life for the crime of breaking Fox's heart, so be it, but he'd be damned if he didn't try to atone for what he'd done.

It was not time to surrender, it was time to fight.

Gaël stumbled to his feet, not yet knowing which direction the path would take him. His mind was only filled with his eventual destination. He made it to the rail, and leapt.

The shock of the water knocked his mind back to the end of his dream. He had no hope of Fox forgiving him. All he wanted was to see his beloved freckled face again. To make sure he was happy and safe.

Gaël resurfaced, gasping, and swam. The *Seahorse* groaned behind him, and the sailors shouted as it listed further. He glanced back once to see some abandoning ship and taking their chances with swimming like him, some battling with the scuttled landing boats. The *Kraken* hung back, not under full sail yet, watching the *Seahorse* sink beneath the waves.

As Gaël neared the *Kraken*'s side, a bullet zinged past him, then another, until the water was peppered with them. Gaël caught one of the grappling ropes hanging off the *Kraken*'s side. The crack of gunfire redirected, picking off other sailors in the water behind him. He didn't question it. Only one path remained for him now, so he climbed.

Gaël fell to the deck, sodden, only to feel the cold press of a pistol barrel against the side of his head.

"Tell me why I shouldn't dump your body back into the sea right now." Gaël looked up to find a bearded man with stern eyes holding the gun.

"Let me join your crew." Gaël's voice did not waver as it had when he'd begged Fox to wait for him in his dream.

The man's eyebrows rose. "Do you know what you're asking?"

As if anyone on the four seas was ignorant to the legends of the Deep Water Demon.

"I know it's my only option."

The bearded man cocked his head to the side. "You think yourself worthy of the Deep Water Demon?" He said it like a man used to striking fear by using the name.

"I'll prove myself. I'll fight anyone on this ship, and win."

A crowd of pirates had gathered to watch this spectacle, the crack of gunfire stilled. Maybe the sailors in the water were already dead. Maybe the pirates were bored. But more distantly Gaël could hear the groan and snap of timbers as the *Seahorse* sank, and the panicked shouts of those who remained alive.

The pirates parted, making way for a tall figure in their midst. The Demon stopped before Gaël as he had before, gazing down his long aristocratic nose. The bearded man kicked Gaël onto his hands and knees, as if prostrating him before a king. Terror shivered through Gaël's body, but when the toe of the Demon's silver-tipped boot lifted his chin, he held the Demon's gaze until the Demon's lips spread into a wicked smile.

"You will fight me."

A gasp rippled through the pirates, and Gaël's heart stuttered as if it would quit on him before he even got the chance to fight. The Demon held out an elegant hand, and a crew member placed a pair of gray leather gloves in his palm.

"Allow me, Captain," the bearded man said, but the Demon cut him off with a now gloved hand.

"Our friend here deserves a chance to live, does he not? He swam all the way here, and no bullet we fired touched him." His gaze swept disapprovingly across the gathered crew, and they cringed back. "Perhaps fate has sent him. Let him up."

The pistol at Gaël's temple withdrew, and the bearded man helped him to his feet.

"Arm him," the Demon ordered, drawing his saber with a flourish. The bearded man sighed, and drew his own cutlass to hand to Gaël.

"I prefer axes," Gaël said. If he was going to fight for his life, he needed to fight at his best.

Another sigh, and a pair of axes were found for him. The assembled pirates cleared a space in the center of the deck.

Screams echoed from the direction of the *Seahorse* as the waves finally swallowed it. The Demon licked his lips as if drinking in their anguish. Gaël tested the heft of the axes in his hands, trying to block out the sounds of the drowning men being sucked down in the ship's wake.

The Demon twirled the saber lazily, then dropped into a fighting stance. Irrational fear threatened to overwhelm Gaël's senses, but he pushed it roughly aside. In its place, determination settled over him like a shroud, loosening his muscles, clearing his mind to focus solely on the task at hand.

Gaël lunged low, shoulders bunching as he slashed at the Demon's legs. The Demon parried easily, the refined steel of the blade sparking against the ax's pitted head. Gaël swung the other ax up under the Demon's guard, narrowly missing gutting him as the taller man danced back on light feet. Gaël kept up his onslaught, and the Demon met every strike with grace and strength. More strength than his elegant frame should have possessed. Gaël got the feeling if he let up for even a moment, the Demon would gain the upper hand and cut his throat.

The Demon never struck back, only met Gaël's attacks until Gaël's brow dripped with sweat, and his chest heaved. Yet the Demon seemed unfazed, not a hair out of place. What kind of man could stand there so unmoved? Could possess such strength?

Gaël retreated to the edge of the circle of onlookers, trying to catch his breath. The polished spurs on the Demon's boots clinked ominously as he circled like a stalking wolf.

"You've lasted longer than most." The Demon seemed almost

pleased. "So I will offer you mercy. If you can land one hit on me, I will let you live."

Hope at the end of this long tunnel. He hadn't been able to land a hit yet, not even close. But if he could manage it, he would live another day to find Fox.

Gaël charged, a roar ripping from his throat. He crossed his axes, aiming low, and the Demon swung his saber down to parry, but at the last second Gaël flipped one of the axes over the back of his hand, and cut up toward the Demon's shoulder. The Demon's eyes sparked, and he twirled away from the cut of the ax. His sword flashed bright into Gaël's eyes, and Gaël stumbled to one knee, his progress halted by the press of the blade at his throat.

He looked up into the Demon's dark, assessing gaze. Gaël remained on one knee like a penitent. At the Demon's mercy.

"What a pity," the Demon drawled.

"Captain..." The bearded man stepped up beside them. "He won."

The Demon's gaze slid to where the blade of Gaël's first ax pressed to his inner thigh, then to the second: its edge glistened with the barest hint of ruby from where it had parted the sleeve of the Demon's immaculate coat.

A slow, vicious smile spread across the Demon's lips. He stepped away, sheathing his sword. His gloved fingertips touched the shallow cut on his arm and came away smeared with blood. Gaël remained on one knee, unsure if the Demon would keep his word.

The Demon touched the blood to his lips. His black eyes sliced to Gaël.

"Welcome to the *Kraken's Fury*." He turned on his heel, coattails flaring behind him, and departed. Gaël got shakily to his feet.

The path ahead of him cleared once again, and this time, he felt in his gut it was the right one.

Chapter 15

GIANT'S BRAWL

HENRI WELLS

Summer, 1663

Henri grit his teeth as the tattoo needle pricked his skin again and again, slowly inking out another geometric scale in the body of the sea serpent now banding his arm. The tattooist didn't glance up from his work as Henri flexed his other hand, easing the tension in his muscles where the other serpent already coiled around his upper forearm, his skin puffy and red where the needle had repeatedly poked him. He'd been here for hours, and his back ached where it rested against the sparingly padded wooden chair. In the end, it would be worth it. The design was almost done.

Looking at his arm now felt like going back in time to when his mother used to roll up her sleeves to knead dough in the bakery. Those were some of the only times he'd seen the tattoos, barely visible beneath their dusting of flour. After the dough had been put aside to rise, he'd trace the patterns of the serpents through the flour, and ask her to tell the story of them again.

"You've heard it so many times, mon cher." His mother would wipe the flour from her skin, and roll down her sleeves, but she always told him anyway. "Once, when the world was only water, there were two great serpents of the sea. One was named La and the other, Fa. They were mates, the only two of their kind, and they roamed the great oceans from north to south, from east to west, chasing the sun and moon across the sky. They roamed in cold and warm water both, and no other creature dared cross them...

"One night as they gazed up at the stars together, a great light streaked across the sky. But they were not frightened, for they had never learned to fear anything. Nothing in this world could hurt them. But the light grew larger and larger and they realized it was a great flaming stone hurtling toward the sea. La dove out of the way, retreating to the deeper water. But Fa wasn't fast enough. The great stone crashed into the sea, trapping Fa's tail between it and the seafloor. The stone's flames boiled the water, sending up a great cloud of steam so La could not see its mate.

"When the steam cloud cleared, La realized that Fa was pinned by the stone, and the sea had boiled away so much that the great mounds and coils of Fa's body stuck out of the water. For the first time in its ancient life, La was afraid. It had never seen Fa hurt before. La tried to move the great stone, but the water was too shallow, and it almost beached itself too.

"By this time it was almost morning. La tried once again to free its mate, but it was no use. In the east, the sun rose. Fa looked at its mate, and for the first time, a creature of this world wept. 'Do not try to free me again, my beloved mate,' Fa said. 'Or you may suffer the same fate. Swim into the deep water, and think of me no more.'

'No,' La said. 'I will stay. I will free you yet.'

"But it was not to be. The sun rose, and crossed the sky as it always did. But this day, Fa's beautiful scaled body was not protected by the cool waters, and the loops and coils of its body began to bake and harden in the sun. By the time night fell, Fa had turned to stone.

"Now La too wept for its dead mate, and vowed that if ever creatures were to live upon Fa's stony scales as they did in the sea, it would honor the children of its beloved and grant them safe passage in its waters.

"And that, mon cher," Henri's mother would say, kissing him on the nose, "is how the Islands were formed. And why Yarene sailors wear the serpent tattoos to show that we are the children of Fa, so La will grant us safe passage."

One of these times when Henri was still quite young, he'd asked, "So Fa and La are like you and Papa?"

His mother had gone still. "How do you mean, Henri?"

"Well you love the sea, Maman. But you're stuck on land. And Papa loves you, but he's always out at sea." He'd blinked up at her for a moment, his eyes suddenly welling with tears. "But then, am I the great stone? Because I've trapped you here?" He'd heard his father say as much one winter night when his parents argued, and he was meant to be asleep.

He's trapped you here. You have no spark left.

"Oh, mon cher." His mother gathered him in her arms, kissing his beaded hair. "Don't you listen to Papa. You haven't trapped me. I chose to be here with you."

THE STING of the needle roused Henri from his thoughts as the tattooist picked out the feathers of the serpent's tail. His mother had never wanted him to get the tattoos, never wanted him to become a sailor, or worse yet, a pirate like his parents.

Henri peered at the tattoo. Only a few more pokes and it would be done. He wondered which was meant to be La and which was Fa, or if it even mattered. As the last dots of ink penetrated his skin, the curtain doorway of the little dockside shop was flung aside, revealing a small man with wild brown hair and a constellation of freckles across his nose and cheeks. The tattooist flinched, poking a dot of ink into Henri's skin where one didn't belong.

"Fred! My favorite artist of the skin!" the freckled man exclaimed, before realizing Fred the dockside tattooist already had a customer in his chair. He smiled wide. "Oh, I'm sorry. I interrupted." But he didn't back out of the tiny shop, which was really only fit for two people at a time, and Henri was larger than most. Instead the man leaned over Fred's shoulder as he etched the final line into Henri's skin.

The freckled man whistled, impressed. "Mighty fine work as always, Fred."

Fred wiped little specks of blood and ink away from Henri's skin with a rag that definitely could've been cleaner.

"That'll be seven coppers," Fred said, ignoring the other man. Henri dug the money out of his belt pouch. It felt a bit light these days. His pay from four months aboard the merchant vessel he'd taken from his hometown had dwindled quickly after only a few weeks here in Kadling Kay. He'd have to find work on another ship soon, hopefully one that would lead him to information about his father. Everything he'd tried thus far had been a dead end.

Henri stood and thanked Fred, eager to escape the suddenly crowded shop. As he edged past the freckled newcomer, chest to chest in the cramped space, he made the mistake of looking down, and was met with a pair of the most brilliantly green eyes he'd ever seen, so bright with mirth he thought it impossible they could ever dim.

The man winked and slipped past Henri farther into the shop, already chattering to Fred about what exactly he wanted and wrestling off his pants before tumbling into the tattooist's chair. Henri averted his gaze and hurried out of the shop, yanking the curtain closed behind him.

"I'm TELLING YOU LADS! The guy was a giant! Taller'n me by two feet at least!" The loud, lilting voice was somehow familiar, but Henri only hunched lower over his ale in his seat at the bar. It had been several days since he'd got his tattoos, and they were still a bit sore. On top of that, he'd stayed on to chase a lead on his father that hadn't panned out, and he'd had no luck finding work since. His coin dwindled by the day. So tonight he was in no mood to give energy or attention to the other loud, obnoxious patrons in the tavern. He'd finish his ale and go to bed so he could get an early start down at the docks tomorrow. Someone had to hire him eventually.

He sipped the one mug of ale he'd allowed himself, tuning out the noise as he made plans for the future. Soon enough he was down to the dregs at the bottom of the clay mug. He slid it over to the other side of the bar and stood. The crowd jostled in every square inch of the tavern room, packed together like fish in a net.

"You give that back!" someone shouted over the din of voices. Henri glanced sideways at a knot of men who were clearly some kind of rogues instead of hardworking sailors. Through gaps in the crowd, he could see a large red-faced man leaning over the table across from a group of three smaller men, who were definitely also up to no good. At the red-faced man's back loomed several large men that could only be described as goons. Muscle-banded arms crossed over barrel chests, scraggly unkempt hair, and brown, rotting teeth.

The noise of the tavern died back slightly at the shout, allowing Henri to hear the next part of the argument. One of the smaller men, his ears dripping with earrings, leaned forward.

"Your father must've been a dog for you to look like that and be this stupid," he said, tapping two fingers on the table arrayed with cards. "You being too dumb to catch my bluffs isn't my problem."

If such a thing were possible, the man's face turned even redder, and he launched to his feet, chair toppling to the floor with a crash. He roared, sweeping an arm across the table and scattering the cards. The three smaller men jumped to their feet as well, squaring off with the wall of much larger opponents. The entire tavern quieted. The anticipation of violence hung in the air. The red-faced man, realizing he now had the attention of the other tavern patrons shouted, "These pirates are cheatin' at cards!"

This proclamation was not met with the outrage he'd obviously been expecting. "They're pirates! What did you expect?" one of the onlookers shouted, earning laughter from the rest of the crowd.

"We didn't cheat," the second pirate said calmly. This one had wavy blond hair, and an innocent face. "You're just bad at this game."

"You cheated me outa my pa's ring!"

"Shouldn't have bet it then." The third pirate, a freckled man who Henri vaguely recognized, flipped a tiger's eye ring into the air and caught it again. "Funny, dogs don't even have fingers."

The red-faced man launched himself over the table with a roar of rage, tackling the much smaller pirate to the floor and grappling for the ring. The one with earrings jumped on his back, but was quickly dragged off by the goons. Before Henri knew it, the entire crowd fell into chaos. It was a tavern full of sailors, after all, and drunken sailors loved nothing more than a good brawl.

A man stumbled into Henri, shoving him up against the bar and quickly disappearing back into the fray. Henri's hand flew to his belt, finding his meager purse, the only money he had to his name, gone.

"Hey!" Henri shouted, plunging into the fray after him, but he hadn't gotten a good look at the thief, and soon lost him. How was he going to afford food tomorrow? All he had was a few honey candies in his pockets, and no one could survive on that. Another body knocked into him, and Henri suddenly found himself in the center of the brawl. He had to get out of here. He couldn't afford to get injured, especially now that he had no money left. He waded through the chaos, ready to fight his way out, and spotted the men who'd started it all.

The three pirates fought like hellions, throwing punches with reckless abandon. The freckled one giggled as one of the goons took a swing at him, missed, and tripped over a fallen chair. Now

Henri recognized the pirate as the green-eyed man from the tattoo shop. Freckles danced away from his opponent, taunting, and backed right into the arms of the red-faced man. He yelped in surprise as a thick arm closed around his throat. The red-faced man drew a wicked knife from his belt and held it to the pirate's throat.

Freckles struggled, driving his elbow into the man's stomach, but he stayed steady, pressing the edge of the blade to his skin.

"Gimme the ring," he growled.

"I lost it when you fucking tackled me!" Freckles shouted back. The red-faced man roared incoherently, a murderous glint in his eye. And before Henri could stop himself, he pushed his way through the crowd and grabbed the large man by the back of his neck.

The man might have been big, but Henri was tall, and no stranger to a hard day's work. He dragged the man away, anger building in his gut. Was a ring freely bet in a game of cards really worth murdering a stranger over? This was a tavern brawl. A place for fists, and feet, and maybe a bottle bashed over someone's head, not deadly weapons. Henri couldn't stand by and watch this tiny man with the mirth-filled eyes get killed for something so trivial.

"Pick on someone your own size," Henri growled. The man struggled in his grip, slashing at his arms with the knife.

"Fox!" The other two pirates rushed over to them. Earrings grabbed Freckles, presumably called Fox, by the shoulder. "Let's get out of here." His ice blue eyes flicked to Henri, who still stood holding the struggling man like an angry scruffed kitten.

In Henri's distraction, the knife connected with his forearm, slashing through his sleeve, and shallowly scoring the skin across his brand new serpent tattoo. Henri released him in shock, and the man rounded on him, slashing again, backing Henri against an overturned table. Shit. He'd gotten himself involved in strangers' affairs and now look what it got him. Blood dripped sluggishly down his arm.

Before the red-faced man could outright stab him, the blond pirate barreled into him from the side, knocking him to the floor.

"Come on!" Fox grabbed Henri by the front of his shirt, almost ripping his father's key right off his neck. Earrings dragged Blondie off their attacker, and all four of them ran to the tavern door, throwing the occasional punch when someone didn't get out of their way fast enough.

The hot, muggy air hit Henri like a wet rag, and all he wanted to do was go back to his small room at the inn and tend his wounds, but the brawl spilled out into the street after them. Fox grabbed him by the sleeve, and they ran.

Fox didn't let go till they reached the docks, stumbling to a halt with labored breath and aching sides. Henri had barely kept up with the fleet-footed pirates, and now he doubled over like the rest of them, gasping to catch his breath. After a few moments, he straightened, intending to take his leave and return to his room at the inn, which he only had for one more night now that all his money had been stolen. But no sooner had he stood to his full height, towering over the three pirates, than Fox squealed in delight.

"It's him!" he crowed to the others. "It's the giant guy from the tattoo shop I told you about!"

Earrings laughed, a bruise blooming along his jaw. "He's hardly two feet taller," he said, piercing blue gaze traveling down the length of Henri's body. "Half a foot, tops." Fox pouted, but Earrings ignored him, offering his hand for Henri to shake. "Thanks for helping us out back there. I'm Rowan. This is Fox. And that's Logan." The blond pirate, his hair short, and darker than Rowan's almost white braid, seemed quieter than the other two, more thoughtful. He nodded in greeting.

"Henri," Henri introduced himself. All three pirates wore a curious mix of clothes and cheap finery, obviously pilfered from various ships and other unsuspecting victims. Fox had the same Laslandish accent Henri had been hearing everywhere since he arrived in Kadling Kay. The other two had a more northerly look about them. Maybe Marran or Avardellan, judging by the paleness of their skin and hair.

Fox drew the gold and tiger's eye ring that had started the whole thing out of his ponytail, and slipped it onto his thumb, though it was clearly much too big for him.

"You told that man you'd lost the ring!" Henri exclaimed.

Fox shrugged. "I hid it." As if stating this obvious fact was enough of an explanation.

"He was about to cut your throat over it!" Why would anyone risk their life for a ring that was probably worth a silver tal at best?

"But he didn't. Thanks for that, by the way. You really saved my ass back there." His green eyes flashed as bright as new spring grass.

"You're welcome," Henri replied.

Fox sidled closer, lips parting, eyelids lowering, and draped himself dramatically into Henri's arms so Henri had no choice but to hold him up.

"You know..." Fox's melodic voice turned sultry. "As a thank you, you can take my ass all the way to bed if you like. A man of your stature"—his gaze roamed down Henri's body—"must have a lot to offer."

Henri almost dropped him in shock.

"I...um..."

"Oi! Lay off the flirting, Fox. You're making our new friend uncomfortable," Rowan commanded, with a slight chuckle. Fox pouted, but nonetheless extricated himself from Henri's arms.

"Fine. Fine." He dusted himself off and turned back to Henri. "What do you say, handsome? Wanna save me from loneliness tonight?"

"Sorry. I..." Discomfort threaded through Henri's chest, but he was nonetheless drawn to the impish, freckled pirate. He cast about for something to distract him, and remembered the piece of hard honey candy wrapped in wax paper in his pocket. "Here." He placed the sweet in Fox's palm and folded his fingers over it.

Fox's chaotic energy stilled, blinking his wide green eyes up at

Henri. "Are you...giving me candy to apologize for not wanting to fuck me?"

"I suppose so," Henri replied, wishing he could sink straight through the dock beneath his feet.

A bright, cackling laugh burst from Fox's mouth, transforming his whole face with joy. The other two doubled over in laughter too, and after a few more moments, giggles bubbled to Henri's lips as well. A spark of comradery lit in Henri's chest, replacing the anxiety of his own awkwardness.

When the laughter died down, Fox turned to Rowan. "I like him. Can we adopt him?"

Rowan wiped a tear of laughter from the corner of his eye as he straightened up. "You looking to join a crew?"

Henri nodded.

"How's your marksmanship?"

"Passable. My linework is good, and I can read and do sums. I'm a fast learner," Henri said. He'd only been a sailor for a few months, but he'd taken to it as easy as breathing.

Rowan gazed at him for a moment, assessing, and seemed to reach a decision. "So whaddya think? Wanna join our crew?"

A curious warmth bloomed from the sparks in Henri's chest. These three men were strange. They were pirates, yet the warmth of friendship between them was clear as day, and despite the initial awkwardness, Henri felt a pull toward them.

"Do you have a ship or do you just start tavern brawls and steal people's jewelry?" he asked.

"We didn't steal it," Logan cut in earnestly. "We actually did win it fair and square."

"And our ship is right there." Henri followed Rowan's pointing finger to a spry little ship two berths down. It looked well kept, and the white lettering on the side proclaimed it the *Siren Song*.

Oh, Henri had heard of that ship. Captained by the...Ghost something. Just a few days ago he'd overheard a probably exaggerated story in the tavern about this ship outmaneuvering a cadre of

Talvan frigates after robbing an armory on the Souna coast. His gaze swung back to Rowan, clearly the leader of this small group. He didn't look like much, but then again, neither did Henri.

Well, it wasn't like Henri had any money or other prospects, and who knew the business of pirates better than other pirates? Maybe this would get him one step closer to finding his father.

Henri found himself smitten with the idea of joining this scrappy little crew. For the first time since his mother's funeral, he felt like he could have a home.

Chapter 16

RUNAWAY GROOM

ROBIN BECKETT

Autumn, 1665

A soft knock sounded on the door of Robin's bedroom, and he glanced up from his notes, realizing the lamp on his desk had guttered low and evening had crept into the rest of the room. Had he missed dinner? Mother would be angry, especially because he wasn't dressed properly and his hair was sure to be a mess from running his fingers through it as he read.

"Come in!" he called, expecting one of the servants to pop their head around the door and summon him to dinner. Or perhaps his mother, come to scold him for being too engrossed in his studies to spend time with his family. Instead it was his little brother, David, who entered.

"Is it time for dinner?" Robin asked, closing his notebook softly on the diagram of the human eye he'd been pouring over.

"You missed it." David leaned against the edge of the desk, reached over, and flipped the notebook back open. It landed on a page detailing the male reproductive system. He grimaced. "I don't know how you can stand to do this doctor stuff. It's gross."

Robin rolled his eyes at this old sentiment from his younger brother, who was due to begin at the Art Academy of Yrenmoor after the new year. Robin himself was a year out of the Royal College of Medicine, and about to finish his apprenticeship. Between three brothers, Robin and David had both exhibited a talent for art from a young age, but as the second son, Robin had been required to put his talents to a use that would bring further status to their family. While David, or Davy as the family affectionately called him, was free to pursue less lucrative endeavors.

"The human body is not gross. You'll have to learn that when they make you draw naked people at the art academy," Robin said, closing the notebook again and hoping his brother didn't see the way his ears reddened at the sight of the diagram he'd so carefully rendered during his school days.

"If it's a girl that won't be so bad. But I'm not drawing a naked bloke. I'm not a poof."

Robin swallowed down the bile that threatened to rise at the venom with which Davy delivered this proclamation. "Why didn't I get called down to dinner?" he asked, so Davy wouldn't expect him to agree with the sentiment.

Davy shrugged. "Father said to let you study since you're almost a full-on doctor."

"I doubt Father used the phrase 'full-on doctor,'" Robin countered.

Davy rolled his eyes. "You're right. He didn't. But he *did* send me up here to get you for tea. Apparently we're expecting guests this evening." He smiled a small, secretive smile as if he knew something Robin didn't.

"This late? Who?"

"Just fix your hair and come down." Davy scoffed with typical younger brother elusiveness. He pushed off the edge of the desk. "And probably put on better clothes too."

ROBIN FOUND his entire family in the front parlor, a fire crackling in the marble fireplace, and a small spread of miniature cakes and the good porcelain tea set laid out on the table between the fashionably arranged settees and chairs. His mother, father, and older brother, Phillip, all looked up when he entered. Davy, unconcerned with whatever the occasion was, continued eyeing the cakes.

Robin stopped inside the door, nerves suddenly climbing up his throat at the sight of the room arranged like this, as if the company they were expecting was very important.

"What's going on?"

"Oh dear, your hair..." his mother tutted, getting up from her seat to come over and smooth his hair. He'd tried to fix it upstairs, but it often had a mind of its own.

"Mother..." Robin protested as she switched from fixing his hair to straightening his jacket. "What's going on?" Why were they all being so elusive? Whoever they were expecting to visit, he was starting to suspect he wasn't going to like it.

"Take a seat, son." His father gestured to an empty spot at the center of the arrangement. Robin eyed him warily and opened his mouth to ask again, but was interrupted by a brisk knock on the front door. His mother squeaked in something like excitement and hustled him to the settee as the footman answered the door.

The servant led a well-dressed older gentleman into the parlor, followed by a woman who was clearly his wife, and a younger woman close to Robin's own age of twenty-four. Robin's breath caught, sudden understanding dawning clear and horrible in his mind.

This young woman was going to be his wife.

As their fathers shook hands, the young woman smiled shyly. She was quite pretty, he had to admit, with fair skin and light brown hair drawn back from her temples with jeweled pins.

"Robin, may I present Lady Marie Collingwood, your fiancée."

Robin did not stand to greet her and kiss her hand. His limbs had gone numb, and he knew if he stood he might fall to the rug and make a fool of himself. Even more of a fool than he looked right now with his mouth hanging open, staring at Marie, who blushed and tucked a strand of hair behind her ear under his shocked regard.

"Ah, he's simply stunned by her beauty." Robin's father chuckled nervously, shooting him a stern look. "Please have a seat." The Collingwoods filtered into the room, Marie ending up on the settee across from Robin.

"Pull yourself together," Davy whispered, nudging him.

Robin nodded absently, but a roaring had begun in his ears. His family began chatting pleasantly with the Collingwoods, like this was just another average tea with family friends. He responded appropriately when addressed, a lifetime of lessons on the manners of polite society taking over his body while he himself retreated in shock.

Snatches of conversation penetrated his skull to make it to his conscious brain.

Spring wedding.

Inheritance.

Townhouse.

Children.

With each detail, he sank lower and lower into himself, his mind racing, as outwardly he smiled and laughed and made polite conversation. They hadn't discussed this, and he hadn't expected it so soon. Not before Phillip married. As the eldest, Phillip should've married first. So why Robin instead? The answer trickled in as slowly as honey. The Collingwoods were clearly minor nobles. If Robin, the middle son, married up, that would open the door for Phillip as heir and eldest to make an even more lucrative match. And why shouldn't Robin be thrilled by the prospect? The Collingwoods were obviously wealthy. Titled. Marie was objectively pretty. She'd been gazing at him with obvious interest all night. The marriage might even come with a title, for all he knew.

The only problem was, Robin liked men.

If his parents knew, they would not even be having this conversation. He'd be out on the streets without even the comfort of their family name. His parents, and the rest of Avardellan society, had made it abundantly clear how they felt about those kinds of people. It hadn't been until Robin escaped from under their thumb at university that he'd realized Avardel was the odd one out in this regard. The rest of the countries that made up the Islands didn't give a flying fig who consenting adults loved. And instead of the disgust with which his family would've reacted to his news, he only felt relief. *He* was one of those people, and ever since then he'd hidden away a part of himself from everyone, including his family.

Somehow, Robin made it through to the end of the tea, and managed to gallantly kiss Marie's knuckles on her way out the door. He muddled his way through his mother's delighted chattering, his father's confident planning for their family's future, and his brothers' playful ribbing. Did any of them even have an inkling that inside Robin was falling apart? That his once peaceful future of quiet bachelorhood was now dark and shadowed by marriage to a person he was incapable of loving?

After it all, Robin stumbled back into his own bedroom, feigning tiredness. His eyes flitted from his bed, to the clothes he'd discarded while changing for tea, to the scattering of notebooks on his desk. All these trappings of his life now shattered beneath the weight of a marriage he should've wanted.

Robin leaned back against the door and wept.

His numb limbs finally gave out, and he slid down the door to lay crumpled on the rug until there were no tears left in his body. Until he was hollowed out and devoid of hope. This felt momentous, an irreversible shift overshadowing all the plans he'd made for his life.

He hadn't asked for much. Hadn't expected to have a great love in his life, or even more than a fling or two when the loneliness became too much. He only wanted to live peacefully with his shameful secret tucked in the back of his mind. He wanted to practice medicine, and dote on his future nieces and nephews, and endure playful teasing from his family about how he'd always been too busy with work to settle down. That was *all* he wanted. All he expected. And now he couldn't even have it.

When all tears were gone, Robin stared into the darkened room he'd grown up in. The room his parents had insisted he come back to after university, till he got his feet under him. Now its shadowed corners and moon-silvered furniture felt foreign to him. Almost hostile. He'd always known he could never tell his family what he was. But now this house felt unwelcoming, as if it had never been home.

He blinked into the darkness, eyes aching, cheeks damp, and for a moment he considered what his life would be like if he followed the path his parents had laid out for him. A townhouse near the hospital, or his own private practice. A proper wife who would host teas and parties waiting for him at home. A child or two if he could manage to grit his teeth through his marital duties. And too much guilt to ever go out and find even the briefest comfort in a man's arms.

It laid itself out clearly before him. He knew most men would kill for a life like that, but to him it would be a prison.

All at once the room felt suffocating. He loosened the collar of his shirt and dashed the back of his hand across his cried-out eyes. He took a few deep breaths, trying to breathe past the panic threatening to overwhelm him again. To think rationally, as he always had.

His parents wouldn't have been able to arrange this quickly. It must have taken weeks to negotiate, which meant they had purposely kept it from him. They'd announced it to him in front of the Collingwoods instead of in private ahead of time. Why? Did they suspect? He could think of no other reason for them to keep it from him. They knew he was too polite to protest in front of the Collingwoods, even if he was shocked. Did they expect him to go along with this without a second thought?

Well why wouldn't they? He'd always been a good, dutiful son.

The thought tasted bitter. He'd always done everything right, and look where it had gotten him.

A sense of determination settled over him. There were only two options. Stay, and accept the fate his parents had made for him. Or go, and take his chances on a life he could build for himself.

One of these choices had already landed him sobbing on the floor of his childhood room. He'd always done everything right, so now, it was time to do something wrong.

DRY BROWN LEAVES skittered across the cobblestones, fetching up against Robin's boots and the corners of buildings as he made his way quickly down the empty street. It was dark, morning still a few hours away, and across the city Robin's family would still be abed, none the wiser that he was not also tucked safely beneath their roof. It had taken Robin an hour to get even this far, and he'd almost turned back countless times. As frightening as the uncertain path ahead was, it had to be better than the sure and slow death that lay behind him.

Robin reached a three-way junction in the street and took the leftmost path, winding through the narrower lane up the hill that culminated at the campus of the Royal College of Medicine. On either side of him loomed stone buildings squished together like books on an overstuffed shelf, each and every one full of overworked students in too-small apartments that their wealthy parents would be appalled at the state of. Up until a year ago, Robin had been one of those students, wiling away the nighttime hours poring over his notes in the common room of the small apartment he shared with his best friend, Benedict Carlyle.

The autumn wind whistled over the roof slates, and Robin stopped at another junction, looking up at the faint candle glow showing between the curtains on the third floor. At first, as Robin packed everything of value into a basket pack he'd found in the kitchens, he'd wondered where he would go. But when he finally stepped out into the night, his feet had taken a familiar route through the streets and canals of Hallenburgh, and now he stood in front of the building where he'd first confirmed he was different from other people. Where he'd first fallen in love.

He stood there in the street, looking up at Benedict's window, and thought about how his life might have been different if the two of them had never met. Or if Benedict had understood Robin's feelings.

Before he could think further on it, Robin bent to retrieve a pebble from the street, and tossed it at the window. It clattered against the glass panes, not loud enough to wake the neighbors, but enough to alert Benedict if he was still awake.

He waited for long moments, feeling almost like a secret suitor waiting for his lover to appear. In another life, if Robin had been braver, maybe that could've been true. Benedict didn't answer, but movement brushed the other side of the curtains. Robin tossed another pebble, and the window opened.

"What?" Benedict called peevishly, leaning on the stone windowsill.

"Ben! Are you going to let me in?" Robin tried to keep his tone light.

With a roll of his eyes, Benedict closed the window, and Robin waited there in the blustery dark till the front door of the building opened.

"Come on," Benedict muttered, gesturing him inside. Robin followed him up the dimly lit stairs to the small apartment they'd shared in their university days, where Benedict now lived alone.

A single lamp lit the small table that had served them both as a desk, now littered with Benedict's unorganized notes, a half-full bottle of brandy, and a silver snuffbox. Benedict lit another lamp and set it on the sideboard.

"So why are you here so late? What's wrong?" Benedict slumped into his chair at the table, his gaze traveling from Robin's red eyes to the heavy basket pack he slid off his shoulder to set by the door.

"I...um..." There was no use hiding that he was running away, but he hadn't thought of what to say when he got here. He couldn't very well tell his best friend that he couldn't marry the lovely Lady Marie Collingwood because he'd been in love with Benedict since they'd met and wasn't attracted to women at all.

"Here." Benedict pushed a cup across the cluttered table and filled it almost to the brim with brandy. Robin usually wasn't one for drink, but he took a small sip. Half to steady his nerves, half to give himself time to think of what to say.

"So," Benedict began when Robin set the cup back on an empty patch of table. "Nervous for your last exam?"

Robin blinked at him. In all the turmoil and panic since learning of the engagement, he'd completely forgotten the exam he was meant to take a week from now, the final piece of schooling to become a full-fledged physician.

"That's not it."

"Well? Spit it out." Benedict grabbed the cup from in front of Robin and took a large swallow, throat bobbing.

Robin hesitated for another moment. Then all at once, sitting here with Benedict in the home they once shared, it all came pouring out. The surprise engagement, his shock, the feeling of being trapped, of panic. Throughout, Benedict listened intently, a small frown on his bow shaped lips. Eventually Robin's flood of panicked words slowed to a trickle and stopped altogether. Benedict sat in quiet contemplation for a few moments, sipping at the brandy.

"I'm not exactly seeing the problem here to be honest," he finally said. His dark eyebrows drew together in concern. "Your parents shouldn't have sprung it on you, but you must've known it was coming eventually."

Panic built again, constricting around Robin's chest like a snake. He couldn't tell Benedict about his feelings, or that he liked men. Especially because he knew Benedict would never reciprocate.

"I just...I can't marry her. You don't know—"

"I do know," Benedict cut him off. The gentle sternness he'd exhibited thus far fell away, replaced by frustration.

Robin blinked at him. "W-what?"

"I know, Robin. I'm not an idiot. I saw you kissing Gavin Burns in the library second year. And I've caught you looking like you wanna kiss me more times than I can count. I was *hoping* you'd finally tell me about it, but I guess that's not going to happen."

Robin's mind spun, and he was quite sure his mouth gaped open in shock. The snake in his chest tightened further, with mortification that Benedict of all people had seen him doing something so shameful. "I...but...why didn't you say anything?"

"'Cause you're my friend, and I was waiting for you to get over it."

"G-get over it?" Robin's stomach dropped, trying to drag his heart along with it.

"Gods, Rob, everyone fools around a bit during school, but you're an adult now. This Marie girl sounds nice enough, so why can't you be content with what you have and try to be normal?"

Try to be normal. Robin had imagined confessing to Benedict a thousand times. If not his feelings, then at least the fact that he liked men, not women. And sometimes in his imaginings the fantastical happened, and Benedict loved him back. But more often than not, Robin's practical brain took over his fantasies, and Benedict said something like this.

I could never love you like that. Why can't you just be normal?

This had happened a thousand times in his mind, but that didn't make it cut any less. What came out of his mouth now was not a sob, as it should have been with his heart on the floor and bitterness rising in his throat, but a chuckle.

Benedict's lips quirked up hesitantly in response, as if he wasn't quite sure what to think.

"You know, you're right, Benny. Maybe I should go back home, and just be normal." The tone of his voice was strange to his own ears, but Benedict, his best friend in the world, didn't seem to notice the bitterness laced through it. He reached across and patted the back of Robin's hand.

"You've had a shock. It's natural to panic a bit when things change." As if it was all done and solved. As if Robin could change his nature like it was nothing. Benedict smiled reassuringly. "Why don't you stay the night on the settee, and think it over? No use walking all the way back across the city at this time of night."

Robin nodded, downtrodden and unable to look Benedict in the eye. Even on his walk here he hadn't been sure what to do, or how Benedict could help him. Perhaps he'd hoped, in the depths of his heart, that he'd have the courage to finally confess his love to Benedict, and they would run away together and start a new life. Any other country would do. None of them cared about this sort of thing like Avardel did.

Of course, that could never have happened. Benedict had known all along Robin had feelings for him, and was waiting for him to get over it. And if Benedict of all people didn't understand him, Robin was truly on his own.

They stayed up a bit longer, Benedict drinking his brandy and chatting happily about how everything would be okay. That if it was really a problem, there was professional help for that sort of thing. Robin would forget all about his schoolboy crushes, and come to love Marie as a man should. Robin listened to it all, still unable to meet his friend's eyes. And after a time, Benedict retired to his bedroom, the faint click of the lock breaking Robin's heart all over again. Robin laid down on the lumpy settee, planning what to do next.

He needed to get out of Avardel as fast as possible. He couldn't stand another day here.

Right before dawn, he rose and splashed water on his face, slung the basket pack onto his back, and made his way down the hill to the docks of Hallenburgh.

Chapter 17

RANSOMED GROOM

ROBIN BECKETT

Autumn, 1665

Cannon fire shattered Robin's uneasy sleep, and he sat bolt upright, bashing his head against the bunk above. *Boom. Boom. Boom.*

The ship shuddered all around him as if the very timbers anticipated imminent demise. Robin fell off the side of the bunk, landing on his hands and knees, then scrambled to his feet, wrenching the door of the cramped cabin open to the corridor. A sailor rushed past, rifle slung over his shoulder.

"What's happening?" Robin called after him. The sailor barely slowed to answer.

"Pirates! Best stay in your cabin, sir. Unless we begin taking on water, stay out of the way." He bolted, leaving Robin clutching the doorjamb, his legs going watery at the words. They'd been at sea for over a week already and were only days away from their destination, Lasland, Robin's hope for a new life.

On the Hallenburgh docks the morning after leaving his family and Benedict behind with no note or explanation, he'd booked passage on the first ship he could find on its way to a different island. A place where he could start anew. A place that did not hold the same restrictive values as Avardel. He'd been sick to his stomach the first few days, so much so that the man who was meant to bunk with him had gone to stay in the crew quarters instead. But in between bouts of puking, Robin had begun to dream of what his life could be in a way he'd never been able to before. Lasland did not have the same qualms as Avardel did. To them, two men in a romantic relationship was as normal as a man and woman.

So he'd wiled away his days and nights at sea thinking of new possibilities for the future. Perhaps he could rent a cottage in a quaint little town, set himself up as a town doctor, and sketch pastoral landscapes in his free time. Perhaps he would meet a handsome man as he bought bread at a bakery one day. Perhaps he would fall in love.

But now, cannon fire shattered that dream, and the ship pitched beneath his feet. He stumbled back into the cabin to sit heavily on the edge of the bed, all those peaceful visions of the future he could've had flashing before his eyes and bleeding away. He should go help with any potential casualties. But he couldn't move. Was it fear that held him here? Or the hopelessness that now loomed large in his mind, blotting out the hope he had let grow like a weed.

The ship shuddered violently; a calamitous crashing noise rent the air, accompanied by panicked shouts. Then all at once, the sounds faded away.

Robin caught his breath. Waiting. Had they gotten away? Had the pirates given up? A small root of hope crept in once again.

The silence stretched long, until finally boots pounded down the corridor. Robin's muscles tensed, and he sprang to his feet. Friend or foe? He cast about for a weapon and found none. A shadow darkened the doorway, and he met the eyes of a man who was horribly, undoubtedly a pirate.

Robin froze, and the pirate grinned, grabbing Robin roughly by the arm and dragging him out into the corridor. Robin wanted to fight, to struggle, to break away and hide in the bowels of the ship. The shock had disconnected his mind from his body, and it would not obey him.

They emerged out into the cold air, wind whipping stinging needles against Robin's face. The black sky seemed to press down upon the deck, suffocating—only held at bay by a ring of guttering torches, orange flames whipping violently in the wind.

"Found this one below," the pirate said, pushing Robin into the group of huddled sailors. The entire crew, some nursing injuries, huddled in the center of the deck surrounded by pirates with swords and axes in their hands. They'd given up with little fight, choosing instead to throw themselves on the mercy of this gang of ruffians in the hopes they would take their loot and go without further bloodshed.

And Robin could see why. The pirates had rammed them. The starboard side was a mess of splintered wood and bodies, a fatal tableau beneath the tentacled figurehead of the pirate ship, which glinted with inset glass and gems. Faced with that, it was no wonder the sailors had surrendered. Bile curdled in the back of Robin's throat as pirates swarmed down to the hold, searching for anything they could get their hands on. The tall, dark masts of the pirate ship loomed, sails blotting out the moon and stars.

The air seemed to sharpen, a shiver rippling through all present on the ship.

"Captain on deck!" a pirate in an old, ruined Marran uniform shouted. A figure stepped onto the deck as if materializing from the night itself. And all at once Robin understood the other reason the crew had succumbed so quickly.

The pirate captain's skin was pale as bone, eyes and hair black as the sky above and water below. The flickering torches cast him in the cataclysmic glow, lending madness to his sculpted face. As he crossed the deck, spurs clinking, terror trailed him like a shadow. A prince of death, at home in the flame-lit night.

He was so beautiful, Robin knew artists back home that would fall to their knees in worship and weep to behold him. That was what some of his fellow captives did now, though their tears were born of fear. And Robin heard the name whispered among them like leaves skittering across cobblestones.

The Deep Water Demon.

The worst pirate in the Islands. The man without humanity or mercy. Yet in the face of overwhelming power, Robin's fellow captives had chosen to surrender their fates to him.

The Deep Water Demon stopped before the captives, dark eyes roving over the bowed heads of their cowering, their praying for mercy.

"Bring me the captain," he ordered, and a muscle-bound pirate with a sharp jaw and short black hair pulled the merchant captain roughly from the crowd.

"P-Please...mercy..." The captain would've fallen to his knees had the pirate not kept him upright.

The Demon's cold gaze swept the other captain from head to toe, his lip curling in distaste.

"Take whatever you want," the captain babbled.

The Demon's hand snapped out, backhanding him, jeweled rings leaving lines of blood across his cheek. The captain stumbled, and the pirate hauled him up again.

"Why do you not fight?" the Demon growled. He sounded almost disappointed they'd surrendered so quickly, that his reputation was such that no one believed they could escape once he had them in his clutches. That there was no violence to be had.

"I-I—" The captain's legs shook, knees practically knocking together.

"What kind of man simply gives up all he's worked for?" The Demon spat at the captain's feet. "Pathetic." A small pocket of silence followed his words, a collective held breath of the captives as the pirate crew continued their vicious looting.

"Throw him overboard," the Demon commanded. Robin gasped, and the captain's legs collapsed beneath him. The muscle-bound pirate let him crumple to the deck. Two other pirates hauled him back up and dragged him to the side without question. Still, he did not fight, only trembled as he wept. What command did the Demon have over the hearts of men, that a man would not even fight for his own life? Was death in the cold embrace of the sea truly less horrible than death at the hands of the Demon?

The pirates dropped cannonballs into the wide pockets of the captain's coat, lashed his wrists together, and shoved him over the rail without preamble. He dropped like a stone into the dark sea. Robin winced at the monstrous splash his body made, and the silence that followed.

The Demon closed his eyes and inhaled deeply. In another man, this may have looked like regret, but on the Demon's face, it was as if he were luxuriating in the murder. He turned back to the captives, dark eyes landing on Robin. Frigid wind sliced through Robin's clothes, leaving him feeling naked under the Demon's cool regard. In two steps the Demon appeared before him, and some corner of Robin's shocked mind registered that the Demon was shorter than him. His instincts screamed at him to flee. To take his chances with the unforgiving sea, which would surely be more merciful than this man. But Robin's limbs remained frozen in fear.

The Demon reached out and took the edge of Robin's collar between graceful fingers. His thumb rubbed over the fabric, the stitching, as if assessing the quality. Their eyes met.

"This man is not a sailor." He addressed the uniformed pirate who'd appeared by his side like a dutiful dog.

"They found him below in a hired cabin," the pirate confirmed.

The Demon hadn't looked away from Robin's face, and Robin felt as if he hadn't breathed in several minutes. His whole being screamed for him to get away. The Demon's fingers strayed to the button at Robin's collar.

"Ivory," he murmured to himself, and turned to the other, muscled pirate. "Bring him to my quarters."

Robin sucked in a sharp breath, terror racing like lightning up his spine.

"Yes, Captain," the muscled pirate said. The Demon stepped away, and the pirate grabbed Robin's arm roughly.

"Come on."

This was it. Would Robin go quietly, weeping as the captain had? Or would he fight?

In the end, he had no strength to do anything but be led like a lamb to slaughter.

The pirate's grip eased slightly once they stepped foot on the pirate ship. They entered a dark corridor, and eventually came to a heavy wooden door. The pirate opened it and ushered Robin through.

The room beyond could not have been more ostentatious had it been in the grandest of mansions back home. But it was not gaudy—the carved wood panels upon the walls had obviously been shaped by a master hand, the furniture fashionable and rich. Opposite from where they'd entered, four panels depicting intricate carvings of sea monsters bookended another door that must have led deeper into the Demon's chambers. Thankfully, the pirate made no move toward it, and instead led Robin to a large table inlaid with a mother-of-pearl map of the Islands. Upon its surface sat a small chest, overflowing with coin and jewelry. A few toppled over stacks of coin sat beside it, as if the Demon had been interrupted in the middle of counting his riches when they'd spotted Robin's unfortunate ship.

The pirate pushed Robin into a seat opposite the chest, then stepped to the side, taking up a position a few feet away like a good soldier.

Robin's breath came in shallow pants, his mind awhirl with speculation about why the Demon had ordered him to be brought here. No sooner did his consciousness snag on one horrible possibility, than one even more horrible conjured in its place.

"Try to calm down. The captain doesn't appreciate weakness." It was the muscle-bound pirate who had spoken, not looking in Robin's direction. He spoke with a deep voice and a softly lilting Laslandish accent, though Robin could clearly see from his dark, angular eyes and tawny skin that he must have originally hailed from one of the countries in the far east across the

Sunrise Sea, both of which had closed their borders to outsiders almost two decades ago.

"W-what is he going to do to me?" Robin stuttered. The pirate's gaze slid toward him.

"Hard to say. But it's a good sign he didn't outright kill you."

Somehow this did nothing to ease Robin's fears. His hands trembled as he raised them to cover his mouth, trying to keep a sob at bay. The pirate seemed to take pity on him, his voice gentling.

"When he comes, show whatever strength you have. He respects the fight."

What kind of strength did Robin have? He was not strong physically. Not brave. The bravest thing he'd ever done was board a ship to start a new life, and it had led him here.

The door clicked open, and Robin's hands trembled harder. He averted his eyes to the table's shiny surface as the Demon's footsteps echoed across the room. Robin felt the Demon settle into the chair opposite him.

"Gaël, the door." The Demon's voice seemed to reverberate through Robin's very bones. The muscle-bound pirate, Gaël, retreated to stand guard. Robin threaded his hands together, knuckles whitening.

Strength. Choose strength.

He raised his eyes to find the Demon already watching him, eyes as cold and dark as a grave. Dread coiled in Robin's gut, and he averted his gaze once again to the table and its piles of shining coin.

"You need not be so frightened," the Demon said. His hands folded on the table, gleaming rings edged with blood. "I do not intend to kill you."

Robin took a deep breath, trying to quiet his nerves, but he said nothing, so the Demon continued. "You come from a wealthy family, do you not? Or did you steal these fine clothes off of someone's washing line?"

Two gunshots echoed into the room from outside. Robin flinched.

"Ignore that. Look at me when I speak to you," the Demon said. With great effort, Robin forced his gaze to meet the Demon's. Would it be better to lie and say he had stolen the clothes and had not a copper to his name? Or admit a wealthy family waited for him back home? The more valuable he was, the greater chance of survival, right?

"Y-yes," he admitted. His fingers began to ache with how tight he clutched them. The Demon smiled, so wicked that Robin half expected his teeth to be sharp.

"Excellent. Where are you from? You sound Avardellan."

"H-Hallenburgh."

"I'm sure your family will be grateful to have you back. For a modest fee of course."

"No!" Robin blurted before he could stop himself. As terrified as he was of this murderous pirate, the thought of going back and being trapped in marriage opened up a deep well of dread in his heart.

The Demon's eyebrows rose. "No? You would not like to be ransomed back to your family? Why is that, pray tell?"

"They are trying to force me to marry and I..." He couldn't quite bring himself to say it even now.

The Demon's eyebrows climbed higher. "Marriage? Is that truly a fate worse than... Ah, I see." Understanding crept into his tone, and Robin felt himself blush to the tips of his ears.

"Well, you have put us both in a predicament. You see, you are useless to me without the prospect of ransom. So what do you propose we do?"

Robin's mind whirled. Was this murderous pirate truly giving him a choice? What did Robin have to offer that would be equal to a potential ransom?

"I-I'm a physician. I could work off the amount they would've paid." Stupid. The Demon would never go for it. But it was the only strength Robin had, the only thing of worth he had to offer. "My things are on the ship, a basket full of the latest teachings of the Royal College of Medicine." A man like the Demon might not care about the health of his crew, but Robin could tell he liked fine things. Robin could be a fine thing. A royally trained physician to be a jewel in his piratical crown.

To Robin's surprise, the Demon leaned forward, interest lighting his dark eyes. "You'd be willing to work for a pirate instead of returning to your family? How intriguing..." He trailed off, obviously searching for a name.

"Robin Beckett." Maybe this was how he could fight for the future he'd only recently begun to dream of. He would dutifully serve the Deep Water Demon until he earned his worth, and if the Demon kept his word, eventually Robin would be free.

"Well Mister Beckett, if I were to take you up on your offer, how does ten thousand silver tals sound?"

Robin inhaled sharply. He was no expert on currency conversions, but even with a generous physician's salary, it would take twenty years to pay off. His family did not have that kind of money to throw around, even with promised marriage ties to nobility. "I-I'm not worth that much," he said quietly. If his parents knew what he was, they wouldn't pay a single copper to get him back.

The Demon smiled that wicked smile again. "How much did your parents stand to gain from your marriage?"

"I don't know. I fled as soon as it was announced." He wouldn't tell him the Collingwoods were nobility. It would only make this situation worse. The Demon chuckled darkly and stood, rounding the table in a few long strides. It took every ounce of Robin's meager strength not to flinch back as he approached.

"I will make you a deal, little doctor. Five thousand tals, and you will serve me for seven years." Robin caught his breath as the Demon leaned close, his nearness as omnipresent as being buried alive. "Of course," the Demon's voice was smooth as silk, "I will give you an opportunity to *earn* your freedom faster." He reached out to stroke Robin's hair, and Robin did flinch then, nearly toppling from his chair in desperation to get away from the Demon's scalding touch.

To his surprise, the Demon withdrew, and returned to his seat on the other side of the table, settling behind the piles of coin like a tyrant king.

"Do you accept these terms, Mister Beckett? Seven years of service, and then you will be free."

"Yes," Robin breathed.

Chapter 18

HUNGER

YVES FRANCOIS LESAUVAGE

Autumn, 1665

Sunlight shattered on the waves of the Broken Sea as the bow of the *Kraken's Fury* cut through them under full sail. The wind favored them, filling the deep blue sails like wine in a cup. Yves sipped it, savoring its swell in his lungs, the scent of danger. Fear.

In the distance, his quarry fled. It was a merchant vessel called the *Fellowship*, entrusted to carry Kefrye's biannual tithe of taxes back to their overlord, the Marran Empire. Yves had already separated her from her naval escort like a wolf isolating the young from the flock. And now the poor thing was on her own. The columns of smoke towering from the charred wreckage of her late protectors still dotted the horizon.

Yves imagined he could still hear the crackle of flames and see the black smoke choking out last night's stars. It had almost been easy to the point of boredom to pick them off one by one. Yves's crew had taken them out with a combination of brute force and flaming arrows. That particular bit of fiery barbarity had been John's idea. But the *Fellowship*, even laden with half a year's taxes and partially crippled by the *Kraken's* previous attacks, had a significant head start and was proving a bit too fast for the *Kraken* to catch up easily. Still, the *Kraken* would run her down eventually. They were so close Yves could practically feel the gold running through his fingers.

"Captain."

John had appeared at his elbow. He handed Yves a spyglass.

"We've got company. Thirty degrees."

Yves raised the spyglass to his eye and instantly spotted a familiar silhouette speeding across the waves. The *Siren Song*, captained by the Ghost Hawk, that little upstart pirate who'd been a thorn in Yves's side for several seasons now. He'd stolen Yves's prizes before they could get far from the coasts. He'd managed feats no other pirate but Yves could pull off, and he'd earned quite a name in a short time. His legends were now on par with the ones told about Yves himself.

But while the legends of the Deep Water Demon were tales of horror, the ones about the Ghost Hawk were all about cleverness. He was a figure that could be the hero if the right spin was put on it; Yves could only be a villain. The Ghost Hawk was the opposite of Yves in almost every way. He'd gained a reputation for quickness, where Yves favored power. He flitted from island to island sticking to the shallows, where Yves lurked in the deep. He was bold, and he was heading directly for the *Fellowship*.

A slow smile curled Yves's lips, and the demon's shadows stirred within him. Yves couldn't wait to crush him.

"It's the *Siren Song*, Captain." John said when Yves handed the spyglass back to him.

"I can see that."

"And it's heading for our quarry."

Yves raised one manicured eyebrow. "Do you imagine I've gone blind in the hour since you spoke to me last?"

John was uncowed as always. He gazed at his captain with those intense brown eyes. "So what are we going to do about it?"

"We're going to take two prizes for the price of one."

. . .

Like many before him, Yves had underestimated the speed of the *Siren Song*, and the tenacity of her captain. Before the sun had sunk much lower, the *Siren Song* fell upon the *Fellowship*.

"We need more speed," Yves growled. There was no more impotent feeling than watching another man swoop in to take a prize he'd already killed for.

"We've got nothing more unless the wind changes," John answered evenly. He didn't seem overly put out by the prospect of losing all that money.

The demon rose up in Yves. He tried to quell it with a deep breath, but it was as if dark water filled his lungs. It was rare, these days, for him and the demon to be in disharmony. Yet still, the hunger for violence threatened to overtake his cooler head. The air tasted of sour defeat, and they could not tolerate it.

The *Siren*'s cannons boomed, the little ship running spry circles around the other. Was the Ghost Hawk toying with them? Or putting on a show for Yves's benefit? Yves couldn't help but admire the Ghost Hawk's tactics. Where other captains might rely on weaponry, the Ghost Hawk kept his ship moving, always shifting his enemy's focus. Never stopping. Never allowing themselves to be subject to the full force of the enemy's guns. The *Fellowship* would no doubt surrender to the *Siren*'s harrying before the *Kraken* could catch up. But they'd never be able to loot the ship quickly enough. Yves would swoop in and ambush him. He would crush the Ghost Hawk beneath his might. Then both ships and their contents would be his, and this vexatious pest would be no more. Perhaps he would even keep the *Siren* as a trophy.

The boom of cannon fire suddenly quieted, and Yves raised the spyglass to his eye once again. The decks of both ships swarmed with activity. One bright-haired figure bounded down from the quarterdeck with the vitality of youth. They were still too far away to see detail, but this had to be the Ghost Hawk.

Anticipation built low in Yves's stomach. The demon hungered for this man. Yearned to break his swift wings and feed his flightless corpse to death, which clawed at Yves's back now more than ever. Even with the blood of the Marran sailors on Yves's hands, death was not sated, but desperate to be fed. And who better to throw into its slavering jaws than this man so seemingly full of life?

Yves would kill the Ghost Hawk by his own hand, and death would curl up at his feet like a sleeping hound.

The *Kraken* sped closer and closer. Yves lowered the spyglass.

"Ready the men for battle," he ordered John, never taking his eyes off the other two ships. "I want minimum damage to the *Siren Song*, and leave the Ghost Hawk for me."

The Ghost Hawk would be his to devour.

"Aye, sir."

No sooner had the words left his lips than the *Kraken*'s massive sails went slack as the wind changed direction. The *Kraken*'s progress slowed. The crew jumped to amend this, trimming sails, adjusting course to try and catch the wind again, but it was no use. They were facing directly into a headwind now, and there was no way to catch it again quickly. The *Kraken*'s progress slowed, then stopped.

Yves's hand tightened on the spyglass, all hope they would catch up with the *Fellowship* and *Siren* vanishing like the wind itself. The *Kraken* was too large and heavy to move effectively with oars. Yves could only watch helplessly as the *Siren* captured his prize. And with every chest of coin the *Siren*'s crew carried into their hold, Yves's rage deepened, and the demon's hunger grew. His hand seized around the spyglass, and he slammed it down into the rail. The wood and brass casing crunched. The glass shattered, driving shards into his flesh. A few crew members nearby flinched, but not John.

Pain washed through his body like a soothing tide, and he clenched his fist tighter, driving the splinters deeper. The demon drank it in but it was only a small drop in the ocean of its vast appetite. It did little to slake his bloodlust.

"There's nothing we can do, Captain." John's voice was low,

like trying to soothe a wild animal. "Let Beckett take care of that injury."

"I'm not leaving the deck."

A short while later, John cleared his throat.

Yves raked his gaze away from the Ghost Hawk robbing him once again. The newest addition to the crew, a tall young doctor with a nervous disposition, stood by John's side. When Yves looked at him, he averted his gaze to the deck. Submissive and frightened.

Yves's lip curled in distaste. When he'd first met Robin Beckett a month ago, and had been convinced to allow him to work off a debt instead of being ransomed, Yves had thought perhaps this man had a fire in his belly. But any intrigue had died quickly, as the man proved to be fearful and demure. Others on his crew had been promising as well. But none could match Yves. None held any interest for him beyond physical transaction. Yves needed someone who could withstand being ripped apart, and no one was enough to pique his interest for long.

Yves's gaze turned back to the distant *Siren*. "It's nothing." He flipped his hand dismissively and a drop of blood flicked off his fingers to land on Beckett's cheek.

"You're bleeding," Beckett said, rather too earnestly, wiping the blood with the cuff of his sleeve. One thing that impressed Yves, the man was not squeamish in the slightest.

"So I am. It's no matter." Yves could already feel the demon's darkness creeping around the edges of the lacerations, attempting to heal him. As soon as he removed the glass, his flesh would close up, and he would be whole again. At least physically.

"Just let him do his job, Captain." John quite obviously barely resisted rolling his eyes. The little shit. He'd gotten too good at reigning Yves in, much to Yves's chagrin.

Without another word, Yves held out his hand, blood dripping freely onto the deck, glass shards glittering in the afternoon sun. John sighed and moved away to talk to the crew. Beckett replaced him at Yves's side. After a moment's hesitation, he took Yves's hand between gentle fingers and began to remove the shards.

Yves didn't take his eyes off the two ships across the water. He didn't react when the first shard slid free of his flesh. The sun slid down the vast bowl of the sky, and the *Siren Song* uncoupled from the *Fellowship*.

A bird winged up from the rigging of the *Siren*, wheeling high before catching the wind and turning toward the *Kraken*. By the time Yves's hand had been bandaged, the vague form of the bird resolved into a gray hawk. The Ghost Hawk's namesake. It screeched, dropping down into range.

"Shoot it down!" Yves shouted, and several marksmen raised rifles to the sky. Shots rang out, and the hawk soared high, then dove through the *Kraken*'s rigging, swooping low enough they could have almost snatched it right out of the air with their bare hands. It released something from its claws, and the object fell, glittering, and clinked onto the deck. The hawk wheeled away before any of them could get another shot off. Gaël picked the object up and held it up to the light.

A single gold coin.

The demon roared to the surface, and Yves barely clamped it down in time to stop a growl from escaping. He stormed down the quarterdeck steps and snatched it from Gaël's fingers. Was it not enough that the Ghost Hawk had swiped another prize from under Yves's nose? Now the little shit was taunting him?

He could not let this slight go unanswered. He could not allow the Ghost Hawk to continue roving unchecked across *his* seas.

The *Siren*'s white sails caught the same wind that kept the *Kraken* in irons, and skipped away over the waves, faster than the *Kraken* could ever hope to follow.

Yves's fist closed around the coin, its golden edges digging into the now healed cuts beneath the bandages.

Next season, he'd be rid of the Ghost Hawk once and for all.

Rowan Faine
Autumn, 1665

"She's back, Captain!" Fox yelled. Members of the *Siren Song* crew that weren't actively engaged in helping the *Siren* flee gathered at the rail to cheer Rowan's pet hawk, Nephele, as she soared back. Triumphant. Rowan grinned as she flared her gray speckled wings to land on the main yardarm and began to preen her feathers.

Rowan pursed his lips, releasing a gentle little trill, and Nephele took off again, gliding down to land on the beaten up leather armor on his shoulder.

"Did you deliver my gift?" Rowan cooed, feeding her a little bit of dried meat. Several crew members gathered around, still riding the high of sweeping a shipful of coin not only from under the noses of the Marran Empire, but also the infamous Deep Water Demon. Rowan himself felt light as a cloud, giddiness threatening to overwhelm him with every yard of open sea they put between themselves and the *Kraken's Fury*.

Nephele's beak preened Rowan's hair affectionately, and he scratched her head in return. He'd have to find a nice juicy rat for her dinner. Or ask Henri to catch her a fish.

"I can't believe we pulled that off." Logan laughed incredulously. The rest of them nodded in agreement. Rowan couldn't quite believe it either. When they'd come across the *Kraken* in pursuit of a lonely ship, he couldn't believe his luck, and moreover, couldn't resist swooping in to take it.

Nor could he resist a cheeky taunt.

Would it get Rowan into trouble later? Probably. Would it be fun as hell until then? Definitely.

CONTENT WARNINGS

General

    Internalized homophobia
    Homophobia
    Unhealthy coping with trauma
    Death of a parent(s) – long-term illness, depression, lost at sea
    Drowning
    Swearing
    Themes of colonialism, human trafficking
    Branding
    Murder
    Graphic violence, blood, and gore
    Hanging / Execution

Sex

    Explicit sex scenes
    Sex under the influence
    Mentions of past sexual abuse
    Uneven power dynamics - dubious consent

For a fully up to date content warnings page, please follow the QR code:

ACKNOWLEDGMENTS

Undefined Tides started out as a few short stories that I wrote for the sole purpose of getting my thoughts straight about events of the characters' pasts while I was writing Demon of the Deep. And...it kind of snowballed from there. I had way too much fun exploring my characters' pasts and watching them meet and interact for the first time.

As always, my biggest supporters and the people I want to thank the most are my beta readers: Emma, Lacey, Lauren, and Chris. Thank you for being so excited to see the boys again. My critique partners, Austin and Erin, also did a lot of heavy lifting for this book in terms of logistical edits.

Additionally, thank you to my editor, Kal Morgan, your feedback is invaluable in making my writing actually readable and publishable. Thank you also to Amphi at Amphi Studios for formatting, and Kelly at Velvet Library for proofreading.

Lastly, I'd like to thank the artists that worked on the beautiful art to accompany this book and bring my characters to life. My cover artist, Maria Arteta. The artist of my author portrait, Gukkhwa (Eunhye Cho). Character art by Vita Divata. Typography, and cover design by Amphi at Amphi Studios. You were all so wonderful to work with, and seeing my characters and vision come to life under your skilled hands has truly been a dream come true.

ABOUT THE AUTHOR

Briar Belmont

Briar Belmont is a spicy romance and romantasy author who debuted in 2024. She's adored reading and writing from a young age and has a soft spot for fairytales and folklore. She can often be found in her garden or curled up with her pets and a good book. *Demon of the Deep* was her debut novel.

Author Portrait by Gukkhwa (Eunhye Cho)

tiktok.com/@briar_belmont

instagram.com/briar_belmont